THE TRUTH BEHIND THE CANVAS

CRAIG SIMPSON

Contents

I

Betrayal

CHAPTER I

When the shadow climbed out of the pit, the woman hardly heard it move behind her. The revolver in her hand was pointed at the eastern side of the sprawling and silent scrapyard, where her eyes meticulously scanned the carcasses of deformed cars stacked like the somber aftermath of a battlefield. Sometimes they looked like subtle shape-shifters, having cannily paused in the midst of their transformation under the intense attention of a stranger intruding into their wasteland. The moon had chosen the cover of a thick menagerie of clouds and all the streetlamps on the street that had led her down here faced away from the scrapyard. Her gaze scoured for the slightest sign of movement in or around the metallic bones jutting out at odd angles.

The shadow stopped in its tracks when she took a few steps closer to the rusting pile of automobiles. She jolted in place when the frenetic growling of dogs cleaved the silent night at its seam. Her head snapped in the direction of the sound, but her fingers had known the feel of her gun long enough not to let it jump free of her grip. The dogs sounded like they were somewhere inside the scrapyard in one of its far corners. Stray mutts? Unlikely, since the municipal hand only recently made a clean sweep of the rising population of homeless dogs in the West Midtown area.

Those dogs must belong to the yard keeper, the thought ran through her head as she decided to take a closer look around the back of the pile in front of her. Holding the muzzle in a straight line, she marched to one corner of the pile and slowly hung her head around it. She mentally slapped herself for wanting to explore this part of the yard. Aisles ran forth between the jagged heaps in five different directions. It was going to take her half the night if she was going to go look down each of them. Besides, she didn't like the idea of getting lost inside the aisles. That is why she had waited out the past half hour in the main clearing close to where she could see the giant magnet puller. That's where the unidentified caller had said she would see the meeting take place. Close to the scrap magnet. But no movement except that of a small eclipse of moths had stirred anywhere around her.

The thirty-three-year-old woman glanced at the steel corpses towering above, some with the front ends facing her, their snouts bent into strangulated sneers. *Could there be someone waiting up there above one of those busted jalopies?* she wondered. After giving it a moment of thought she decided there was no way anyone would risk climbing up that stack of rattletraps. So what should she do now? Maybe make her way back to her car and call Steve. She had been in two minds before heading down here whether or not she should let him know where she was going before settling on later.

Fingers quietly closed on her shoulder and she turned around with such force that the man had to fall back two steps to avoid a collision. The woman's eyes narrowed as she aligned her gaze with the sight of her gun. He quickly held up both hands in front of his face.

"It's me," the man said.

Her eyes widened. "Steve? What the heck?" Her posture relaxed.

"Sorry if I gave you a scare, but I didn't want anyone else hearing me call out to you."

"There is no one else here," the woman said with a blasé look in her eyes. Then they sharpened. "How'd you know where to find me?"

The darkness had grown a little thicker, but she didn't miss the grin starting at the corner of his mouth. "Steve," she said, the realization dawning on her. She hadn't been able to place the voice of the man who had called her, but she had been in too much of a hurry to cogitate on it.

"It was me who called you," Steve said.

"You sly dog," she said. "Since when did you get to be such a sneaky little fiend?"

"Hey," Steve shrugged, "I've been watching this place since yesterday morning. Remember the manager denied any green van leaving this yard the day the body was found? Well, I spotted a green Mercedez Sprinter leaving here today around 11 a.m."

The woman didn't seem to be listening "Where were you hiding all this time?"

"Oh…" Steve turned to look at a murky spot in the ground about twenty yards away from where they stood. "In that sand pit over there."

The woman began walking toward the chain-link fence, heading up to the place whence she had entered earlier.

"Hey where you going?" Steve said and began following her. "Wait, there's something I need you to see. I think we may just have hit pay dirt."

The woman stopped and rolled her eyes. "What is it now?"

Steve beckoned with his finger, his voice a tender nasal tease. "Come look for yourself, Liv."

The woman, still in a huff, walked up to the lip of the pit and looked down. It was too gloomy for her to make out the bottom clearly but she thought she saw something moving there. "What's down there?" she said. The next moment she was sure she saw a pair of bloodshot eyes looking up from below. "Hey, di—" was all she was able to say without looking back. The bullet tore straight though the back of her skull and she toppled forward in stunned shock.

Max Worthington shouted "No!" in his sleep before toppling out of his bed in a confusion of sheets and sweat. He flopped around wildly, trying to free himself of the tangle of fabric, until his face showed. "No!" he cried again. "That's not how I want the story to end."

He got to his feet in a huff, peeled off his undershirt, and walked straight to his typewriter in the other room wearing nothing but his terribly slackened underpants. There it was, the half blank page jutting out the top of his Olympia model with the last line he had been trying to finish: *Sometimes they looked like subtle shape-shifters...*

"I will not let Liv Hargison die at the end like that," he announced to the page that he had started last evening and which was supposed to be the start of the ending chapter of the novel he was currently working on. As soon as he had started to type the unfinished line his phone had burred.

Felicity had wanted to find out if he was up for dinner at La Tavola di Atlanta, but he had politely declined.

Returning to his work desk, which boasted both a desktop replacement laptop and the Olympia, he had spent too much time mulling how to proceed. The phone call had categorically disrupted the feverish pace he had been going at. At times, he could not help playing the perfectionist, even though he hated it worse than the words of his mother telling him he was barely serviceable at anything while growing up. He might have opted writing multiple endings to the novel but the call he had received from Redbrick the day before had effectively preempted that tactic. And now he was in a tight spot.

Max Worthington stared absently through the window of his garden apartment, trying to remember what day it was when he had spoken to the lady at Redbrick Editions. He picked up his phone and saw it was a Thursday, so they had had the suavely intractable hound ring him up on Tuesday. He had not shifted from the word processor on his computer to his typewriter until then; hoping that hopping over would bring about a miraculous shift in affairs. But he had hardly been tearing up the asphalt down to the finish line.

Bloody snakebit Tuesday! He had been looking at the blinking cursor; then at the keyboard, as he stroked a straggly bit of hair on his forearm that looked too tangled. He had taken a deep breath, then creased his brow, splayed his fingers an inch above the keyboard and softly curled them onto the keys again, and repeated the whole ball again, right before his phone threw the bad iron at him.

They had special people, trained in the deadly art of hounding a writer, set to work on you, he thought. *Get him to finish that book, don't rest until he gets that last word on the damned page.* Those were her orders, and she saw to it that they were carried out religiously.

"Yes, I am working on it. I should say I am almost done. It might not take more than another week," he had said on the phone, in the best business-like tone he could muster after being so rudely interrupted.

"Mr. Worthington, you sure? You just said it 'might' not take. So, it just might, if that's what you meant." She could have mothered a battalion of disciplined men.

"Uhm…" Max looked back into the room where he kept his computer. He scratched the side of his thigh distractedly, then cleared his throat as he found his thoughts again. "Miss Romana, I did not mean there was a foreseeable chance of delay…" (*Shit, he thought closing his eyes. Can't you just understand what I am saying, lady?*). "Make it 'it should not take more than a week' — that is what I meant. You could safely count on it." And then he'd smiled, hoping no hint of sarcasm had crept into his voice.

"Okay, Mr. Worthington. I wish you all the best. But you must understand we are bound by contract, and there are time-frames which need compliance."

It's a book, dammit, not your laundry with the wash-dial telling you when it gets done. Time-frame? Better start talking mind-frame, woman.

"I know. I thank you for the kind reminder," he said. "Now the sooner I get back to the manuscript, the better chance there is of me finishing it within, uhm, the stipulated time-frame."

There had been a minute of silence on the other side. It looked like she had smelled sarcasm in what he just said after all. "ALL RIGHT. I will get back to you later. Thank you. Do keep the changes recommended by the developmental department in mind as you finish your manuscript."

That had sealed any chances he may have had to move on with his writing on Tuesday.

Other thoughts had begun to crowd his head then. "I know I shouldn't have signed that deal with these people," he said aloud as he poured out a drink. "I might as well tell them I want out."

But it was true that these publishers were his best shot in a long time. They could pull strings in the market, and he should count himself lucky for landing a deal with them.

Yet, the thought about walking away from the deal nagged him. "Okay, now look, Mr. I'm-the-Next-Great-American-Author, quit your bellyachin' and get it done, you hack," he had mimicked the sound of the woman on the phone. "Your job right now is not worrying about whether or not you should be in a deal at all. Your job is sitting your ass in your chair and getting to the last line of that manuscript."

And at present, putting his phone down, he repeated, "Still I am not letting Liv die. So that means more time to figure out the ending, right?" He drew in a barrelful of breath and shouted away the quiet of his apartment. "*Right?*"

That is when his phone buzzed again. Breathless from the antic he'd just performed, he stared at the reminder blinking in the screen. "Shit!" he said. He'd forgotten the meeting today at the Redbrick office in Inman Park.

There was plenty of time to shave and bathe and horse around for some time before he drove the old model faded vermillion Fairlady 300ZX parked out front into the lush and leafy suburbs east of town. A half hour later, Max stepped out of the bathroom dripping and barely mulled over the choice of casual slacks to go with a slightly loose but sprightly looking flannel shirt. When his reflection looked out from the bulky cheval mirror that had survived down his mother's side of the family as a redoubtable heirloom, he looked ready to sit face to face with the publisher with an air of grounded certainty. Right, that's what he needed—a confidence that would linger in the air like a firm whisper, instead of shouting.

He set the coffee on the stove before walking out into the backyard to retrieve the newspaper. The one thing he had never been able to accustom himself to, digitally, was reading the news. He was aware that even in this Grant Park neighborhood, his was perhaps one of five residences passing which the paperboy still braked on his way down the street each morning. This area of town was supposed to cling to the old ways a little more perkily than the rest of the city.

As he sat munching on his toast, the mug of coffee steaming quietly beside him, he thought about how the arrangement on the breakfast table would not be so meager had it been one of Felicity's nights staying over.

The fresh ink faintly smudged his fingers as he unfolded the newspaper, and began to skim over the front page. The headlines were a predictable mix—politics, local news, and the latest developments from the wider world. The lead story was about the mayor's latest efforts to address the city's ever-growing traffic problem, a task as Herculean as it was thankless. The mayor had proposed yet another round of expansions to the MARTA transit system, met with the usual chorus of skepticism and cautious optimism. Max's lips curled into a thin smile; he'd seen these stories before—different names, same promises. Atlanta had its share of the nation's troubles, and the paper reflected that.

The story on the right caught his eye next—a piece on the Falcons' preseason hopes, their star quarterback recovering from an injury that had nearly derailed last year's campaign. The sportswriter's tone was cautiously hopeful, as if trying to will a winning season into existence. Max took a sip of his coffee, considering the team's chances. He wasn't much of a football man, but even he knew how desperate this city was for a championship.

As he flipped to the back page, the mood shifted with the stories becoming more intimate, closer to home. There was a small feature on a new farm-to-table restaurant opening in the Old Fourth Ward, the chef a local boy who'd trained in New York before coming home to bring a taste of Manhattan to the South. He thought about whether Felicity would want to try this place out.

Next to it, a column about the burgeoning film industry in Atlanta—the city had become the "Hollywood of the South," with more and more productions choosing its streets as their backdrop. A photo of a film crew setting up in front of the Fox Theatre caught his eye; it was a familiar sight these days.

The obituaries snuggled in one corner of the page, just as they always did—trying to be a sober reminder of the passage of time. Max tried to visualize how his own obituary might be phrased one day. He imagined the neat columns of type, with the words carefully chosen by some distant relative or hurried journalist.

Max Worthington, age 72, passed away quietly at his home in Atlanta, surrounded by an impressive collection of half-read books and an array of coffee mugs that never quite made it back to the kitchen. A man of few words but many opinions, Max was best known for his ability to solve crossword puzzles faster than anyone in his neighborhood, though his solutions were often met with puzzled looks. He spent his career in finance, where his greatest achievement was mastering the art of looking busy without actually doing much. In his later years, he dedicated himself to perfecting the art of procrastination, a skill he honed to such a degree that it's rumored he delayed his own death by sheer force of habit. He is survived by his cat, Max, who is expected to inherit the lion's share of his estate, which consists largely of the aforementioned coffee mugs and a collection of well-worn slippers. Funeral services will be held when convenient, though knowing Max, it will likely be later rather than sooner.

A soft chuckle broke the stillness of the kitchen. Not bad, was it? Even though he didn't have a cat and he'd never spent any worthwhile time of his life working in finance. And could he not come up with a better name for the cat than naming it after himself? Besides, while mashing together truth and jest, the description about his estate leaned wholly to the latter. Even so, who wouldn't want to be remembered with a smile?

Max got up and his thigh hit the edge of the table. The inadvertent jerk rocked the coffee mug and the next instant the remaining black liquid was soaking the side of the folded newspaper like a mechanic's rag.

He hurriedly righted the mug, picked up the paper and began to lightly slap it with one hand. Then he moved over to the kitchen counter and slapped the paper on the inside of the sink. Just as he was tracing a finger gingerly over the soggy, drooping dog's ear of a paper, something on one of the inside pages caught his attention.

Spreading the paper over the counter, he paused at a headline that proclaimed: **Exclusive Auction to Feature Rare and Historic Artworks.** The article was tucked away near the middle of the page. It was the kind of story easily overlooked by most readers, but something about it drew him in.

He leaned closer, skimming the details. The auction was set to take place on August 30 at one of the city's more prestigious galleries. It promised to be a significant event for collectors and enthusiasts alike. The list of items to be auctioned was impressive—antique furniture, rare books, and a selection of fine art. Each of the paintings boasted a history as varied as the brushstrokes that brought it to life.

It was the mention of a particular painting that gave Max pause. He read the column.

"Among the featured items is a painting titled *The Silent Watch,* an enigmatic work by an artist from the early 19th century. This piece, with its haunting portrayal of a lone figure standing guard over a windswept landscape, has remained in a private collection for decades, rarely seen by the public. The provenance of *The Silent Watch* suggests a storied past, and its appearance at auction is expected to draw considerable interest from collectors."

Max felt a faint tug at the edges of his memory; something about the name *The Silent Watch* niggled at him, but he couldn't quite place it. He reread the passage, trying to conjure up an image of the painting in his mind, but it eluded him, like a half-forgotten dream. The description of the lone figure in the windswept landscape seemed oddly familiar, yet distant, as if it belonged to a different time, a different life.

He left the paper where it was, turning away from the counter with a thoughtful frown. There was something about that news, something he should remember. But what was it? The answer hovered just out of reach, like the figure in the painting, standing watch over memories that refused to surface.

Max shot a glance inside the ceramic coffee pot to see it was empty and stepped into his study, looking to pick up his cross-body messenger bag. He noticed a photograph laying face-down under the corner of a shelf from where it had fallen. Stooping to pick it up in a hurry, he bumped his head against the shelf.

"Ouch," he said. "Sorry I put your picture in this place. Let's find you a cozier spot to settle in." Wryly massaging the side of his head, he looked at the woman looking out from the silver frame with a mellow affection stealing across his face. He stared at those intense eyes. He had known the woman behind those eyes for more than four years and she still didn't fail to stir the emotions that he sometimes suspected time had run aground.

All at once the light in the study dulled as the sun was momentarily blinded by clouds. The long shadow flitting across the walls took him to the place where doubt had dropped upon his heart like grapnel. *We always have the finest talent when it comes to being cruel to ourselves*, he thought.

He heard his own voice echo off the walls of his apartment. "You think it's so easy, don't you?" His words a yell, raw with frustration. "You can just pick up a camera, click a button, and there it is! A perfect shot...a perfect *moment*. But writing likes to give you a hard time wanting to have that perfect moment. It's messy..." Hearing the word *messy* rolling off the tip of his tongue had put an edge to his frustration. "Sometimes it feels like I'm bleeding onto the page." Gosh, the least he could do while trying to tell her about his feelings was let Hemingway get in the way.

Felicity had said nothing for a long time. Right when he thought the inscrutable expression on her face would make him walk out of the apartment, she'd spoken calmly. Yet he could feel the tenterhook jabbing at his own anger. "You think I don't struggle? That it's easy for me? You have no idea what it's like to look through that lens and wonder if you're seeing the world as it really is or just how you want it to be."

That's what he'd felt like: was he seeing their relationship like it really was or just how he wanted it to be.

Stung by her words he'd retreated and buried himself in his work, shutting her out. For days they barely spoke. The silence between them was like thick ice and he was sure he sometimes heard something ticking underneath it. But the ticking had faded and Felicity had eventually packed a bag. She went back to her own place but didn't stay away long.

A week later, she'd shown up at his door. "I can't do this without you," she'd simply said, and Max had known then that he couldn't do it without her either. His last book had tanked, and the pressure of trying to produce something new, something better, was nearly driving him mad. Felicity was there to offer her support, but he had felt suffocated. The pain of bearing the weight of her expectations, or worse, her pity could knock his confidence into a small deadly space.

But she challenged him, pushed him to dig deeper, even when it hurt. Especially when it hurt. He knew that the work he could be most proud of had come from those moments when she'd refused to let him take the easy way out.

Max sauntered over to another shelf with a much wider ledge and placed the photograph inside a broad gap between a severely read and reread Faulkner and a half-finished Jeffrey Archer.

Felicity had always possessed a certain magnetism. The olive in her complection was Italian and the hint of blue in her eyes was Irish. She often wore the waves of her hair loose around her shoulders. Her sharp features were softened only by the curve of her lips and the small, almost imperceptible dimple that flashed with her smile. She was older than him by a few years, and that added to her allure. He enjoyed being around a woman who had experienced a bit more of the world than he had.

Now, as he looked at her picture, he couldn't imagine what his life would have been like without Felicity. She brought a sense of order where forces threatened to spiral him out of control. Her clothes neatly folded in the drawers, her older camera gear organized with military precision, even the way she always remembered to water the plants— things he would never have bothered with on his own. Felicity wasn't here now, but she was never really gone. Life with Felicity was far from perfect, but it was real.

A small smile tugged at his lips as Max traced the edge of the photo frame with his finger. His phone buzzed with a message from Liam Corcoran at Redbrick. He scooped up his bag and answered the message on his way out.

Standing by his car with the keys jangling in his hand, Max absorbed a little of the Atlanta sun beating down on the asphalt. Perhaps today was going to be another August scorcher. He was about to climb into his Nissan when a yelp from across the street caught his attention.

A girl, no more than eight, had tumbled off her bike. Max had seen her around the neighborhood. Her pigtails were askew, and she was struggling to get up. Max didn't hesitate. His loafers slapped against the pavement as he sprinted across the street.

"You okay there, kiddo?" Max said as he held out a hand to help her to her feet.

The girl sniffled, brushing gravel from her palms. "I think so. Thanks, mister."

"What's your name?"

"Mackenzie," she mumbled.

"Well, Mackenzie, looks like you took quite a spill. How about we get that bike of yours upright?"

As Max righted the small purple bicycle, Mackenzie's eyes widened. "My mom's gonna kill me. Look at my new shorts!"

Max chuckled. "Don't worry. A little dirt never hurt anyone. You just be more careful next time, alright?"

Mackenzie nodded as a smile wobbled across her little mouth. Max gave her a reassuring pat on the shoulder and turned to head back to his car. He was about to step off the curb when a sleek black Ford cruised by, forcing him to pause.

The driver's face snagged Max's attention like a fishhook. Close-cropped salt-and-pepper hair, a hawk-like nose, and eyes hidden behind mirrored aviators. A thin scar reached from the temple almost down to his chin, like some cruel signature carved by fate.

Max's brow furrowed. He knew that face. But from where? A hotel lobby? Some upscale restaurant? The nagging feeling of familiarity itched at the back of his mind as the car glided past.

Shaking off the odd sensation, Max crossed back toward his front porch and slid into the driver's seat. The leather was warm against his back as he backed out onto the street and slowly pulled away. His thoughts drifted to the drive up to Inman Park, all the while that stranger's face lingering in his mind's rearview mirror.

CHAPTER II

David Hollister reclined in his leather chair, feet propped on the mahogany desk that dominated his penthouse office. Floor-to-ceiling windows offered a panoramic view of Atlanta's skyline; synchronous with the concrete testament to his real estate empire. He flipped idly through a hardcover novel, sneering at the author photo on the back flap.

"Max fucking Worthington," he muttered, tossing the book aside. It slid across the polished wood, nearly toppling a crystal tumbler of bourbon. "Writing pretty words while I build empires. What a waste."

A knock at the door interrupted his brooding. "Come in," he barked.

His assistant, a rail-thin man with darting eyes, entered. "Mr. Hollister, the Governor's on line one."

David's lips curled into a predatory smile. "About time." He snatched up the phone. "Governor! How's the family?"

As he spoke, David's free hand toyed with a letter opener, its blade glinting in the afternoon sun. The conversation was brief, peppered with insider jokes and thinly veiled threats.

"Of course, I understand the delicacy of the situation," David purred into the phone. "But let's not forget who financed your last campaign. I'm sure we can come to an arrangement that benefits us both."

When he hung up, his eyes gleamed with satisfaction.

"Cancel my dinner plans," he told his assistant. "Seems I'll be dining at the Governor's mansion tonight."

The assistant hesitated. "Sir, about the zoning issue in Buckhead…"

David waved a dismissive hand. "Consider it handled. The right palms have been greased."

"But sir, the environmental impa—"

"Did I stutter?" David's voice turned to ice. "Handle it. Or I'll find someone who can."

The assistant paled. "Yes, Mr. Hollister. Right away."

Alone again, David swiveled to face the window. His reflection stared back at him: silver-streaked hair, deep-set eyes, cold and calculating. But it was the scar that drew the eye; a thin, jagged line that ran from under his chin along his right jawline, curving to join with the corner of his mouth. It was like a permanent sneer etched into his skin; a memento from his wilder days, when he'd do anything for a thrill, or a profit. His features were handsome in a severe way. They could lend his most charming grin a feral shadow, as if there was a different face comfortably tucked behind what met the eye.

He thought back to his first real estate deal, how he'd leveraged his parents' fortune and connections to muscle out the competition. It had been ruthless, bordering on illegal, but it had worked. That was all that mattered in the end.

"You've come a long way, Davey boy," he murmured to his reflection. "From trust fund brat to king of the city."

His gaze drifted to a framed photo on his desk. Two families posed together at some long-ago garden party. The

Hollisters and the Worthingtons, all smiles and summer whites. David's hand clenched involuntarily.

The rift had started small. A misunderstanding over property lines, a perceived slight at a charity gala. But it had festered, growing into a chasm of hatred that spanned generations.

"Dad," David addressed the younger version of his father in the photo. "You were always too weak to do anything about it. But I'm not weak."

He picked up Max's novel again, flipping it open to a random page. The words blurred as memories surfaced. Hushed conversations, shady deals in back alleys, the occasional body that needed to disappear. Atlanta's glittering facade hid a rotten core, and David had his fingers in all of it.

"I built this city," he murmured, "and I'll be damned if I let a Worthington tear it down."

He hurled the book across the room. It hit the wall with a satisfying thud, pages fluttering.

David reached for his phone again, punching in a number from memory. "It's me," he said when the line connected. "I need you to dig up everything you can on Max Worthington. And I mean everything. Tax records, medical history, what kind of fucking toothpaste he uses. I want to know it all."

He paused, listening to the voice on the other end. "Price is no object. Just get it done."

As he hung up, David allowed himself a cold smile. Max Worthington might be the darling of the literary world, but David would make sure his next bestseller was a tragedy— his own.

The intercom buzzed. "Mr. Hollister? Your 3 o'clock is here. Mr. Bridges."

David straightened his tie, schooling his features into a mask of affable charm. "Send him in."

The door opened, and a portly man in an expensive suit entered. "David! Good to see you, my boy."

"Senator," David greeted, shaking his hand firmly. "Always a pleasure. Drink?"

As he poured two glasses of bourbon, David's mind raced with possibilities. Every connection, every favor owed, every dirty secret; all weapons in his arsenal against the Worthingtons.

"To progress," he toasted, raising his glass.

The Senator clinked glasses, oblivious to the storm brewing behind David's eyes. "To progress."

As they settled into their meeting, David's gaze flickered to Max's discarded novel. Soon, he thought. Soon, I'll write your coda, Max. And it won't be a happy one.

CHAPTER III

Max Worthington stepped out of the elevator onto the 7th floor of the Redbrick Editions building in Inman Park, Atlanta. The smell of fresh paint and new carpet assaulted his nostrils, a stark reminder that the publishing house had only recently moved into these swanky new digs. He adjusted the collar of his shirt, more out of habit than necessity, and approached the reception desk.

Behind it sat a woman who looked like she'd stepped out of a 1950s librarian catalog. Horn-rimmed glasses perched on a thin nose, mousy brown hair pulled back so tight it looked painful, and a high-collared blouse that screamed: I've never had fun in my life. Boy what it would be like if she said yes to someone taking her for a racy joyride.

"Hello, Mr. Worthington. May I help you?" Her voice was as colorless as her appearance.

Max leaned on the desk, flashing his most charming smile. "I have an appointment with Liam Corcoran."

She blinked at him, unimpressed. "One moment, please."

As she picked up the phone, Max found himself wondering what she'd look like with her hair down, maybe in something less…restrictive. There was something about her face that said she had been in the habit of keeping a tight lid on hidden talents. He shook his head, banishing the thought. Getting involved with publishing staff was a recipe for disaster, no matter how intriguing the package.

"Mr. Liam will see you now. Third door on the right."

Max nodded his thanks and headed down the hallway. He couldn't shake the feeling that her eyes were boring into his back as he walked away. Brilliant front desk coverup, for sure.

Liam Corcoran's office was a testament to old money trying to look modern. Sleek furniture clashed with antique bookshelves, and a state-of-the-art computer sat next to an unused vintage typewriter. The man himself was a similar study in contrasts: silver hair and deep laugh lines framed sharp eyes that rarely missed anything.

"Max, you old son of a bitch!" Liam boomed, rising from behind his desk. "Get in here and sit down."

Max grinned, clasping Liam's hand in a firm shake before settling into one of the plush chairs facing the desk. "Liam. Place looks good. How's the view treating you?"

Liam waved a dismissive hand. "Can't complain. Beats staring at a brick wall all day. But enough small talk. Where's my goddamn book?"

And there it was. Max's smile faltered for a moment before he recovered. "It's coming along. Just need to iron out a few kinks in the plot, you know how it is."

"Bullshit," Liam said, but there was no real heat behind it. He'd known Max too long for that. "You haven't written a word, have you?"

Max spread his hands in a gesture of mock surrender. "You got me."

The man behind the desk bunched up an exultant fist. "Come on, you got the end in sight. Nothing to hold you back now."

Max scratched the jutted lower lip of his parted mouth. "But I've been thinking about it. A lot."

"What happened after the last talk we had about your lead character…uhm, what's her name? Yeah! Liv."

Max gave his head a slow, deliberate shake. "If I kill her now, it will have consequences when I sit down to write the sequel. Besides, it's too easy."

"We'll figure a way to bring her back to life if we need to." Holding his palms outward, Liam slowly moved them apart like he was introducing a late night special show to an auditorium filled with shadowy, expectant faces. "Unlike what everyone assumed after the conclusion of the last story, Liv Hargison did not meet her fate. She is back, and this time she's sharp as a wolf on the scent of her prey."

"Yes, I'm happy that Redbrick had its last big hit with a paranormal romance."

"Kill her, Max. Make it easy on yourself."

"Too much of a cheap shot, if you ask me."

Liam leaned back in his chair, studying Max with those piercing eyes. "You know, I remember when you first walked into my office. Fresh out of college, full of piss and vinegar, waving that manuscript around like it was the second coming of Hemingway."

"And you told me it was derivative crap," Max said, chuckling at the memory.

"It was," Liam agreed. "But there was something there. A spark. That's why I took a chance on you after starting Redbrick."

Max nodded, suddenly serious. "I know, Liam. And I appreciate it. I really do."

"Then show me," Liam said, leaning forward. "You've got talent, kid. Real talent. But talent without discipline is worse than useless. It's a goddamn tragedy."

Max shifted uncomfortably in his seat. He'd heard this speech before, or variations of it, from teachers, agents, and now publishers. But it hit different coming from Liam.

"I know I'm behind," Max admitted. "But I've got ideas. Big ideas. I just need a little more time to—"

"Time?" Corcoran interrupted, his voice rising. "Time is the one thing we don't have, Max. The deadline's in six weeks. Six weeks to get the hardback version out there. And you haven't written a single fucking word?"

Max opened his mouth to protest, but Corcoran held up a hand, silencing him.

"No, don't give me excuses. I've heard 'em all before. Writer's block, personal issues, Mercury in retrograde—it's all bullshit. You know what the difference is between a professional writer and an amateur? Professionals write. Even when they don't feel like it. Especially when they don't feel like it."

Liam's words stung, but Max knew he was right. He'd been coasting on his early success for too long, relying on his natural talent and charm to smooth over the gaps in his work ethic. But charm only got you so far in this business.

"You're right," Max said quietly. "I've been slacking. But I promise you, Liam, I'll have something for you. Soon."

Liam's expression softened slightly. "I hope so, kid. For both our sakes. This industry's changing. It's not like the old days when we could nurse a writer along for years, waiting for their magnum opus. We need product, and we need it now."

Max nodded, feeling the weight of expectation settle on his shoulders. He was about to respond when something on Liam's desk caught his eye. A newspaper, folded open to show an advertisement for an upcoming auction.

There was something familiar about one of the items pictured. A painting. Max leaned forward, squinting at the image.

"What's got you so interested?" Liam asked, following Max's gaze.

"That painting," Max said, pointing. "I could swear I've seen it before."

Liam picked up the paper, glancing at the advert. "This old thing? It's part of the Millbrook estate sale. Guy was a big collector, died without heirs. Whole collection's going up for auction in about two weeks."

But Max was barely listening. His mind was racing, trying to place where he'd seen that painting before. Then it hit him like a thunderbolt.

"Holy shit," he breathed.

"What?" Liam asked, alarmed by the sudden change in Max's demeanor.

Max stood up abruptly, snatching the newspaper from Liam's hands. "I've got to go. I'm sorry, Liam, but this is important. I'll call you later, okay?"

Before Liam could respond, Max was out the door. He barely noticed the librarian-like secretary's startled look as he rushed past her to the elevator. His mind was focused on one thing: getting home as fast as possible. The painting in the auction ad. It was identical to the one his parents had owned. The one that should be safely tucked away in the safe in his garden apartment. But if that was true, how could it be up for auction?

As the elevator descended, Max's mind raced through possibilities, each more unsettling than the last. Was he simply losing his mind, seeing connections where none existed?

He burst out of the building onto the bustling streets of Inman Park, barely noticing the curious glances from passersby. His car was parked a block away, and he set off at a brisk pace, weaving through the lunchtime crowd. Atlanta in August could be a sweltering mess, and by the time Max reached his car, his shirt was sticking to his back. He cranked the AC as soon as he got in, but the discomfort from the weather was the least of his worries.

CHAPTER IV

The man sat in his nondescript sedan, parked half a block away from Max Worthington's garden apartment in Grant Park. The afternoon sun cast long shadows across the tree-lined street, providing an extra layer of concealment.

He checked his watch and it showed 2:17 p.m. Perfect. Max wouldn't be back until four hours later, and even then he'd be stuck in Atlanta's notorious rush hour traffic for at least another hour, probably cursing the day he decided to live in Grant Park and visit for work in Midtown. That gave plenty of time for the job. Still, that didn't mean he shouldn't make it as soon as he could.

He reached into the glove compartment and pulled out a pair of thin, supple leather gloves. As he slipped them on, he couldn't help but marvel at how easy this was all turning out to be. People like this writer lived in a bubble of perceived security. They never imagined that someone might be plotting to take what was theirs.

The man stepped out of the car with a canvas messenger bag slung over his shoulder. To any casual observer, he looked like just another resident probably coming home from work. He strolled down the sidewalk, eyes forward, posture relaxed. Nothing to see here, folks.

As he approached Max's building, he felt the familiar surge of adrenaline, the heightened awareness that came with the job. Every sense was on high alert, scanning for potential threats or complications. But the street was quiet. A couple of kids were playing basketball farther down the block. Their shouts and the rhythmic bounces of the ball provided a mundane soundtrack to the stranger's decidedly non-mundane activities.

He climbed the steps to Max's front door, fishing a key out of his pocket as he went. Taking a moment before he reached the threshold, he gave a cheery wave at the mechanical eye trained on the porch.

"Can't see what's really there, can you?" he said to the camera.

The key slid into the lock smoothly, turning without a hint of resistance. The man allowed himself a small smile. The door swung open silently. The hinges didn't squeak just as the intruder had expected. Max Worthington had only oiled them last week.

The intruder stepped inside and closed the door behind him. The cool air of the apartment washed over his face, a stark contrast to the muggy Atlanta heat outside. He stood still for a moment, letting his eyes adjust to the dimmer light, listening for any unexpected sounds. The apartment was silent as a tomb. Only the subdued whir of the second camera as it changed angles to look at him. The man smiled up at it and said, "Hello, Max. I'm here."

He moved through the space with ease, his footsteps muffled by the plush carpet. The layout was exactly as had been described — living room to the left, kitchen straight ahead, bedroom and study to the right. Silently, he headed for the study and as he entered, his eyes immediately locked onto the bookcase on the far wall. It looked ordinary enough

— rows of hardbacks and paperbacks, a few framed photos, some random knick-knacks. But this man knew better.

He approached the bookcase, running his gloved fingers along the spines of the books on the third shelf from the bottom. When he reached *Shall We Tell the President?* he paused. This was it. The trigger for the hidden mechanism. He pulled the book towards him, feeling a slight resistance before hearing a soft click. The entire right side of the bookcase swung outward an inch or two. He grinned. Some people really were predictable. With a gentle tug, the stranger opened the false panel fully, revealing the safe nestled in the wall behind. It was a decent model; not top-of-the-line that you'd need a stethoscope to crack.

Good thing he had come prepared.

He pressed his ear against the cool metal of the safe door, fingers resting lightly on the dial. Slowly, deliberately, he began to turn it, listening intently for the telltale clicks that would betray the combination. It was a skill that called for patience and precision and he'd had ample of chances in life to get nimble at it. The first number came easily. The second took a bit more finesse, but soon enough, 7 fell into place. Third one followed, then 2, and finally, 5.

With each number, the man, his breath held artfully still, felt a small thrill of satisfaction. This was what he lived for — the challenge, the risk, the sheer exhilaration of doing what most people thought impossible. That's why he had taken on the job himself instead of charging a surrogate.

As he reached the final digit, he heard a soft, definitive click. A smile tugged at the corners of his mouth. Bingo.

With a gentle pull, the safe door swung open to reveal its contents. The trespasser allowed himself a moment of quiet triumph. Another lock picked, another barrier overcome. It was almost too easy, even after all this time.

The interloper's heart rate picked up as he peered inside. There it was, wrapped in protective cloth, just where it was supposed to be. He reached in and carefully extracted the object before setting it gently on the desk nearby. From his messenger bag, he produced a nearly identical package — same size, same protective wrapping. He placed it inside the safe, positioning it exactly as the previous one had been.

Next, the man turned his attention to the rest of the safe's contents. He rifled through the documents and quickly located the ownership papers. He pocketed these, along with a few other official-looking documents. Better to take too much than too little.

Now came the moment of truth. The stranger unwrapped the original painting, his breath catching slightly as the still vibrant colors came into view. It was beautiful, no doubt about it. More importantly, it was valuable. To the right buyer, at least. He examined it closely, checking for any signs of damage or wear. Finding none, he carefully re-wrapped it and placed it in his messenger bag.

A quick glance at his watch. 3:15 p.m. Still plenty of time, but no reason to dawdle.

He closed the safe, spun the dial, and swung the false panel back into place. He made sure *Shall We Tell the President?* was positioned exactly as it had been before. Then he took a step back, surveying the room.

Everything looked undisturbed. Perfect.

The stranger retraced his steps through the garden apartment, pausing at the front door to listen for any activity outside. Hearing nothing alarming, he slipped out, and locked the door behind him.

The walk back to his car felt longer somehow, the weight of the painting in his bag seeming to grow with each step. But the man's outward demeanor remained calm and casual, so he'd strike anyone looking at him as just another guy heading home. The next instant he heard tires screeching to a halt. He almost flew off his feet as his leg knocked hard into the front fender of a car. Quickly shooting out a hand to keep himself from barreling over the vehicle's hood, he managed to right himself before the weight of the messenger bag could swat him to the ground. Snapping his head away from whoever was behind the wheel, he keeled away from the headlights' glare. *No running,* he mentally reminded himself as he ignored the words of the agitated driver, who was driving with the brights on in broad daylight.

As he slid into the driver's seat of his sedan, he allowed himself a moment of satisfaction. In and out in less than an hour. No alarms, no surprises, no complications, except the boneheaded chump who'd nearly run him over. But he was okay. It was almost too easy.

He started the engine and pulled away from the curb, to quickly merge into the late afternoon traffic. As he drove, his mind wandered to the next steps. The buyer was already lined up. Some rich tech bro with more money than taste, eager to impress his friends with a piece of "real art". The ownership papers would seal the deal, providing a veneer of legitimacy to the whole transaction. His phone buzzed. He glanced at it, seeing a text from an unknown number.

"Package secure?"

He smiled. Right on schedule.

"All good," he texted back. "Delivery tomorrow as planned."

He tossed the phone onto the passenger seat and focused on driving. No sense in taking unnecessary risks now, not when everything was going so smoothly.

Driving through the familiar streets the man couldn't help but feel a twinge of…what was it? Not quite regret. He'd left that emotion behind a long time ago. But something adjacent to it. A faint echo of the person he might have been, in another life. He shook away the thought. This was who he was now: Art thief extraordinaire, besides other impressive vitae in his repertoire of tricks; most of which came off without any hitches when required. The man who could steal your most prized possession right out from under your nose, and leave you none the wiser.

Besides, it wasn't like Max Worthington would miss the painting. Not really. To him, it was just a memento, a relic of his dead parents. He probably hadn't looked at the thing in years.

No, the trespasser was doing him a favor, really. By the time Max realized the painting was gone — if he ever did — the burglar would be long gone.

As he pulled onto the highway, the stranger allowed himself a small chuckle. Poor Max. The guy had no idea what was coming his way. But then again, that was the nature of the game. There were players, and there were marks. And Max Worthington? He was definitely a mark. The Atlanta skyline loomed in the rearview mirror, a glittering monument to ambition and greed. It was a city of strivers and climbers; everyone looking for their big break, their chance to make it to the top. Well, this man had had found his. It might not be legal, might not be moral, but it was his. And he was damn good at it.

He merged into the fast lane, pushing the sedan to its limits. The sooner he got the painting secured, the better. There was still work to be done; calls to make, arrangements to finalize. The heist might be over, but the job wasn't finished. Not by a long shot. He moved through the city like a wolf in the forest. The instinct guiding him was raw, primal, and unerring.

As the city receded behind him, the man's mind drifted to his source. They had played their part perfectly, feeding him the information he needed bit by bit. Everything had carefully been filed away for future use. The girl he was seeing was caught up in something she didn't understand. But collateral damage was part of the price of doing business in his world. You couldn't make an omelette without breaking a few eggs, as the saying went. And this omelette? It was going to set him up for life.

The safe house slowly came into view. It was an unremarkable suburban home, the kind you'd drive past a thousand times without ever really noticing. The sedan pulled into the garage, and the door rolled down behind him with a reassuring finality. He sat in the car for a moment, hands still on the wheel, breathing deeply. The adrenaline was starting to wear off, leaving behind a bone-deep weariness. But there was no time to rest, not yet.

He grabbed his bag and headed inside. The house was sparsely furnished, just the basics needed for a short stay. He made his way to the bedroom, where a small safe was bolted to the floor of the closet. With practiced movements, he opened the safe and carefully placed the painting inside. The ownership documents went in too, along with the other papers he'd taken from Max's safe. Better to keep everything together.

As he closed the safe, the man caught a glimpse of himself in the mirror hanging on the closet door. He looked ordinary. Just another middle-aged guy, a little worse for wear maybe, but nothing special. Nothing that would make you look twice if you passed him on the street.

And that, he knew, was his greatest asset. In his line of work, being forgettable was a virtue. Now the mask could come off.

He leaned closer to the mirror, fingers finding the nearly invisible seam along his hairline. Deftly, he began to peel away the high-tech silicone mask. It was a miracle of modern technology that could alter a person's features so subtly, so completely, that even a trained observer would be hard-pressed to spot the deception. Anonymity was more than just a virtue. It was survival.

As he removed the gossamer-thin material, it was as if years melted away from his face. The nondescript, forgettable features gave way to something altogether more striking. The man in the mirror now was David Hollister in the flesh; his true visage a stark contrast to the everyman disguise he'd worn moments before. Deep-set eyes, cold and calculating, stared back at him from the reflection. They were the eyes of a predator, always watching, always assessing.

David ran a hand over his face, feeling the familiar contours. The mask was a necessary tool, but there was always a sense of relief when he could shed it, could be himself again; for better or worse.

He carefully folded the silicone mask and tucked it away in a hidden compartment of his bag. In the wrong hands, it could be incriminating evidence. In his, it was nothing less than a license to disappear, to become anyone he needed to be. With one last glance at his true face in the mirror, David turned away.

He walked back to the living room, collapsing onto the worn sofa with a sigh. One last thing to do before he could call it a night. He pulled out his phone and dialed a number from memory.

It rang twice before a gruff voice answered. "Yeah?"

"It's done," David said simply.

A pause, then: "Any complications?"

"Smooth as silk. Got the painting and the papers. We're good to go."

Another pause, longer this time. David could almost hear the gears turning on the other end of the line. "Alright," the voice said finally. "Stick to the plan. I'll be in touch."

The line went dead. David tossed the phone onto the coffee table and leaned back, closing his eyes. He would be in the wind before anyone knew what had happened. It was a good plan. A solid plan. The kind of plan that had served him well over the years; allowing him to stay one step ahead of the law, always just out of reach.

As he sat there in the quiet of the safe house, a nagging doubt began to creep in. Something about this job felt different. Off, somehow. Maybe it was the personal connection. He'd never stolen from someone he knew before, even tangentially. Or maybe it was something else, something he couldn't quite put his finger on. He shook his head, trying to dispel the unease. It was just nerves, he told himself. Post-job jitters. Nothing to worry about.

CHAPTER V

As he drove back to his place in Grant Park, Max's mind wandered back to the painting. He remembered the day his parents had brought it home, some pretentious modern surrealist art piece that his teenage self had scoffed at. But over the years, it had grown on him. After their death, he couldn't bear to part with it, even though he knew it was probably worth a small fortune.

Traffic on the connector was unusually dense. Max drummed his fingers on the steering wheel, frustration mounting with each passing minute. He considered calling his friend at the Atlanta PD, but what would he say? *Hey, I think someone might have stolen a painting from my safe, but I'm not sure, and I haven't actually checked yet?*

No, he needed to see for himself first.

Finally, after what felt like hours but was probably only thirty minutes, Max pulled into his street. As soon as he did, he instinctively geared down, and the next moment his foot was thrusting into the brake pedal. "Hey, you almost ended up on my hood!" Max called out as the man with the portly messenger bag stooped his head and quietly bailed.

Nosing into his driveway, Max was out of the car before the engine had fully died, fumbling with his keys as he approached the front door.

Cool and quiet the way he left it, the house was a stark contrast to the chaos swirling in his head. Max made a beeline for the study, where the safe was hidden behind a false panel in one of the bookcases. His hands shook slightly as he clicked the combination on the dial. 3-7-9-2-5. The same as always. The safe door swung open with a soft hiss.

Max held his breath as he reached inside, pushing aside stacks of documents and a small jewelry box. His fingers brushed against the familiar texture of canvas wrapped in protective cloth. Relief washed over him as he pulled the painting out. It was here. Safe and sound. He unwrapped it carefully, studying the swirls of color that pulled the mind into a deeply unsettling place. His fingers traced the edges of the worn frame. *The Silent Watch* depicted a scene that had always daunted and perplexed him, yet he couldn't look away. The desolate landscape stretched under a brooding sky, where the windswept grass whispered a secret and at the center of this bleakness stood the figure. A young boy, no older than ten perhaps, dressed in the tattered garments of a bygone era. His clothes, a mix of browns and grays, hinted at a time of hardship, perhaps a century past. The boy's expression was unreadable. That face was a mask of stoic determination belying youth. He stood with an old wooden staff, worn smooth from use, planted firmly in the ground. Eyes, shadowed beneath a ragged cap, seemed to follow the viewer, conveying a watchfulness that transcended the canvas. Though the wind whipped around the lone figure, rustling his clothes and tousling his hair, the boy remained unmoved. It looked like he was rooted to the earth itself. The haunting loneliness…the eternal vigil over a world that had forgotten him…yet, there was something in the boy's stance.

It was something that wasn't afraid of standing up to time and fate.

But as Max stared at it, a new worry began to gnaw at him. If this was here, then what was the painting in the auction? A copy? But who would copy such an obscure piece of art?

Max rewrapped the painting and placed it back in the safe, his mind buzzing with questions. He needed answers, and he knew just where to start looking. Pulling out his phone, he dialed a number he hadn't used in years. It rang three times before a gruff voice answered. "Pearson Auction House, this is Tom speaking."

Max took a deep breath. "Tom, it's Max Worthington. I need a favor."

There was a pause on the other end of the line. "Max? Jesus, it's been what, three years?"

"At least," Max agreed. "Listen, I saw an ad for the Millbrook estate auction. There's a painting I need information on."

He could almost hear Tom's frown through the phone. "You know I can't give out details on consignors, Max. That's confidential information."

"I'm not asking for names," Max said quickly. "Just… provenance. Where did this painting come from? When did Millbrook acquire it?"

Another pause. "This isn't like you, Max. What's going on?"

Max hesitated. How much should he reveal? "It's complicated, Tom. But I think…I think there might be some funny business going on with this painting. Maybe a forgery, maybe something worse."

Tom sighed heavily. "Jesus, Max. You always did know how to make things interesting. Alright, I'll see what I can dig up. But I'm not promising anything, you hear me?"

"That's all I'm asking," Max said, relief evident in his voice. "Thanks, Tom. I owe you one."

"You owe me several," Tom grumbled. "I'll call you back when I have something."

The line went dead, and Max slumped back in his chair. He glanced at the safe, then at the crumpled newspaper still clutched in the other hand.

Something wasn't adding up, and Max had a sinking feeling that this was just the tip of the iceberg. His parents had never been art collectors in the true sense of the word. Where had they gotten that painting? And why did someone else have an identical one?

As he sat there, staring at the auction ad, a new thought occurred to him. Maybe this was it. The story he'd been struggling to write. A mystery wrapped in family secrets and high-stakes art deals.

Max reached for his laptop, fingers hovering over the keys. For the first time in months, words began to flow. The cursor blinked, then moved, and a rudimentary picture of intrigue and deception began to unfold on the blank page.

In the back of his mind, a small voice reminded him of Liam's warning. Six weeks. The deadline loomed large, but for once, Max wasn't worried. He had a feeling this story was going to write itself. As the afternoon light faded into evening, Max barely noticed the time. He was lost in the world he was creating, a world where nothing was as it seemed and every stroke of the sentence hid a secret.

The shrill ring of his phone startled him out of his writing trance. Max glanced at the clock, surprised to see that hours had passed. He grabbed the phone, heart racing when he saw Tom's number on the display.

"Tom? What did you find out?"

There was a long pause before Tom's voice came through. It was low and serious. "Max, you need to be careful. This painting…there's something not right about it. The provenance is a mess, full of gaps and contradictions. And the last recorded owner before Millbrook? He disappeared three years ago. Never found."

Max felt a chill run down the side of his body. "What are you saying, Tom?"

"I'm saying watch your back," Tom said. "Whatever you're mixed up in, it's bigger than some art world shenanigans. This has the vibe of something dangerous."

As Max hung up the phone, his eyes drifted back to the safe where his parents' painting lay hidden. What had they gotten him into? And more importantly, what was he going to do about it?

He spent the next five minutes pacing, running his hands through his hair, trying to make sense of what Tom had just told him. But none of it added up. He stood in the dim light of his living room, staring at the floor. Moving back to the spot in the bookcase, his hands were already starting to shake. The safe was still half-open. Its heavy steel door yawned wide as if mocking him. He pulled out the painting and propped it gently against the couch, careful not to let the frame brush against the edges. *The Silent Watch* glinted in the warm glow from the lamp.

Max stood there for a moment, staring at it. The boy in the painting, pale-faced, tattered clothes, his staff planted into the earth. The windswept landscape was so bleak it made you shiver. Max had grown up hearing his parents talk about it as if it were some rare treasure. It was part of his family, part of his past.

His finger traced the bottom of the frame, as if some hidden clue would reveal itself. "This can't be a fake," he muttered under his breath. "No way."

He turned it around and scanned the back, his eyes flicking over the old, yellowed canvas and the faded ink stamps. The gallery logo, the date, everything seemed in order. But Tom wouldn't have said anything unless he was sure. Max knew that about him. If Tom was spooked, there was a reason for it.

"Dammit," Max sighed, raking his fingers over his scalp. "How the hell did I get here?"

He dropped into the nearest chair, staring blankly at the painting. The room was too quiet, save for the low hum of the fridge in the kitchen. It was surreal, the whole thing. One minute, he was juggling deadlines and manuscript rewrites; the next, he was mixed up in some mystery about a painting he thought had been nothing more than a family heirloom. He tapped his knuckles on the table, a soft rhythm that kept up with the pulse in his temples.

"Let's see it, then." He leaned closer and studied the frame again. There had to be something off, something subtle. He pulled his phone out and snapped a picture, wanting to send it over to Tom. Maybe there was something the old friend hadn't mentioned yet, some detail he missed in the rush of warning Max. But he decided against sending the picture to his friend for now. Instead, he slouched back. Tom's words kept replaying. 'Bigger than some art world shenanigans.' A knot was forming in his center. He didn't need this. Not now, with the deadline for his next book looming. He was supposed to be typing out chapters, not unraveling mysteries tied to his parents' past.

"Alright," he said out loud, almost daring himself to dig deeper. "Let's figure this out." He wasn't about to be one of those guys who just let a mystery hang over their heads.

Max grabbed the edge of the frame and inspected it more closely. Maybe there was a discrepancy in the brushwork, or something with the colors that didn't match the original. His mom had drummed into him a love for fine art, but hell if he knew the technical aspects behind it all. That was what experts were for. He flipped it back over and ran his hands over the canvas surface, feeling for any unusual bumps or irregularities. It felt perfect.

It didn't make sense. How could this be a fake? How could the art world's best appraisers not catch it? His parents had claimed it to be a priceless artifact. And he had kept it tucked into the safe for years. And maybe it had been priceless, until someone swapped it. Max's chest tightened.

He stood up suddenly and walked over to the window. The evening shadows had grown longer, stretching across the street. His eyes scanned the neighborhood as if the answers might be waiting out there, beneath the oak trees swaying gently in the humid air. There wasn't a soul around, just the occasional distant sound of a car rolling past.

"Goddamn painting's gonna drive me nuts." He muttered the words like a prayer, hoping some divine intervention would drop an answer into his lap.

Then like a match flaring in the haze, the memory struck him. The man who had almost tumbled on top of the Fairlady's hood when he turned the corner of his street. The bag under the stranger's arm did look like it held something large and solid, didn't it?

"Jesus Christ," Max said.

Turning back to the room, Max knew one thing for sure: whatever had just fallen into his lap wasn't going to let him go without a fight. *The Silent Watch* might have been more than just a painting to his parents—it could be the key to something far darker than he'd imagined.

And he wasn't sure he was ready for where that key might take him. Or was he?

One thing was certain: his deadline with Liam Corcoran was the least of his worries now. Max Worthington had stumbled into a mystery that threatened to upend his mundane life. And he had an elusive but discreetly approaching feeling that solving it might just cost him what he was ready to shell out.

CHAPTER VI

David Hollister stood at the window of his penthouse suite, gazing out at the sprawling city skyline. The setting sun cast a golden glow across the city, but David's mind was far from the picturesque view. His fingers drummed an impatient rhythm on the crystal tumbler in his hand, the amber liquid within barely disturbed by the motion.

A soft knock at the door broke his reverie. "Come in," he called, not bothering to turn around.

The door opened, and the crisp click of heels on hardwood announced the arrival of his secretary, Evelyn. "Mr. Hollister, I have the final details from Sotheby's regarding the auction."

David took a slow sip of his drink before turning to face her. Evelyn stood poised, tablet in hand, her expression neutral but expectant. He gestured for her to continue.

"They've completed the preliminary authentication process for The Silent Watch. All the paperwork checks out, and they're moving forward with the next steps."

A thin smile crossed David's face. "Excellent. And the publicity?"

Evelyn swiped through her tablet. "As per your instructions, we've kept it low-key. Just enough to attract the right bidders without causing a stir."

"Good, good," David murmured, turning back to the window. "The last thing we need is some art world frenzy drawing unwanted attention."

"There is one thing, sir," Evelyn added, a note of hesitation in her voice.

David's shoulders tensed. "What is it?"

"Sotheby's is pushing for a more...comprehensive marketing strategy. They believe the painting could fetch a significantly higher price with broader exposure."

David's grip tightened on his glass. "No," he said firmly. "We stick to the plan. Too much publicity and someone might start asking the wrong questions. We need this to be clean, quick, and quiet."

Evelyn nodded, making a note on her tablet. "Understood, sir. I'll convey your decision to Sotheby's."

"See that you do," David replied, his tone leaving no room for argument. "Now, what's the latest on the authentication process?"

Evelyn consulted her notes once more. "The preliminary examination has been completed. The canvas and pigments are consistent with the period, and the brushwork matches known examples of the artist's technique. They're moving on to more advanced tests. Spectral imaging, x-ray fluorescence, that sort of thing."

David nodded, a sense of satisfaction settling over him. "And the provenance?"

"All in order, sir. The paper trail we...established...holds up to scrutiny. Millbrook was a close friend of your father's and he wasn't survived by any heirs. He named you as the legatee of his art collection. But no evidence of him ever owning that painting exists. We nicely sold the papers a bill of goods with that estate sale story. As far as anyone can tell, The Silent Watch has been in your family's private collection for generations."

A chuckle escaped David's lips. *Generations. If they only knew*, he thought.

He turned back to Evelyn, his eyes sharp. "And what about our friend, Mr. Worthington? Any rumblings?"

Evelyn shook her head. "Nothing concrete, sir. He seems to be keeping a low profile since the…incident."

"Good," David mused. "Let's hope it stays that way. The last thing we need is Max causing a scene before we can offload this masterpiece."

He drained the last of his drink and set the glass down on a nearby table. "Alright, Evelyn. Set up a meeting with the Sotheby's team for tomorrow. I want to go over every detail of this auction myself. No surprises, no slip-ups."

"Of course, Mr. Hollister. I'll make the arrangements right away."

As Evelyn turned to leave, David called out, "Oh, and Evelyn? Make sure our friends at Sotheby's understand the importance of discretion in this matter. A generous bonus for a smooth transaction might help drive the point home."

Evelyn nodded, a knowing smile on her lips. "Consider it done, sir."

With that, she left the room, leaving David alone with his thoughts and the glittering cityscape beyond.

The following afternoon found David striding through the halls of Sotheby's Atlanta office, Evelyn two steps behind him. The hushed atmosphere and tasteful decor spoke of old money and valuable secrets; a world David had long since learned to navigate with ease.

A tall, elegantly dressed woman met them at the entrance to a private viewing room. "Mr. Hollister, welcome to

Sotheby's. I'm Victoria Kensington, head of our Impressionist and Modern Art department. It's a pleasure to finally meet you in person."

David shook her hand, his grip firm and his smile calculated. "The pleasure's all mine, Ms. Kensington. I trust everything is in order for our little unveiling?"

Victoria nodded, gesturing for them to enter the room. "Indeed it is. We've taken every precaution to ensure the utmost discretion, as per your request."

The viewing room was softly lit, with a single painting displayed on the far wall. As they approached, David felt a familiar thrill course through him. There it was — *The Silent Watch*, in all its glory. The muted colors and haunting stillness of the scene debunked the rough journey that had brought it to this moment.

Victoria began her presentation, her voice taking on the measured tones of an experienced art expert. "As you can see, Mr. Hollister, The Silent Watch is a prime example of the artist's later period. The use of light and shadow, the subtle interplay of colors—it's truly a masterpiece."

David nodded, his eyes never leaving the painting. "And the authentication?"

"Ah, yes," Victoria said, moving to a nearby table where several documents were laid out. "We've completed our thorough examination, and I'm pleased to say that everything checks out. The canvas and pigments are period-appropriate, the brushwork is consistent with the artist's known technique, and our advanced imaging tests have revealed no signs of forgery or alteration."

She handed David a thick folder. "Here's the full report, along with the provenance documentation you provided.

Everything is in order, tracing the painting's history from its creation to its place in your family's collection."

David leafed through the papers, feeling a quiet satisfaction take hold. Everything was falling into place perfectly.

"Excellent work, Ms. Kensington," he said, handing the folder to Evelyn. "Now, about the auction itself. I trust you understand my desire for a more restrained approach?"

Victoria's smile faltered slightly. "Yes, Mr. Hollister. Though I must say, with a piece of this caliber, we typically recommend a more robust marketing strategy. The potential for breaking records is significant."

David's eyes narrowed. "I appreciate your expertise, Ms. Kensington, but I prefer to keep this sale…selective. Quality over quantity, you understand."

Victoria nodded, though her expression suggested she wasn't entirely convinced. "Of course, Mr. Hollister. We'll tailor our approach to your specifications. We've already begun reaching out to a curated list of potential bidders. They are collectors and institutions with both the means and the appreciation for a work of this importance."

"Good," David said. "And the reserve price?"

"We've set it at $15 million, as you requested. Though given the painting's provenance and condition, we expect it to far exceed that figure."

David allowed himself a small smile. "Let's hope you're right, Ms. Kensington. Now, walk me through the security measures you have in place."

For the next hour, Victoria detailed the extensive precautions Sotheby's would be taking to protect *The Silent Watch* in the lead-up to the auction. Climate-controlled storage, 24/7 surveillance, limited access — no expense had been spared.

As the meeting drew to a close, David felt a sense of anticipation building. Soon, very soon, this last loose end would be tied up, and he could move on to bigger things.

"One last question, Ms. Kensington," he said as they prepared to leave. "Have you had any inquiries about the painting's recent history? Any…unexpected interest?"

Victoria looked slightly puzzled. "Nothing out of the ordinary, Mr. Hollister. Is there something specific you're concerned about?"

David waved his hand dismissively. "No, no. Just being thorough. You can never be too careful with a piece like this, can you?"

As they left Sotheby's and climbed into the waiting town car, Evelyn turned to David. "Everything seems to be proceeding according to plan, sir."

David nodded, his mind already racing ahead. "So far, so good. But we're not in the clear yet. Keep a close eye on any chatter in the art world, Evelyn. If Max Worthington so much as sneezes in the direction of this auction, I want to know about it."

"Of course, Mr. Hollister. And if he does make a move?"

David's eyes hardened, his voice dropping to a dangerous whisper. "Then we'll have to remind him of the consequences of poking his nose where it doesn't belong. One way or another, The Silent Watch will be nothing but a memory soon enough."

As the car pulled away from the curb, David allowed himself a moment of quiet satisfaction. The game was afoot, and he intended to see it through to its lucrative conclusion— no matter the cost.

CHAPTER VII

Max Worthington was surrounded by pulp with his laptop open before him. The study, usually a bastion of order and refinement, now looked like the aftermath of a paper hurricane. Stacks of files teetered precariously on every available surface and sticky notes made a rainbow of colors on the walls. Frustration and the scent of stale coffee hung heavy in the air.

Max swept a hand through his disheveled hair, his eyes bloodshot from hours of intense focus. On the screen before him, a complex web of connections sprawled out — a digital corkboard of suspects, leads, and dead ends. At the center of it all was an image of *The Silent Watch*, the painting that had vanished from his grasp like some dream upon waking.

He leaned back in his chair, the leather creaking in protest, and rubbed his tired eyes. The theft had been clean, professional; no broken windows, no tripped alarms, nothing out of place except for the inimitably crafted copy on the wall where *The Silent Watch* had never hung before. It was as if the real painting had simply decided to walk out on its own.

Max had been at this for many hours now, trying to piece together who could be behind the theft and what they might want with the painting. The logical part of his brain told him that involving the police would be the sensible thing to do.

But something—call it pride, stubbornness, or a nagging suspicion that this went deeper than a simple burglary—kept him from making that call.

He clicked through a series of documents. Insurance records, provenance papers, recent sales of similar works. Nothing jumped out at him, no smoking gun that pointed to a clear suspect or motive. Max had called in favors from contacts throughout the art world, discreetly inquiring about any whispers of *The Silent Watch* hitting the black market. So far, nothing but radio silence.

"They can't legally sell it," Max muttered to himself, a mantra he'd repeated countless times over the past few days. "They'd need my approval for any above-board transaction."

And yet, the painting remained stubbornly missing, with no ransom demands or attempts at negotiation. It was as if *The Silent Watch* had simply vanished into thin air.

Max stood up, stretching muscles stiff from hours of inactivity, and walked to the window. Long shadows spilled across the neighborhood from the late afternoon sun. Somewhere out there, his painting was hidden away, waiting to be found.

He turned back to his desk, eyes falling on a framed photo of himself and Felicity, taken at a gallery opening last year. They were both smiling, caught in a moment of genuine happiness. Max felt a pang of guilt. He'd been so consumed by this investigation that he'd been neglecting her, brushing off her concerns with vague excuses about work stress.

Sighing, Max returned to his laptop, pulling up the security footage from the day of the theft. He'd been over it a hundred times, but something kept drawing him back. The two cameras showed nothing out of the ordinary—no mysterious figures, no unexplained gaps in the timeline. And yet, the painting was gone.

As he watched the footage again, a thought struck him. What if the thief hadn't broken in at all? What if they had already been inside the house?

Max's mind raced, considering the possibilities. The house staff? The only long-term employee was Guadalupe, the quadragenarian who visited twice a week mainly to do the laundry alongside some work in the kitchen. But she'd been thoroughly vetted. Guests from the dinner party the night before the theft was discovered? Possible, but unlikely—the alarm would have been set after they left.

Unless…

Max froze, a chill plying his spine. Unless someone had stayed behind, hidden away until the house was quiet. Or unless someone had let them in later.

He shook his head, trying to dispel the thought. No, that was paranoia talking. He trusted his staff, his friends. This line of thinking would only lead to madness.

And yet, the seed of doubt had been planted.

A soft knock at the door jolted Max from his thoughts. "Come in," he called, hastily minimizing the windows on his laptop.

The door opened, revealing Felicity, her camera bag slung over one shoulder. Her eyes widened slightly as she took in the chaos of the room. "Wow, looks like a tornado hit in here. Everything okay, Max?"

Max forced a smile, hoping it didn't look as strained as it felt. "Hey, Fel. Yeah, just…doing some research for a new acquisition. You know how I get when I'm on the trail of something good."

Felicity raised an eyebrow, not entirely convinced. She made her way carefully through the paper-strewn floor, perching on the edge of the desk. "Must be some acquisition."

Max's smile faltered for a moment. Of course she knew. Felicity had been there through the whole ordeal with *The Silent Watch*. He'd confided in her about the theft, sworn her to secrecy while he tried to handle things on his own. And now here he was, lying to her face.

"I haven't seen you so worked up before," she said. "It's been almost two weeks. You need to stop thinking about what happened, you know."

Max leaned back, pouting a smile. "It's not what you think, darling."

"What is it then?"

"It's nothing that exciting, really," Max said, standing up and stretching in an attempt to appear casual. "Just got a bit carried away. How was your shoot?"

Felicity's eyes lingered on him for a moment, a flicker of something passing across her face. Concern? Suspicion? But then it was gone, replaced by her usual warm smile. "It was great, actually. Got some amazing shots of the new exhibition at the High Museum. Want to see?"

Max nodded, grateful for the change of subject. As Felicity pulled out her camera and began showing him the photos, he felt a wave of guilt wash over him. He hated keeping things from her, but he told himself it was for her own protection. The less she knew about his investigation, the better.

As they scrolled through the images, Max found his mind wandering. There was something about Felicity's latest work—the composition, the play of light and shadow—that reminded him of *The Silent Watch*. One photo, in particular, caught his eye: a striking black-and-white shot of an empty frame hanging on a gallery wall.

"This one's interesting," Max said, tapping the screen. "What made you take this shot?"

Felicity leaned in, her shoulder brushing against his. "Oh, that one. It's part of a series I'm working on. 'Absence and Presence.' I'm exploring the idea of negative space, what's not there being just as important as what is."

Max nodded, a strange feeling settling in his stomach. "It's…evocative. Makes you wonder about the story behind the missing painting."

"Exactly," Felicity said with a voice soft. "Sometimes what's not there tells us more than what is."

Their eyes met for a moment, and Max felt as if he were standing on the edge of a precipice. There was something in Felicity's gaze. A depth. A knowing. It both drew him in and set off warning bells in his mind.

"Max? Earth to Max." Felicity's voice cut through his rushing thoughts. "You still with me?"

Max blinked, realizing he'd completely zoned out. "Sorry, Fel. I guess I'm more tired than I thought. The photos are beautiful, really. You've outdone yourself."

Felicity set the camera down, her expression softening. "Max, what's really going on? And don't tell me it's just work stress. I know you better than that."

For a moment, Max was tempted to come clean, to spill everything about his investigation and his fears. But the words caught in his throat. Instead, he reached out and took Felicity's hand, giving it a gentle squeeze.

"It's nothing you need to worry about, I promise," he said, hoping his voice sounded more convincing than it felt. "Just some…business complications. Nothing I can't handle."

Felicity held his gaze for a long moment, and Max had the unsettling feeling that she could see right through him. But then she nodded, squeezing his hand in return. "Okay. But you know I'm here if you need to talk, right? About anything."

Max nodded, a lump forming in his throat. "I know, Fel. Thank you."

As Felicity gathered her things to leave the room, Max felt the weight of his secrets pressing down on him. He watched her go, fighting the urge to call her back, to confess everything.

But he didn't. Instead, he turned back to his laptop, to the endless web of clues and dead ends. Somewhere out there, someone had his painting. And Max was determined to find out who, and why.

The door closed behind Felicity with a soft click, leaving Max alone with his thoughts once more. He stared at the screen, the image of the empty frame from Felicity's photo burned into his mind. Absence and presence. What's not there being just as important as what is.

With a sudden burst of energy, Max began sorting through the papers on his desk. There had to be something he was missing, some detail that would blow this whole thing wide open. He pulled up financial records, cross-referencing them with known art thieves and fence operations.

The sky outside darkened as night fell over Atlanta. Max barely noticed, his focus entirely on the task at hand. He was so close, he could feel it. The answer was right there, just out of reach.

And then, buried in a stack of old correspondence, he found it. A letter from six months ago, inquiring about the possibility of loaning *The Silent Watch* for a private exhibition. The letterhead bore the logo of a company Max didn't recognize: Hollister Enterprises. Max's heart pounded as he quickly looked up the company. High-end investment firm, specializing in art and antiquities. CEO: David Hollister.

The name rang a bell. Max vaguely remembered meeting Hollister at a charity auction last year. Charming man, with a keen eye for art and a seemingly endless bank account.

Could this be the lead he'd been looking for? Max's fingers flew across the keyboard, digging deeper into this Hollister's background. Nothing overtly suspicious came up, but there was something about the man's rapid rise in the art world that set off Max's instincts.

He was so engrossed in his research that he almost missed the soft ping of an incoming email. Max glanced at the notification, his breath catching in his throat as he read the subject line: "Regarding 'The Silent Watch'."

With trembling fingers, he opened the email. It was short, just a few lines:

Mr. Worthington,

I believe we have a mutual interest in a certain piece of art. If you wish to discuss its return, come alone to the Piedmont Park Conservatory tomorrow at noon. Tell no one.
A friend.

Max leaned back in his chair, his mind reeling. This was it. The break he'd been waiting for. But who was this "friend"? And could he trust them? He glanced at the framed photo of himself and Felicity, torn between his promise to keep her out of this and his desire to confide in her. But no, he'd come this far on his own. He couldn't risk involving her now.

Decision made, Max began preparing for the meeting. He had no idea what tomorrow would bring, but one thing was certain: he was one step closer to bringing *The Silent Watch* home. But a voice in his head abruptly spoke up: Max Worthington, sometimes the price of knowledge can be higher than we anticipate.

CHAPTER VIII

The crack of a shotgun shatters the crisp autumn air as the clay pigeon explodes into fragments. David Hollister lowers the weapon, a grin spreading across his seventeen-year-old face as he watches.

"Nice shot, son," Robert Hollister calls out from behind him. "You're a natural."

David turns, basking in the rare praise. His father stands on the manicured lawn of their estate, martini in hand despite the early hour. Beside him is Harrison Worthington, Max's father, his own drink untouched.

"Thank you, sir," David says, puffing out his chest slightly. "I've been practicing."

Harrison Worthington clears his throat. "Speaking of practice, Robert, have you given any more thought to my proposal? The joint venture could be quite lucrative for both our families."

It hardly takes a moment for Robert's expression to sour. "Harrison, we've been over this. The Hollister name stands on its own. We don't need to partner with anyone, especially not..." He cuts himself off, but the implication hangs heavy between them. Especially not the Worthingtons.

Harrison's jaw tightens. "I see. Well, if that's how you feel, perhaps it's time we discussed the property line issue.

Your new stable is encroaching on our land by a good ten feet."

"Nonsense," Robert scoffs. "I had the best surveyors in Atlanta out here. That land is ours, fair and square."

"Your surveyors," — Harrison spits the word — "must have been as drunk as you are now. I won't stand for this, Robert. Either we come to an agreement, or I'll be forced to take legal action."

David watches the two men with growing unease. He's never seen his father's business associate, and friend, speak to him like this before. His father's face flushes an ugly shade of crimson. "Is that a threat, Worthington? You'd sue me over a few feet of godforsaken Georgia clay?"

"It's not about the land, Robert." Harrison's voice is low and dangerous. "It's about respect. Something you seem to have forgotten."

Robert's grip tightens on his glass. For a moment, David thinks he might throw it. Instead, his father's lips curl into a sneer. "Respect? That's rich, coming from new money like you. How many generations have the Worthingtons been in Atlanta? Two? Three? My family helped build this city."

Harrison's eyes have narrowed. "And my family is helping to drag it into the future, while you cling to your outdated ideas and your dwindling influence. Face it, Robert. The world is changing, and you're being left behind." The words cling to the air like gunpowder smoke. David holds his breath, waiting for the explosion. It comes in the form of a laugh — harsh and bitter from his father's throat. "Get off my property, Harrison. And take your holier-than-thou attitude with you. We're done here."

Harrison straightens and smooths down his jacket. "Indeed we are. Don't say I didn't try to be reasonable, Robert. You'll be hearing from my lawyers."

As Harrison strides away, David catches a glimpse of movement near the house. Max Worthington, barely fourteen, stands on the porch. He has been watching the scene with wide eyes. Their gazes meet for a brief moment before Max ducks back inside. Robert drains his martini in one gulp, then hurls the empty glass against a nearby oak tree. It shatters with a sound not unlike the clay pigeon.

"Dad?" David ventures cautiously. "What was that all about?"

His father's eyes are cold when they meet his. "That, my boy, was the end of a mistake. I should never have let the Worthingtons get so close. They're not our kind, David. Remember that."

David nods slowly, committing the words to memory. "Yes, sir. I understand." But he doesn't, not really. Not yet. It is going to take years for the true impact of this day to sink in, for the seed of resentment to take root and grow into something dark and twisted. All he knows in this moment is that something has changed, irrevocably. And that Max Worthington, the quiet boy who always has his nose in a book, is somehow at the center of it all.

The unbidden memory faded, leaving David staring at his reflection once more. He stood before the full-length mirror in his penthouse suite, adjusting his Brioni tie with practiced precision. The charcoal Tom Ford suit hugged his frame perfectly. It was a testament to both his physique and his tailor's skill. At fifty-two, he cut an impressive figure — salt-and-pepper hair artfully tousled, jawline still sharp despite the encroaching jowls of middle age. His lips curled into a mirthless smile.

"Well, Dad," he murmured while his gaze drifted to the framed garden party photo on his dresser, the same one that had occupied his desk for years. "I may not have dragged Atlanta into the future, but I've damn sure made it mine." David's hand clenched involuntarily as the memory of that day thirty-five years ago lingered in his mind.

A discreet chime from his phone pulled David from his reverie. He glanced at the screen: it was a message from his ever-efficient secretary.

Car waiting downstairs. Auction for our Lot starts in 45 minutes.

David pocketed the phone, giving himself one final once-over in the mirror. Today was the culmination of years of planning. After laying the groundwork so carefully, he would watch Max Worthington's world begin to crumble today. He was going to savor every moment of it. "Showtime," he said to his reflection, and strode out of the penthouse.

The auction house hummed with anticipation. Well-heeled patrons milled about, sipping champagne and eyeing the lots with carefully cultivated nonchalance. David moved through the crowd with the ease of a shark gliding through a school of fish. He nodded to acquaintances and exchanged pleasantries when necessary.

His eyes scanned the room, noting the key players. Victoria Kensington stood near the podium, looking resplendent in a tailored navy suit. She caught his gaze and offered a small nod. David returned it with a gracious smile.

Their backroom agreement had paid off for both, so long as it stayed off the record.

He spotted his plants: Jerome Blackwell, moving forward from one of the rear rows and Anastasia Chen behind him. Both were legitimate collectors, known for their deep pockets and competitive streaks. Neither had any idea of the role they were about to play in David's grand design. As he made his way to his seat in the front row, David's eyes ranged over the room. With a methodical sharpness his brain sorted through the faces. He calculated everything like a hunter stalking unseen prey. The vast hall was a hive of wealth and ambition barely contained by Sotheby's tasteful decor.

David settled into his chair, adjusting his cufflinks — a habitual gesture that doubled as a subtle signal to the head of the Impressionist and Modern Art department. There was an almost imperceptible nod from her side. Everything was in place.

When the last attendee took their seat, David let a wave of quiet pride wash over him. Months of precise planning had culminated in this room. The defining moment was at hand. Soon, the first domino in his grand design would fall and Max Worthington wouldn't even be here to witness it.

The auctioneer, a distinguished gentleman with a crisp British accent, stepped up to the podium. The murmur of conversation died down as he cleared his throat.

"Ladies and gentlemen, welcome back after the recess. Now, we will move towards a truly remarkable piece up for auction today. A long-lost masterpiece recently rediscovered and authenticated. Lot 42: The Silent Watch by Theodore Hart."

A hush fell over the crowd as the painting was unveiled. Even David, who had seen it countless times, felt a small thrill at the sight. The young boy in tattered clothes, his staff planted firmly in the dusty ground, seemed to stare out at the assembled bidders with a mixture of defiance and weariness beyond his years.

"We'll start the bidding at fifteen million dollars," the auctioneer announced. "Do I hear fifteen million?"

Jerome Blackwell's hand shot up immediately. "Fifteen million," he called out, his voice carrying easily across the room.

David leaned back in his chair, affecting an air of casual interest. His gaze flickered to Anastasia Chen, seated three rows behind Blackwell. Right on cue, her paddle rose.

"Sixteen," she said coolly.

The bids escalated like a verbal volley between Jerome and Anastasia. Seventeen million. Nineteen million. Twenty-five million. Everyone present in the room listened, captivated. David's face was a mask of mild curiosity as he watched the exchange with growing satisfaction. To anyone observing, he would have appeared to be nothing more than another interested party, perhaps considering a bid of his own. In reality, he was surrounded by a masterclass of greed and manipulation and he was the one pulling the strings. As the bidding approached forty million dollars, David glanced across the room at Victoria.

"Fifty million dollars," Victoria called out, her crisp voice cutting through the tension.

A ripple of excitement ran through the crowd. David allowed his eyebrows to raise slightly, the picture of surprised interest. Beneath the surface, he was gloating. *Dance, puppets, dance.*

Jerome Blackwell hesitated for just a moment before raising his paddle again. "Fifty-five million."

"Fifty-eight," Anastasia countered immediately.

The bidding war raged on, the price climbing higher with each exchange. David could almost taste the change in the room as the buzz of excitement hardened into a taut, almost suffocating tension. This wasn't just an auction anymore — it had transformed into a high-stakes standoff, where egos and fortunes hung in the balance.

As the bidding approached sixty-nine million dollars, David gave a subtle signal to his third plant in the audience. It was time to push things over the edge.

"Seventy-five million," a new voice called out. Heads turned to see a distinguished-looking woman in her sixties, dripping in old money and confidence.

Jerome and Anastasia exchanged glances, both looking slightly shell-shocked by the sudden leap in price. The auctioneer, to his credit, barely missed a beat.

"Seventy-five million to the lady in the third row," he confirmed. "Do I hear seventy-five point one?"

There was a moment of electrified silence. David held his breath, waiting to see if his precise and covert campaign would pay off.

Jerome Blackwell squared his shoulders. "Seventy-five point six," he said, his voice tight with determination.

The room collectively exhaled. The game was still on.

"Seventy-six point seven," Anastasia Chen countered, her cool facade beginning to crack under the pressure.

"Eighty million," the newcomer called out.

The bidding continued its frenzied ascent, pushing past eighty-five million, then ninety. David watched with carefully concealed glee while his pawns danced to his tune, driving the price of the painting to dizzying heights.

As the bidding approached ninety-three million dollars, David allowed his thoughts to drift momentarily to Max Worthington. He imagined the novelist in his shabby apartment, blissfully unaware that his family's legacy was being auctioned off to the highest bidder. The thought sent a thrill of vindictive pleasure through him.

"Ninety-nine point five million," Anastasia Chen called out, her voice wavering slightly.

There was a pause, heavy with anticipation. Jerome Blackwell looked conflicted. His hand twitched toward his paddle before falling back to his side.

"Ninety-nine point five million," the auctioneer repeated. "Going once…"

David held his breath, his heart pounding in his ears. This was it. It was happening.

"Going twice…"

The room was silent, save for the barely audible rustle of fabric as people leaned forward in their seats.

"Sold!" The crack of the gavel was like a gunshot. "To the lady in the fourth row for ninety-nine point five million dollars."

A smattering of applause broke out, tinged with an undercurrent of awe at the astronomical price. David allowed himself a small, satisfied smile as he joined in the clapping. Phase one of his plan was complete. As the crowd began to disperse, chattering excitedly about the unexpected bidding war, David weaved his way toward Victoria

Kensington, who was already engaged in conversation with the winning bidder.

"…truly remarkable piece," Victoria was saying as David approached. "You've made an excellent investment, Mrs. Chen."

Anastasia Chen beamed, flush with victory. "Thank you, Ms. Kensington. I can't wait to see it hanging in my gallery."

David cleared his throat softly. "Pardon the interruption, ladies. I just wanted to offer my congratulations on a truly thrilling auction."

Victoria turned and her smile widened. "Mr. Hollister! I'm so glad you could make it. What did you think of our little show?"

"Absolutely riveting," David replied smoothly. "Mrs. Chen, allow me to add my congratulations. You've acquired a true masterpiece."

Anastasia preened under the attention. "Thank you, Mr. Hollister. I must admit, I got caught up in the excitement. But when you see a piece like that, you simply can't let it slip away."

David's smile never wavered. *Oh, if you only knew.* Out loud, he said, "I couldn't agree more. In fact, I was hoping I might have a word with you about the painting. Perhaps over drinks?"

Anastasia's eyes lit up at the prospect of discussing her new acquisition with such a well-known patron of the arts. "I'd be delighted," she said. As David led Anastasia away, his mind was already racing ahead to the next phase of his plan. They made their way to the champagne bar, where David signaled for two glasses. As the bubbles fizzed in their flutes, he turned to Anastasia with a conspiratorial smile.

"You know, Mrs. Chen, I have a particular interest in works from the American Provincial period. I'd love to hear your thoughts on The Silent Watch. What drew you to it?"

Anastasia sipped her champagne, considering a suitable reply. "There's a rawness to it, a…vulnerability. The boy's stance is defiant, but his eyes…they tell a different story."

David nodded, impressed despite himself. "Perceptive. You have quite an eye."

"One doesn't build a collection like mine without developing an eye," Anastasia said with a hint of pride in her voice. "But I sense you have more than a passing interest in this piece, Mr. Hollister. Am I right?"

Clever woman, David thought. *This might be more fun than I anticipated.*

"You are," he admitted, lowering his voice. "In fact, I have some information about The Silent Watch that might interest you. Information that could significantly increase its value."

Anastasia's eyes narrowed slightly. "Go on."

David's voice barely exceeded a whisper as he said, "What if I told you that this painting has a secret? A hidden provenance that ties it to one of Atlanta's oldest families?"

He watched as curiosity and greed warred in Anastasia's eyes. Hook, line, and sinker. "I'm listening," she said.

As David began to weave a blend of truth, lies, and tantalizing half-truths, exhilaration surged in him. This was what he lived for: the thrill of the con, the dance of deception. And with each word, he was drawing the net tighter around Max Worthington.

Enjoy your blissful ignorance while you can, Max, said a voice inside David's head. *Your world is about to come crashing down, and you won't even see it coming.*

With a smile that didn't quite reach his eyes, David raised his glass to Anastasia. "To new partnerships," he said smoothly. "And to the secrets that bind us."

As their glasses clinked together, David allowed himself a moment of pure, unadulterated triumph. The game was afoot, and he was holding the next card ready in his hand. For now, David Hollister intended to drink in every ounce of the victory he'd waited so long to taste.

Let Max Worthington try to write his way out of this one.

CHAPTER IX

Max Worthington's coffee was growing cold beside him as he stared at the newspaper. The words on the page seemed to mock him. They were twisting reality into an incomprehensible knot. There, in black and white, was an announcement of the sale of *The Silent Watch* at Sotheby's. The same one that belonged to him. The absurdity of it all made his head spin.

"This is impossible." The words were a hoarse whisper as he ran a hand through his disheveled hair.

His mind raced back to the day of the auction. He'd meant to go, to confront whoever was behind this madness. But fate, it seemed, had other plans.

"Come on, Max! Live a little." Felicity had laughed two days ago. Her nakedness was partially covered under the sheets, her hair stuck to her damp neck after the past hour they'd spent grinding the bedsprings with gusto.

Max hesitated. "I don't know, Fel. I've got a lot on my mind. I've got to do something about the deadline with Redbrick and bloody soon. Then this whole painting business. Bad timing." He mournfully shook his head. "But I'm not that concerned about the theft as I am about finding the perfect way to keep my main character from getting a bullet in her head." He hoped he sounded natural conveying it was the manuscript preoccupying his thoughts instead of the heist, not the other way around.

As she tugged on his arm, her eyes had sparkled with the indulgence of having his company. There was no way he should miss out on the new fusion restaurant that had opened downtown. "All the more reason to take your mind off things for one night. You've been obsessing over this for weeks. One dinner won't hurt." Her mouth pouted playfully.

He sighed, feeling his resolve weaken. "Alright, alright. One dinner."

The evening had started pleasantly enough, especially since he didn't find as many cars on the roads as he had expected. Two taller buildings seemed to scrunch the restaurant between them like an old postcard. No sooner had they stepped through the meager façade into the much roomier interior than the exotic aromas wafting from the kitchen were enticing him. Max found himself relaxing in his chair as the atmosphere around him buzzed with a mollified energy. Felicity's infectious laughter had momentarily pushed his worries aside.

"Try this," she insisted, holding out a forkful of something unidentifiable but delicious-looking. "It's their signature dish."

Max had obliged, savoring the explosion of flavors. "Wow, that's intense," he managed to say as he reached for his water. As the night wore on, a creeping discomfort began to settle in Max's stomach. By the time they were driving back from the restaurant, he was sweating, and his insides were churning ominously.

The next morning — the day of the auction — Max awoke to a stomach that felt like it was trying to turn itself inside out. He barely made it to the bathroom before violent nausea overcame him. Hours later, pale and shaky, he finally managed to check his phone. His heart sank as he saw the time. The auction had started over an hour ago.

"Dammit!" he croaked, his throat raw. He'd missed his chance.

And now Max was staring at the newspaper, cursing his luck and that ill-fated dinner. He crumpled the paper in frustration, then smoothed it out again, his eyes drawn to the auction details. The painting had sold for an astronomical sum — far more than he'd ever imagined it was worth.

His phone buzzed, startling him. It was a text message from an unknown number: "Don't forget Piedmont Park." Max's pulse quickened. The mysterious e-mailer. He glanced at his watch. 11:30 a.m. He had just enough time to make it. Grabbing his jacket, Max hurried out the door. The drive to Piedmont Park was a blur of green lights and impatient lane changes. As he pulled into the parking lot, the car's clock ticked over to 11:58.

Max jogged into the park, his eyes scanning the landscape. Piedmont Park stretched out before him. It was a verdant oasis in the heart of Atlanta. The air was alive with the scent of magnolias and freshly cut grass. On any other day, he might have paused to admire the way the sunlight dappled through the canopy of old oak trees, or how the distant Atlanta skyline provided a striking contrast to the natural beauty. But his attention was focused solely on finding his mysterious contact. He made his way down the main path, passing joggers and dog-walkers. Everyone was oblivious to the tension coiled within him.

As the path curved around the Lake Clara Meer, Max's phone rang. He answered without checking the caller ID.

"Mr. Worthington," a distorted voice crackled through the speaker. "Walk towards the Cherry Blossom grove. When you see the large weeping willow, stop in front of the rhododendron bush to its left."

The line went dead before Max could respond. He quickened his pace, his heart pounding in time with his footsteps. The cherry trees were just past their peak bloom, a few pale petals still clinging stubbornly to their branches. Max spotted the willow. Its long tendrils swayed gently in the breeze. Next to it, a dense rhododendron bush stood, with its dark green leaves concealing whatever — or whoever — might be hiding behind it.

He approached cautiously, stopping a few feet from the bush. "I'm here," he called out, trying to keep his voice steady. There was a moment of silence, broken only by the distant laughter of children on the playground. Then, a voice emerged from behind the foliage, low and gravelly.

"Mr. Worthington. I'm glad you could make it."

Max's eyes narrowed, trying in vain to catch a glimpse of the speaker through the leaves. "Who are you? What do you know about my painting?"

A dry chuckle. "Who I am is irrelevant. What matters is that we both want the same thing. To see The Silent Watch returned to its rightful owner."

"And that would be me," Max said firmly.

"Would it?" the voice said. A hint of amusement colored the words. "The newspapers seem to think you've sold it."

Max clenched his fists. "That's a lie. The painting was stolen from me. I would never sell it."

"I believe you," the voice said softly. "But belief and proof are two very different things, Mr. Worthington."

"What do you want?" Max said, frustration edging into his tone. "Why all this cloak and dagger routine?"

There was a rustling from behind the bush, as if the speaker had shifted position. "I have… a vested interest in seeing justice done. Let's just say that the individual behind the theft of your painting has wronged me as well."

Max's mind raced. "You know who stole it? Tell me!"

"Patience, Mr. Worthington," the voice cautioned. "This is a dangerous game we're playing. The man we're dealing with, he's not someone to be trifled with."

"I don't care how dangerous he is," Max growled. "That painting is all I have left of my family's legacy. I need to know who took it."

There was a long pause. When the voice spoke again, it was quieter, almost hesitant. "Your father… he never told you about the feud, did he?"

Max blinked, caught off guard. "Feud? What feud?"

"Ah," the voice sighed. "It seems there's much you don't know. Your father and the father of the man who orchestrated this theft; they had a bitter rivalry that stretched back decades. A rivalry that, it seems, has been passed down to the next generation."

Max's mind reeled. His father had never mentioned any feud. But then again, there was so much about his family's past that remained a mystery to him.

"Who is this man?" Max pressed. "If this is about some old grudge, I deserve to know."

"Knowledge can be a dangerous thing, Mr. Worthington," the voice warned. "But perhaps… perhaps it's time you learned the truth. Meet me here again in three days. Come prepared for a long conversation. And watch your back. You're not the only one looking for answers."

Max had had enough of the cryptic responses. "No," he said as he took a step towards the bush. "I'm not waiting three more days. You're going to tell me everything you know. *Right now!*"

He reached out to push aside the branches, determined to confront his mysterious informant face-to-face. But as his hand touched the leaves, there was a sudden flurry of movement. A figure burst from behind the bush, shoving Max backward. He stumbled, nearly losing his footing on the uneven ground. By the time he regained his balance, the stranger was already sprinting away, weaving between trees and startled park visitors.

"Hey!" Max shouted, giving chase. But the man was fast, and clearly knew the park's layout better than Max did. After a few minutes of pursuit, Max found himself alone on a quiet path, out of breath and no closer to answers.

Frustrated and more confused than ever, Max made his way back to his car. His mind churned with questions. Who was the mysterious informant? What did he know about the theft? And most pressingly, who was this unknown rival, carrying on a feud Max knew nothing about?

Over the next few days, Max threw himself into his investigation with renewed vigor. He pored over old family documents, searching for any hint of the feud the stranger had mentioned. He decided to reach out to some distant relatives who might be willing to help, or so Max thought. He could do little more than simply hope someone might shed light on this chapter of his family's history.

Max sighed, rubbing his temples as he scrolled through his contacts. His eyes landed on a name he hadn't called in years. His father's cousin, technically, but the boisterous Texan had always insisted on "Uncle."

"Well, desperate times," Max muttered to himself as he hit the call button.

The phone rang three times before a deep, twangy voice boomed through the speaker. The man at the other end asked who was calling before Max introduced himself.

"Well, I'll be damned! If it ain't little Maxie Worthington! What in tarnation you callin' for, boy? Someone die?"

Max couldn't help a chuckle. "No, Uncle Hank, everyone's fine. Well, as far as I know. Actually, I'm calling because I need some information about Dad. And Grandpa."

"Harrison and ol' Teddy? Shoot, what you wanna know about them two ornery cusses for?"

Max hesitated, unsure how to broach the subject. "Uncle Hank, did you ever hear anything about a… uhm, a feud? Between our family and someone else's?"

There was a long pause on the other end of the line. Then, "Boy, you best pour yourself a drink. This gonna take a while."

Max obliged, grabbing a bottle of bourbon from the cabinet. "Okay, I'm armed and ready. Spill it, Uncle Hank."

"Now, you gotta understand, this all happened way back when. Your grandpappy Teddy, he was slicker than a greased pig in a mud wrestlin' contest. Made his fortune in oil, but folks always whispered he had some, shall we say, creative accountin' practices."

Max took a swig of bourbon. "Are you saying Grandpa was a crook?"

"Crook's a mighty strong word, Maxie. Let's just say he knew how to work the system better'n a cow knows how to swat flies with its tail. Anyhoo, there was this other fella, name of Jeremiah Blackwood. He and your grandpappy were thicker than thieves. Right up until they weren't."

"What happened?"

Uncle Hank chuckled. "What always happens, boy. Money and a woman. See, there was this pretty little thing named Rosalie. Your grandpappy and ol' Jeremiah both had eyes for her. But she only had eyes for one thing: cold, hard cash."

Max leaned forward, intrigued. "So… what? She played them against each other?"

"Like a fiddle at a square dance. Ended up marryin' Jeremiah, but not before she got your grandpappy to invest in some cockamamie scheme of hers. When it all went belly-up, Teddy lost a fortune. He was convinced Jeremiah and Rosalie had set him up."

"And had they?"

"Who knows? But your grandpappy sure thought so. Swore he'd get revenge if it was the last thing he did. And lemme tell you, Teddy Worthington could hold a grudge longer than a camel can go without water, as they say."

Max took another gulp from the glass, his mind racing. "But what does this have to do with Dad? Or me, for that matter?"

"Well, now, that's where things get interesting. See, your daddy Harrison, he didn't want no part of this feud nonsense. But Jeremiah's boy, Clayton, he was cut from the same vindictive cloth as your grandpappy. Kept the bad blood going, even after the old timers were pushin' up daisies."

"Clayton Blackwood," Max repeated, scribbling the name down. "You think he might still be carrying on this grudge?"

Uncle Hank's laugh crackled through the phone. "Boy, if that man ain't still nursin' that grudge, I'll eat my hat. And let me tell you, this ain't no flimsy baseball cap. We're talkin' a genuine, ten-gallon Stetson."

Max couldn't help but smile. "I appreciate the intel, Uncle Hank. But why didn't Dad ever tell me about any of this?"

"Your daddy, bless his heart, he thought he could leave it all behind. Moved y'all out to Atlanta, tried to start fresh. But you know what they say: you can take the boy out of Texas, but you can't take Texas out of the boy."

"So you think this Clayton Blackwood might be behind, uhm, recent events?"

"Recent events? Boy, you in some kind of trouble?"

Max hesitated. "It's complicated, Uncle Hank. Let's just say someone's stirring up old ghosts."

"Well, butter my butt and call me a biscuit! You watch yourself, you hear? Them Blackwoods, they're slipperier than a pocketful of pudding. And meaner than a mama wasp when you poke her nest."

"I'll be careful," Max promised. "Thanks for the history lesson, Uncle Hank. I owe you one."

"Aw, hell, boy. Family don't keep score. But if you're ever down Texas way, you best come by for some real barbecue. That stuff y'all call barbecue up in Atlanta? That's just sad."

Max laughed. "Will do, Uncle Hank. Take care."

As he hung up the phone, Max was thinking he had names now, and the outlines of a story. But somehow, he felt like he had more questions than ever. He stared at his notes, the names Jeremiah Blackwood and Clayton Blackwood standing out in bold letters. Somewhere in this tangled history lay the key to understanding why his painting had been stolen. And maybe, just maybe, the clue to getting it back. Or did it? No way to say for sure at the moment. A few other relatives he managed to contact knew nothing; or claimed to know nothing. The family records were frustratingly vague; full of hints and allusions but no concrete information. It was a dead end at every turn.

Max even tried to trace the e-mail and the phone number the stranger had used to contact him, but both led nowhere. It was as if the man had appeared out of thin air, only to vanish just as quickly.

As another day passed, Max found himself back at square one. He had no new leads, no clearer understanding of who might have stolen the painting or why. All he had was a growing sense of unease and a nagging feeling that he was missing something crucial.

He stared at his reflection in the bathroom mirror, noting the dark circles under his eyes and the worried crease in his brow. "What am I not seeing?" he muttered to his haggard doppelganger. The face in the mirror offered no answers, but Max's resolve hardened. When he returned to Piedmont Park, he would finally get the answers he needed.

As he climbed into bed that night, exhaustion finally overcame his racing thoughts. Max couldn't shake off the feeling that a dramatic change had hurled itself into his life.

For better or worse, the truth about *The Silent Watch* and his family's past would finally be within reach. Soon, his dreams filled with shadowy figures, whispered secrets, and the haunting image of a young figure standing alone in a windswept landscape. While Max Worthington slept, the boy's silent watch was never-ending.

CHAPTER X

The intermittent flicker of The Velvet Lounge tossed a tranced glow on to the rain-slicked street. David Hollister pushed through the heavy oak door, his eyes scanning the dimly lit interior. The bar had long served as a crossroads for Atlanta's power players, where expensive whispers negotiated fortunes and shrewd tongues bartered secrets over glasses of aged whiskey.

David made his way to the bar, his Italian leather shoes barely making a sound on the polished hardwood floor. He nodded at the bartender, a tall man with a neatly trimmed salt-and-pepper beard.

"Macallan 18, neat," David said, his voice low and controlled.

The bartender placed the amber liquid in front of him without a word. David took a sip, savoring the smoky flavor as he checked his watch. 9:45 p.m. The call would come soon.

As if on cue, his phone vibrated in his pocket. David pulled it out, glancing at the unknown number before he answered. "Yes?" His tone was clipped and businesslike.

A gravelly voice responded, "Back alley. Five minutes."

The line went dead. David downed the rest of his whiskey in one gulp, left a crisp hundred-dollar bill on the bar, and made his way towards the rear exit.

The alley behind The Velvet Lounge was a stark contrast to the opulence inside. Dumpsters lined one wall, as their pungent odor mixed with the humid Atlanta air. A single flickering streetlight cast long shadows to create pockets of darkness. The place was perfect for striking a profitable deal. David leaned against the brick wall, as his hand instinctively reached for the gun holstered beneath his tailored jacket. He didn't have to wait long.

A silhouette materialized from the gloom. David watched as each precise, deliberate step the figure took reminded him of a history steeped in crime. The man was of average height, but his presence seemed to fill the alley. The fedora pulled over his eyes obscured most of his features.

"You're the one who called about The Silent Watch?" The man's voice was a low rumble.

David nodded, pushing himself off the wall. "That's right. I trust you've done your homework?"

The man's chuckle was devoid of humor. "I always do. Close to a hundred million at Sotheby's. Set to be shipped to some rich widow in Monaco next week. You want me to make the switch before it leaves Atlanta."

Not Monaco, exactly. But it suits both of us if that's what you believe, David thought.

"Correct," David said, donning an incredibly impressed face. "I have the replica in my car. It's good enough to fool anyone who isn't looking too closely."

The man raised an eyebrow. "And how do you know it'll fool me?"

David smirked. "Because you're not here to appreciate art. You're here for the payday."

"Fair enough," the man conceded. "Let's see it."

David led the way to his car, a sleek black Audi parked in the shadows at the end of the alley. He popped the trunk, revealing a large, flat case. With practiced ease, he opened it to reveal a painting that was, to the untrained eye, identical to *The Silent Watch*.

The man leaned in with narrowing eyes as he studied the forgery. "Not bad," he muttered. "Who's your guy?"

"That's not your concern," David replied sharply. "All you need to know is that it'll pass muster long enough for us to be in the wind with the original."

The man straightened up and nodded slowly. "Alright. What's the timeline?"

David closed the trunk, his movements deliberate. "The painting ships out next Tuesday. You'll have a 48-hour window to make the switch at the secure storage facility. I'll provide you with the details of the security system and guard rotations."

"And my cut?"

"Ten percent of the sale price," David said, his tone brooking no argument. "Nine-and-a-half million. More than enough to disappear for a good long while."

The man whistled low. "That's some serious cash. But why me? A job this big, you could have your pick of crews."

David's eyes hardened. "Because you're the best. And because after that stunt you pulled in Chicago, you need this score as much as I do. Don't think I don't know about the heat you're under."

The man stiffened, his hand twitching towards his coat. David tensed, ready for anything, but after a moment, the man relaxed.

"You've done your homework too, I see," he said with a grudging respect in his voice.

"Always," David replied. "So, are we in business?"

The man was silent for a long moment. Finally, after weighing his options he nodded. "We're in business. But if this goes south—"

"It won't," David cut him off. "Not if you're as good as they say you are."

The man smirked. "Oh, I'm better." He gestured towards the trunk. "I'll take that now. Need to study it, make sure I know exactly what I'm looking for when I'm in there."

David hesitated for a split second before nodding. He opened the trunk again and carefully handed over the case containing the forged painting.

"I'll contact you with the final details in 72 hours," David said. "After that, radio silence until the job is done. Understood?"

The man tucked the case under his arm. "Crystal clear. See you on the other side, Mr. Hollister."

With that, he melted back into the shadows, leaving David alone in the alley. The distant sound of sirens echoed through the night. It was a reminder of the thin line they were walking. David took a deep breath, straightened his tie, and headed back towards The Velvet Lounge. The pieces were in motion now. Soon, he'd have his reckoning with the novelist, indelibly claiming the fortune that rightfully belonged to the latter. Or did it?

As he reached for the door, a flicker of doubt crossed his mind. Was he really going to trust this unknown man with such a crucial part of his plan? But then he remembered the look in the man's eyes. The hunger for that big score. *No*, he thought, *this would work.* It had to.

As the heavy door swallowed him back into the world of whispered deals and cunning promises, the only evidence of the meeting in the alley was the lingering scent of expensive cologne and desperation.

Hanging low, the moon was a pale sentinel watching over the city's shadowy underbelly. A sleek black sedan cruised silently through the industrial district, its headlights off, guided only by the ambient glow of distant streetlamps. The face of the assigned man behind the wheel was a mask of concentration.

He parked the car in a secluded spot, hidden from the main road by a row of shipping containers. A fortress of brick and steel loomed before him. The Sotheby's warehouse guarded millions in precious artwork. Including his target. The man checked his watch. 2:43 a.m. Perfect. He reached into the glove compartment and pulled out a small, matte-black handgun. In a single fluid motion, he screwed on a sound suppressor, the metal cool against his fingers.

"Showtime," he muttered, and slipped out of the car.

The perimeter was quiet, save for the distant hum of the city. As he approached the warehouse, he spotted his first obstacle: a lone security guard making his rounds. The guard moved with the lethargic gait of someone counting down the minutes until their shift ended.

The man melted into the shadows, his breath steady, waiting for the perfect moment. As the guard passed by, fumbling with his flashlight, the robber struck. It took one calculated move to wrap an arm around the guard's neck, and apply the baffling pressure to the carotid artery. The guard's eyes widened in shock. His mouth opened in a silent gasp before consciousness slipped away.

"Nothing personal, pal," the man whispered, as he lowered the limp watchman to the ground. He quickly dragged the unconscious man back to his car, and popped open the trunk. With a grunt of effort, he hefted the watchman inside, pausing only to remove the man's uniform and ID badge.

Back at the warehouse entrance, now clad in the guard's attire, the robber swiped the stolen ID card. The lock disengaged with a soft click. He slipped through, eyes adjusting to the dusk-like ambiance that greeted him inside.

Rows upon rows of crates and shelves stretched out before him. It was a labyrinth of priceless art. The robber's eyes narrowed. Somewhere in this maze was his prize, but first, he needed to find the registry. He moved swiftly through the warehouse, footsteps echoing softly in the cavernous space. Near the back, he found what he was looking for: a small office, its window casting a faint glow. He tried the door. Locked. With a smirk, he pulled out a set of lock picks. Seconds later, he was inside. The office was cramped, dominated by a desk cluttered with paperwork and a humming computer. He slid into the chair, and fingers began flying over the keyboard.

"Come on, come on," he muttered, scrolling through shipping manifests. His eyes lit up. "Gotcha." The Silent Watch. Crate 247B. Aisle 12, Row 5.

Memorizing the location, the robber erased his digital footprints and slipped out of the office. He navigated the maze of shelves with purpose now, counting off aisles until he reached his destination.

There it was. Crate 247B. His heart raced as he approached the spot. The culmination of weeks of planning was now within reach. With steady hands, he pried open the crate, revealing the paintings nestled inside. And there it was. Even in the dim light of the warehouse, its beauty was evident. The man allowed himself a moment of appreciation before getting to work.

From the slim briefcase he'd brought along, he produced the forgery David had given him. It was good, he had to admit. In the low light, it was nearly indistinguishable from the original. Nearly. With painstaking care, he removed the authentic painting from its packing, replacing it with the fake. Every crease in the protective wrapping, every piece of tape, had to be perfect. One misplaced detail could unravel everything.

Minutes ticked by, each second an eternity as he worked. Finally, he stepped back, surveying his handiwork. To the untrained eye, nothing was amiss. The crate looked exactly as it had before he'd opened it. He allowed himself a small smile of triumph as he secured the real Silent Watch in his briefcase. He'd done it. Now, all that remained was to—

A noise. Faint, but unmistakable. Footsteps.

The robber froze, and his hand instinctively moved to the gun at his hip. He'd accounted for every variable, or so he'd thought. But now, as the footsteps grew closer, he realized he'd made a critical error.

The night shift wasn't over.

He ducked behind a nearby shelf, heart pounding. The footsteps drew nearer, accompanied by the crackle of a walkie-talkie.

"Hey, Jim, you there? Haven't heard from you in a while. Everything okay?"

The lurker cursed silently. Jim must be the guard currently taking an involuntary nap in his trunk. He had seconds to make a decision. As the approaching guard rounded the corner, he stepped out, adopting a casual stance.

"Hey there," he said, pitching his voice low. "Radio's acting up. Been meaning to check in."

The guard squinted, clearly not recognizing him. "Who are you? Where's Jim?"

The robber's hand tightened on his concealed weapon. "New guy," he said smoothly. "Jim wasn't feeling well, so they sent me to cover. Guess they forgot to radio it in."

The guard's eyes narrowed further with suspicion. "I'm gonna need to see some ID, buddy."

Time slowed to a crawl. He knew he had a choice to make. In the space of a single breath, he drew his weapon. The other man's eyes widened, as his hand flew to his own holster. But he was too slow. Two muffled shots rang out, barely louder than a cough. The guard crumpled to the ground, with a look of disbelief frozen on his face.

The robber stood there for a moment, the gun still raised, his breath coming in short gasps. This wasn't part of the plan. This changed everything. Forcing himself to focus, he dragged the body behind a row of crates close to the entrance of the warehouse. He had minutes, at most, before someone came looking. He returned to grab his briefcase and made his way swiftly towards the exit, every shadow now a potential threat.

As he emerged into the cool night air, he fought the urge to run. Calmly, steadily, he walked to his car, and opened the trunk. The first guard was still there, unconscious but alive. The robber hesitated for a split second before making his decision.

He couldn't leave witnesses.

When he drove away from the warehouse, his hands were gripping the steering wheel so tightly his knuckles were white. In the trunk, two bodies lay still and cold.

As he merged onto the highway, his phone rang. David.

With a deep breath, he answered. "It's done," he said, his voice remarkably steady.

"Excellent," David's voice crackled through the speaker. "Any complications?"

The driver's eyes flicked to the rearview mirror, half-expecting to see flashing lights. "Nothing I couldn't handle," he replied. "But we've got some cleanup to take care of."

There was a pause on the other end of the line. "How much cleanup?"

"Two bodies' worth."

Another, longer pause. When David spoke again, his voice was ice cold. "I see. Take care of it. Permanently. Then meet me at the usual spot. We need to talk."

The driver tossed the phone onto the passenger seat. This job had just gotten a lot more complicated. And a lot more dangerous. As he drove through the night, The Silent Watch safely hidden in his briefcase, he shook off every other feeling and reminded himself he had a job to finish. And two bodies to dispose of before the sun rose over Atlanta.

The abandoned factory loomed against the pre-dawn sky, a hulking silhouette of rust and broken windows. David Hollister stood in its shadow, his eyes scanning the empty lot. The air was thick with anticipation and the acrid smell of industrial decay. A set of headlights pierced the darkness, and David's hand instinctively moved to the gun concealed beneath his jacket. A black sedan rolled to a stop a few yards away. The engine cut off, plunging the scene back into silence.

The driver's door opened, and the man David had entrusted with the heist stepped out. Even in the dim light, David could see the tension in the man's shoulders, the wariness in his movements. He carried a slim briefcase in one hand, holding it close like a lifeline.

"You're late." David's voice cut through the stillness.

The man shrugged, his face impassive. "Had some loose ends to tie up."

David's eyes narrowed. "The bodies?"

"Taken care of," the man replied in a flat tone. "They won't be found."

A moment of silence stretched between them, heavy with unspoken questions. Finally, David nodded. "Let's see it, then."

The man approached, placing the briefcase on the hood of his car. With a glance at David, he popped the latches. The lid swung open, revealing the prize nestled within.

Even in the weak light of dawn, The Silent Watch seemed to glow. The brushstrokes, the play of light and shadow, the haunting gaze of the subject—it was all there, exactly as David remembered from that fateful day in Max

Worthington's study. A surge of emotion welled up in David's chest. Triumph, exhilaration, a savage joy that threatened to overwhelm him. His hands trembled slightly as he reached out, fingers hovering just above the canvas.

"Beautiful, isn't it?" he murmured, more to himself than his companion.

The man grunted noncommittally. "It's a nice picture. Nicer with the price tag attached."

David shot him a sharp look, then smiled. "Of course. Your payment." He reached behind a stack of planks and produced a second briefcase. "As agreed. Ten percent of the auction price. All of the nine and a half."

He placed the briefcase next to the painting and opened it. Neatly arranged stacks of hundred-dollar bills filled the interior. The other man's eyes widened almost imperceptibly.

"Count it if you like." There was a note of challenge in David's voice.

The man shook his head. "I trust you. Professional courtesy."

David's nod was an appreciation of the man's composure. "You've done well. Better than I expected, given the complications."

A shadow passed over the man's face. "Yeah, well, shit happens. Nothing I couldn't take care of on my own."

"Clearly," David said. He closed the briefcase containing the painting, lifting it with a reverence usually reserved for holy relics. "Our business is concluded. I trust you'll be disappearing for a while?"

The man picked up the briefcase full of cash. "That's the plan. Somewhere warm, I think. No extradition."

"A wise choice," David said. He extended his hand. "It's been a pleasure doing business with you."

The man hesitated for a moment before shaking David's hand. "Likewise. Though if it's all the same to you, let's not do it again."

David gave a chuckle. "Agreed."

They parted ways, and each man returned to his respective vehicle. As David slid into the driver's seat of his luxury SUV, unfiltered triumph washed over him, and he relished the moment. Phase two of his plan was complete. The real Silent Watch was in his possession, and by the time anyone realized the switch had been made, he'd have erased all the trails that might lead to his doorstep. He started the engine, the painting secure beside him. As he pulled away from the abandoned factory, his mind was already librating around the next stage of his plan. How far was the day when he would watch Max Worthington's downfall like the brilliance of a star fading into the vast, indifferent night?

In his rearview mirror, he saw the black sedan heading in the opposite direction, carrying a man whose name he'd never known towards a new life bought with blood money. For a brief moment, David felt a twinge of what they'd done. The lives altered, ended even, in pursuit of his grand plan.

But then the feeling passed, replaced by a cold determination. He was too close to his goal now to let sentiment get in the way. Max's family had taken everything from his family once. Now it was David's turn to return the favor.

The sun was rising over Atlanta as David merged onto the highway, The Silent Watch riding shotgun like a silent co-conspirator. In a few hours, the city would be waking up, going about its business, unaware of the drama that had unfolded in its shadowy corners. David smiled to himself. Let them go about their mundane lives. He had bigger things to attend to. The next phase of his plan awaited, and with it, the sweet promise of revenge.

As the city receded behind him, David felt a sense of destiny settling over him. The trap was set for Max Worthington. The SUV sped on, carrying a man consumed by vengeance. The silent watch had begun, and David Hollister intended to see it through to its logical conclusion.

CHAPTER XI

Max Worthington stood before the weathered brick building, squinting against the harsh Atlanta sun. The faded gold lettering on the second-story window read Callahan Investigations. He took a deep breath, and steeled himself for the conversation ahead.

The stairwell smelled of stale cigarettes and lemon-scented cleaner. Max's footsteps echoed as he climbed, each step feeling heavier than the last. He'd known Jimmy Callahan since his days pounding the streets as a beat reporter, long before Jimmy had traded his press pass for a detective's badge. Now, with Jimmy in private practice, Max hoped his old friend could shed some light on the theft that had upended his life.

Max rapped his knuckles against the frosted glass door. A gruff voice called out, "It's open."

Jimmy Callahan's office was a study in organized chaos. Case files teetered in precarious stacks, sharing space with empty coffee cups and a well-worn baseball mitt. The man himself sat behind a battered desk, his salt-and-pepper hair disheveled, tie loosened. He looked up with a crooked grin spreading across his face.

"Well, I'll be damned. Max Worthington, as I live and breathe. To what do I owe the pleasure?"

Leather whined under his weight as Max sank into the chair across from Jimmy. "I need your help, Jimmy. Professional capacity."

Jimmy's eyebrows shot up. "That bad, huh? Last I checked, you were spinning yarns, not living 'em."

"Yeah, well …" Max ran a hand through his hair. "Things have taken a turn."

"Alright, spill it. What's got you looking like you've seen a ghost?"

Max leaned forward, elbows on his knees. "Someone broke into my place. Stole a painting. Family heirloom, worth a small fortune."

Jimmy whistled low. "Damn. When?"

"Been a little over three weeks. But here's the kicker — there's no sign of forced entry. And the painting was in a safe."

"So either you've got one hell of a cat burglar, or…"

"Or it was someone who knew the combination," Max finished.

Jimmy's eyes narrowed. "You tell anyone that combo?"

Max shook his head emphatically. "Not a soul. That's what's driving me crazy."

"What about security footage?"

"Two cameras. One on the porch, one in the main hallway. Nothing out of the ordinary on either."

Jimmy drummed his fingers on the desk. "Could've been tampered with. There are ways to loop footage, make it look clean."

Max's heart sank. "Christ, I didn't even think of that."

"Hey, that's why you came to the professional, right?" Jimmy flashed a reassuring smile. "What else you got for me?"

Max hesitated, then decided to lay it all out. "I got an email. Anonymous. Told me to go to Piedmont Park Conservatory."

Jimmy's chair squawked like some old, bad-tempered Maude as he leaned back into it. "And?"

"And I went. Met a guy. Well, sort of. He stayed hidden, talking from behind some bushes. Said the person who wronged me had wronged him too."

"Well, that's cryptic as hell. He give you anything useful?"

Max shook his head. "Not really. Mentioned some old family feud I can barely remember. Wanted to meet again in a few days."

Jimmy's brow furrowed. "You planning on going?"

"I don't know. Seems like my only lead at this point."

"It's risky, Max. This guy could be involved in the theft, setting you up for God knows what."

Max nodded, a grim smile on his face. "Trust me, I've thought about that. But I'm out of options here."

Jimmy sighed, leaning forward. "Alright, what's your next move then?"

"There's something else." Max's voice was tight. "The painting … it showed up at auction. Sotheby's. Sold for a fortune."

Jimmy's eyebrows darted up like startled fish breaking the water's surface. "Jesus. Someone's got brass ones, I'll give 'em that. You know who bought it?"

Max nodded. "Woman named Anastasia Chen. Lives in Buckhead, from what I can tell."

"And let me guess, you're thinking of paying Ms. Chen a visit?"

"Got it in one."

Jimmy shook his head. "Max, I gotta ask, what's the endgame here? Even if you track down this Chen woman, it's not like you can just take the painting back."

Max's jaw clenched. "I don't know, Jimmy. But it's the only thread I've got. Maybe I can convince her it was stolen, get her to cooperate somehow."

"That's a hell of a long shot, my friend."

"You got a better idea? Because I'm all ears."

Jimmy held up his hands in surrender. "Hey, I'm not trying to rain on your parade. Just want you to be careful. This whole thing stinks to high heaven."

Max stood, his expression a mix of determination and desperation. "I appreciate the concern, Jimmy. Really. But I need to see this through."

Jimmy rose as well, coming around the desk. He clapped a hand on Max's shoulder. "I know you do. Just … watch your back, alright? And keep me in the loop. I'll do some digging on my end, see if anything shakes loose."

Gratitude was evident in his eyes as Max gave the detective a nod. "Thanks, Jimmy. I owe you one."

"Ah, just dedicate your next bestseller to me. That'll square us up."

As Max turned to leave, Jimmy called out, "Hey, Worthington?"

Max paused at the door, looking back.

Jimmy's expression was deadly serious. "There's more going on here than meets the eye. Be careful who you trust."

With a final nod, Max stepped out into the hallway, Jimmy's warning sounding in his mind. As he descended the stairs, he couldn't shake the feeling that he was stepping into something far bigger, and far more dangerous than a simple art theft.

Max Worthington's faded vermillion Fairlady 300ZX purred to life. The engine's low rumble matching the tension coiled in his gut. He'd spent the better part of two days tracking Anastasia Chen's movements, finally being able to piece together fragments of high-society gossip and carefully placed phone calls. Fortune, it seemed, was on his side. Ms. Chen was hosting a charity auction for some up-and-coming artists at her Buckhead estate.

Getting on the guest list had required a touch of ingenuity and a hefty dose of brass. Max had reached out to an old college friend, now a rising star in Atlanta's art scene. A few white lies about wanting to cover the event for research on his next novel, and Max found himself with a plus-one invitation burning a hole in his pocket. As he navigated the winding streets of Buckhead, the mansions loomed like medieval fortresses behind wrought-iron gates, Max couldn't shake the feeling that he was in over his head. But the thought of *The Silent Watch*, his family's legacy, hanging in some stranger's home steeled his resolve.

The Chen estate sprawled across several acres, a modernist marvel of glass and steel nestled among old-growth trees. Max handed his keys to a valet, straightening his borrowed Armani jacket before approaching the entrance. A burly man with an earpiece checked his name against the list, eyeing him with a hint of suspicion before he waved him through. The foyer opened into a vast, two-story great room. Floor-to-ceiling windows framed a view of the distant Atlanta skyline, while clusters of the city's elite mingled around displays of avant-garde sculptures and vibrant canvases. As Max snagged a flute of champagne from a passing waiter, his eyes scanned the crowd.

And then he saw her.

The woman cut through the room like a shark through still waters. Her presence commanded attention without her seeming to notice it. The black cocktail dress hugged curves that made Max's mouth go dry, but it was the intelligence glinting in her dark eyes that truly arrested him. She was mid-conversation with an older couple when her gaze locked onto Max. A flicker of curiosity crossed her features.

Max took a steadying breath and made his approach. Anastasia excused herself from her previous conversation, meeting him halfway.

"I don't believe we've been introduced." Her voice was a melodic contralto. "I make it a point to know all my guests."

Max flashed his most disarming smile. "Max Worthington. I'm afraid I'm here under slightly false pretenses. I'm a friend of Daniel Cho. When he mentioned your event, I couldn't resist the opportunity to see your collection firsthand."

Recognition dawned in Anastasia's eyes. "Max Worthington? The novelist?"

Max nodded, a hint of self-deprecation in his smile. "Guilty as charged. Though I assure you, I'm much less interesting than my characters."

Anastasia's laugh was rich and genuine. "Oh, I doubt that very much, Mr. Worthington. Come, let me give you the tour. I'm always curious to hear how a writer's eye interprets art." As they moved through the gallery, Max found himself genuinely captivated; both by the art and by Anastasia herself. She was knowledgeable, passionate, and possessed a wry sense of humor that kept him on his toes. It was almost enough to make him forget his true purpose.

Almost.

"I have to say," Max ventured as they paused before a particularly striking landscape, "your taste is impeccable. I'd love to hear about some of your recent acquisitions."

Anastasia's eyes lit up. "Oh, where to begin? Just some days ago at Sotheby's, I managed to snag the most exquisite piece. The Silent Watch. Are you familiar with it?"

Max's heart hammered against his ribs, but he kept his voice steady. "I've heard of it, yes. Quite the coup, from what I understand."

"It was a bit of a bidding war," Anastasia admitted with a hint of pride in her voice. "But well worth it. The emotional depth in that painting … it's unlike anything I've seen."

"I'd love to hear more about the auction," Max pressed gently. "Was it as cutthroat as they say?"

Anastasia laughed. "Oh, you have no idea. There was this one man, David Hollister, I think his name was, yes, who seemed determined to outbid everyone. But in the end, I just wanted it more."

Max filed the name away, careful to keep his expression neutral. The name rang a bell. That name had cropped up somewhere only recently. He'd think about that later. "Sounds thrilling. I don't suppose the artist was there?"

"Oh, the artist lived a long time ago. No, it was all done through proxies. Quite mysterious, really. Adds to the allure, don't you think?"

Max nodded, his eyes drawn to Anastasia's profile as she gazed at a nearby sculpture. The soft gallery lighting accentuated the elegant curve of her neck, the high cheekbones that spoke of aristocratic heritage. When she turned back to him, her dark eyes sparkled with mischief.

"You seem quite interested in the auction, Mr. Worthington. Planning on making some acquisitions of your own?"

Max chuckled, allowing himself to relax into the flirtation. "Please, call me Max. And I'm afraid my budget is more 'starving artist' than 'esteemed collector'. Though I must admit, the company alone makes me wish I could be a regular on the circuit."

Anastasia's laugh was musical, as her hand came to rest lightly on Max's forearm. He couldn't help but notice how perfectly manicured her nails were, a deep red that matched her lipstick.

"Flattery will get you everywhere, Max," she purred. As she shifted her weight, Max's gaze was drawn to the enticing curve of her hips, brought out by the sleek lines of her dress. He forced his eyes back to her face, hoping she hadn't noticed his wandering attention.

"Speaking of the auction," Max ventured, "you mentioned a David Hollister? I'm not familiar with the name."

Anastasia's brow furrowed slightly. "To be honest, I don't know much about him. We chatted briefly after the bidding. He seemed … intense. Disappointed about losing the painting, obviously, but there was something else. Almost like he took it personally." She shrugged, the movement causing the strap of her dress to slip slightly off her shoulder. All of a sudden, her eyes pinned down a thought that had been dodging her. "Oh, actually, he's the one who sold it. He was the last owner. But enough about him. I find you far more intriguing, Max."

Max felt a flush of heat at her words, at once thrilled and unnerved by her forwardness. "I'm flattered, truly. Though I have to ask, isn't your husband going to mind you lavishing attention on another man?"

David Hollister, the last owner? Max thought. *How in the fucking world could this possibly be real?*

Anastasia's smile took on a wistful quality. "My husband is … away. Business, always business. Sometimes I think he forgets he has a wife at all." Her eyes locked onto Max's, filled with an unmistakable invitation. "But let's not talk about him. Tell me, Max, what inspires a novelist like yourself?"

Max opened his mouth to respond, his mind racing to find a balance between maintaining his cover and pursuing the information he needed. But before he could utter a word, a waiter approached, whispering something in Anastasia's ear. She frowned slightly, then turned back to Max with an apologetic smile.

"I'm afraid duty calls. But please, enjoy the rest of the evening. And Mr. Worthington?" Her hand brushed his arm, the touch electric. "I'd love to continue our conversation sometime. Perhaps over dinner?"

Max's pulse quickened. "I'd like that," he said, meaning it despite himself. As Anastasia glided away, Max's mind raced. The name David Hollister, the mysterious proxy sale. Pieces were falling into place, but the picture they formed was still maddeningly unclear. He made his way through the rest of the party on autopilot, exchanging pleasantries and dodging questions about his next book. When he finally escaped into the cool night air, relief washed over him.

Max slid into the driver's seat of his Fairlady, but didn't start the engine. Instead, he pulled out a small notebook, jotting down everything he'd learned. The timeline was starting to take shape, but crucial questions remained. How had David Hollister gotten his hands on the painting? And why go through the trouble of an auction, rather than a private sale?

Lost in thought, Max didn't notice the pair of hands protrude through the shadows of a nearby hedge. The soft click of a camera shutter was lost in the general bustle of a few departing guests.

As Max finally pulled away from the Chen estate, his mind churned with possibilities. He'd gotten what he came for — confirmation that *The Silent Watch* had indeed passed through Sotheby's. But Anastasia's easy charm and obvious interest gnawed at him. Was she truly ignorant of the painting's history, or was this all part of some larger game? One thing was certain: he was treading in dangerous waters. The affluent neighborhood receded in his rearview mirror, and Max couldn't shake the feeling someone was watching him. The stakes in this game were surely higher than he had initially imagined.

Max Worthington's fingers drummed an impatient rhythm on the arm of his weathered leather chair. His eyes darted between the silent phone on his desk and the antique grandfather clock in the corner of his garden apartment. Its steady ticking seemed to mock him, each second stretching into eternity.

Three days had passed since his enigmatic encounter in Piedmont Park. Three days of questions multiplying like weeds in his mind, choking out any semblance of peace. The mysterious e-mailer had promised answers, a key to unlock the spiraling madness his life had become since *The Silent Watch* vanished.

As the clock hands inched towards noon, Max's resolve hardened. Message or no message, he would return to the park. He couldn't afford to let this lead slip away.

The drive down to Piedmont Park was a blur of green-dappled sunlight and racing thoughts. Max parked his Fairlady, its faded vermillion paint glaringly at odds with the lush surroundings. He made his way down the familiar paths, eyes scanning for any sign of his elusive contact. The cherry blossom grove lay before him, a riot of pale pink as its petals danced on the breeze. At its heart stood the massive weeping willow whose branches drooped to create a verdant sanctuary. To its left, the rhododendron bush where the stranger had hidden during their first meeting stood silent and empty.

Minutes stretched into an hour as Max paced the area, his phone clutched in his hand like a lifeline. No call came. No shadowy figure emerged from the foliage. Frustration gnawed at him, mingling with a growing sense of foolishness. Had he imagined the whole thing?

Dejected, Max turned to leave. As he passed a nearby bench, a voice froze him in his tracks.

"Mr. Worthington."

The words were muffled, barely above a whisper, but unmistakable. Max's head snapped towards the source. A figure sat on the bench, face obscured by a newspaper. Slowly, deliberately, the paper lowered. Max's breath caught in his throat. On his face the man wore an amalgam of colors and intricate design. Clearly of Chinese origin, the mask was unlike anything he'd ever seen. The base was a deep, lustrous red, with swirling patterns of gold and black creating the illusion of scales. Fierce, slanted eyes peered out from behind it. The haunting sharpness of that stare sent a shiver down Max's spine. The mask's most striking feature was its lower half — a gaping maw filled with razor-sharp golden fangs, giving the wearer the appearance of a snarling dragon.

Max glanced around. The grove was deserted. The only sounds were the rustle of leaves and the distant laughter of children on the playground. Swallowing hard, he lowered himself onto the bench beside the masked stranger.

"You're late." The man's voice sounded like a low growl to Max.

Max's jaw tightened. "I've been here for over an hour. You're the one who didn't show up where we met last time."

A dry chuckle emanated from behind the mask. "Expecting the expected is a fool's game, Mr. Worthington. I thought a writer of your caliber would understand that."

Max bit back a retort. He needed answers, not a verbal sparring match. "You said you had information. About the old feud in my family."

The dragon's eyes seemed to narrow behind the mask. "Ah, yes. The sins of the fathers, visited upon the sons. Tell me, what do you know of your family's … history?"

Max hesitated, then decided to lay his cards on the table. "Not much. I called my Uncle Hank in Texas after our last meeting. He mentioned some names. Jeremiah Blackwood, Clayton Blackwood. Something about my grandfather Teddy losing a woman to Jeremiah, bad blood that carried down through the generations."

The masked man remained still, but Max sensed a shift in his demeanor. "Blackwood," he mused, mocking the name like a bad punchline to an old joke. "A red herring, Mr. Worthington. Your Uncle Hank, well-meaning as he may be, is chasing ghosts. The real story, the one that matters, began right here in Atlanta."

Max leaned forward, his heart racing. "What do you mean?"

"I'm talking about a feud between titans, Mr. Worthington. Your father, Harrison, and another man. A 'pillar of the community,'" — Max could hear the sneer in his voice — "who saw your family as interlopers. New money, threatening the old order."

Images flashed through Max's mind. Half-remembered conversations overheard as a child, tension at family gatherings that he'd never understood. "Who was this man?"

"Robert," the stranger said, the name laden with meaning. "Robert Hollister."

Max's breath caught. "Hollister? As in David Hollister?"

The change was instantaneous. The masked man stiffened, his head snapping towards Max with predatory focus. "Where did you hear that name?" he demanded.

Max's mind raced. He couldn't reveal his encounter with Anastasia Chen, not without exposing his own investigation. "I... I've been doing some digging of my own," he said carefully. "The name came up in connection with the theft of my painting."

A long moment of silence stretched between them. When the masked man spoke again, his voice was tight, controlled. "It seems you've been busy, Mr. Worthington. Perhaps too busy for your own good."

"What does David Hollister have to do with all this?" Max pressed.

The stranger's posture changed, becoming guarded. "Our time grows short," he said, rising from the bench. "But know this: the feud between Harrison Worthington and

Robert Hollister ran deeper than you can imagine. Land disputes, business rivalries, old money versus new… it was a powder keg waiting to explode."

Desperation clawed at Max and he stood as well. "Wait! You can't leave now. What happened? How does this connect to the theft of my painting?"

The masked man took a step back. "The past never truly dies, Mr. Worthington. It sleeps, waiting to be awakened. Your father's actions set something in motion, something that's been building for years. The theft of your painting? Merely the opening move in a game you don't yet understand."

"What game? Who's behind this?" Max reached out, his fingers closing around the stranger's arm.

In a blur of motion, the masked man twisted away. Max, driven by frustration and a burning need for answers, lunged forward. His hands found purchase on the edge of the mask, tugging at it. A sharp pressure against his ribs stopped him cold. Max looked down to see the gleam of a pistol's muzzle pressed against his side.

"I wouldn't," the masked man said, his voice low and dangerous.

Max slowly raised his hands, and backed away. "Who are you?" he whispered.

With a quiet slickness the stranger holstered his weapon. "A ghost," he replied. "A shadow of the past, here to right old wrongs." He took a step back, then paused. "We'll meet again, Max Worthington. When the time is right. Until then, watch your six. The game is far from over."

With that, he turned and strode away, quickly vanishing among the trees. Max stood rooted to the spot, while his mind reeled. The scent of cherry blossoms hung heavy in the air. It made for a sickly-sweet counterpoint to the bitter taste of fear that rose in his throat. As the masked man's footsteps faded, Max sank back onto the bench, his legs suddenly weak. The peaceful park around him seemed transformed. Shadows lurked behind every tree, secrets whispered over the breeze. He'd come seeking answers, but was left with more questions than ever. The theft of *The Silent Watch* must merely be the tip of a very dangerous iceberg. As Max finally got up to leave, he thought about the masked man's parting words.

The game is far from over.

There was no mistaking the sinking feeling that he was playing for stakes far higher than a stolen painting. And he was already in too deep to fold.

CHAPTER XII

Max Worthington had always thought he could separate fact from fiction. It was his job, after all. But right now, fact and fiction were a knot he couldn't untangle, a snarl of clues, dead ends, and something deeper — something he was missing. And he hated missing things. The papers were still running the costly auction of the painting, and the mystery that had been slowly tightening around his neck was starting to feel more like a noose.

David Hollister. That name kept coming back to him. The man was powerful, untouchable even, and Max didn't have proof. Not yet. But he knew. His gut told him it was Hollister who must be behind the theft of *The Silent Watch*.

It had been around four weeks since the auction at Sotheby's and almost four days since he had walked away from Anastasia Chen's estate in Buckhead and felt those eyes on him, though he hadn't seen anyone. He wasn't being paranoid, he knew that. Someone was tailing him. He just didn't know who. Felicity had been around more often lately, trying to coax him back to his book, but even her soothing voice couldn't keep his mind from spinning in overdrive.

Tonight, he was supposed to meet an 'insider'. Someone who claimed to have answers about the painting. The email had come from an untraceable source. "I have information about Hollister's connection to the auction. Meet me at 10 p.m. at Steel River warehouse on the edge of town. Come alone." It stank of a trap, but Max's curiosity — and desperation — had gotten the better of him.

He glanced at the time on his dashboard: 9:52 p.m. He was already late.

The road stretched long and empty ahead of him, the main meat of the town shrinking in his rearview mirror as he neared the desolate industrial district. Max reached for his phone, hesitated, and then dialed.

"Callahan."

"Jimmy, it's Max. Listen, I got a tip. Somebody claims to know about Hollister's involvement in the auction."

There was silence on the other end, just the crackle of the phone line. Max could almost hear Jimmy's brain working through the name. It didn't take long for it to click and when Callahan spoke again, he sounded like he'd swallowed nails and liked the taste. "You mean *David* Hollister, right? The same one?"

Max nodded even though Jimmy couldn't see him. "Yeah, him."

Jimmy let out a low whistle, followed by the faint sound of a cigarette being lit. "Damn, Max. You realize what you're walking into, don't you? That guy's not just some local businessman. David Hollister's practically the king of Atlanta. Runs in all the high-end circles. Art, finance, government. Hell, he's got fingers in more pies than you can count. You don't mess with him unless you're looking to be waist-deep in trouble."

"I know," Max said. "I looked him up earlier. Saw how quickly he's risen in the art world. Plus, he's tied to some big-money real estate deals downtown. He moves fast, doesn't leave much behind."

"Yeah, and I bet there's a whole lot he's hiding behind that shiny exterior. If this is the same Hollister, you're in deeper than you think, man."

"I figured as much," Max muttered, as he gripped the steering wheel a little tighter. "That's why I've got to check this out. Whoever sent me this email mentioned Hollister by name. They said they have dirt on him, something about his connection to the auction."

There was another pause on Jimmy's end. "And you're going to the meeting? Just like that?"

"Yeah," Max replied, determination creeping into his voice. "Steel River Warehouse. 10 p.m. I'm running late as it is, but if there's any chance this leads to something, I have to go."

"You sure this isn't a setup?" Jimmy asked, his voice dropping lower.

"I'm sure it is," Max admitted. "But I can't sit around waiting for answers anymore. This whole thing is closing in too fast. If Hollister's involved, I need to know what he's hiding."

Max could hear the faint drag of a cigarette before Jimmy said, "Max, be careful. Hollister's got more connections than a damn spider web. He doesn't let anyone dig around in his business. And from what I've heard, when people start asking questions about him, they don't usually stick around long enough to get answers. You sure you don't want backup?"

"I'll be fine," Max said, more to convince himself than Callahan. Then he sighed. "I just want to check it out. But I wanted someone to know, just in case …"

"Max …"

But Max hung up before Jimmy could try to stop him. He didn't need to hear it. He already knew the risks.

The warehouse loomed ahead like a behemoth, its windows blacked out and the only light coming from a flickering streetlamp that looked like it was losing its battle with time. Max pulled his car into the shadows and killed the engine. He waited for a moment, watching, listening. The air was thick, humid, and the kind of silence that wasn't really silent hung around the place. It was like the city itself was holding its breath.

It's a trap, Max thought, sliding his gun into the back of his jeans. Still he stepped out of the car. The night closed in around him as he approached the side entrance, the metallic clink of his boots echoing off the corrugated walls. The door was already cracked open, with a sliver of darkness beckoning him in. He paused, glanced around — nobody in sight — and pushed the door wider.

The inside was worse than he'd imagined. Shadows curled around the edges of the room, thick and uninviting. He could hear the faint drip of water from somewhere overhead, the sound of something scurrying in the dark. A lone light bulb hung from the ceiling, swaying ever so slightly, casting long, distorted shapes across the concrete floor.

"Hello?" His voice sounded too loud in the empty space.

Nothing. Just the soft hum of the flickering bulb.

Max took a step forward. Then another. He could feel it now, a change in the air, like a storm brewing in the black belly of this abandoned place. His instincts screamed at him to turn around, but before he could react, the light bulb snapped off and he was plunged into darkness.

"Damn it," Max cursed, reaching for his phone. But the signal was gone, just static on the screen. He fumbled for the gun tucked into the back of his waistband when the lights suddenly flared back on — blinding him this time — and the very next instant he saw them.

Three men. No, four. No faces he recognized, but their posture was unmistakable. They were pros. The kind who didn't hesitate, didn't miss. And they had him boxed in.

"Well, well, if it isn't the man of the hour."

Max turned to see a tall figure stepping out from behind the shadows. One of the men? No. This one was different, dressed in an impeccable suit with a smirk that curled like smoke. He had the easy confidence of someone who knew they had already won.

"Max Worthington," the man said with a low chuckle. "Mr. Hollister sends his regards."

Max's pulse quickened. So this was it. Hollister had set him up. "You don't want to do this," Max said, trying his best to keep his voice steady.

The man shrugged. "It's not personal, just business."

Two of the goons stepped forward, reaching for him. Max moved quickly, backing away, as his mind ticked louder and closer to the brink each passing moment. The door was too far, the windows boarded up. He had seconds, maybe less.

That is when Max's eyes flicked to the ceiling, spotting the ventilation shaft just a few feet above. Desperate, he moved, quick and fluid, grabbing a nearby metal barrel and flipping it on its side. The men were on him, but Max was faster. He hoisted himself up, grabbed the edge of the vent, and swung his legs inside just as one of the men lunged.

"Get him!" the leader barked, but Max was already pulling himself through the narrow shaft.

The sound of footsteps echoed behind him as he crawled forward, heart pounding in his chest. He knew they wouldn't give up that easily, but he also knew these kinds of buildings. The old industrial design had one weakness: the ventilation system that connected the entire structure. He kept moving, the sound of his breath and the clatter of the men below chasing him through the maze of metal tunnels. All at once, voices drifted up through the grate ahead, low but distinct. He stopped, straining to hear.

"They should've just killed him," one of the men grumbled.

"Orders are orders. Hollister wants him alive, for now."

Max's blood ran cold. Hollister had plans for him, bigger than just removing him from the picture. But why?

A noise from the other side of the vent drew his attention. He froze. The sound of something — or someone — moving. Before Max could react, the grate ahead of him swung open, and he tensed, expecting one of the goons.

But it wasn't.

The figure crouched in the shadows, the face partially obscured by a hood, and Max couldn't quite make him out. The stranger motioned for Max to follow him without a word. Max hesitated. He didn't know if he could trust this man — he didn't even know who he was. But there wasn't time to argue. The goons were closing in, and this mysterious figure seemed to know the way out. He followed.

They emerged through a side entrance, and Max whipped his head this way and that to find himself in a narrow alley behind the warehouse. Max glanced over his shoulder, expecting to see the men following them, but the alley was clear. The stranger turned to face Max, his features hidden in the shadows. For a moment, Max thought he recognized something in the man's face, but the thought slipped away before he could grasp it.

"Who are you?" Max asked, his voice hoarse.

The man didn't answer. Instead, he gave Max a nod, then melted into the darkness before Max could stop him.

Max stood there, heart racing, breath coming in shallow gasps. He was out alive but he had more questions now than ever before. Someone had helped him, but why?

And more importantly, how did they know to be there?

Max didn't return home. Not yet. He drove in silence, replaying the night in his head. He had been so close to walking into Hollister's hands, so close to being wiped off the map like so many others who had crossed the man. But someone had pulled him back.

By the time he parked in front of Jimmy Callahan's place, it was well past midnight. He wasn't ready to explain everything yet, but Jimmy needed to know what had happened.

Max knocked on the door, feeling the night press down on him. The door opened, and Jimmy stood there, bleary-eyed but alert, like he always was in the early hours.

"You look like hell," Jimmy muttered, stepping aside to let him in.

"You should see the other guy," Max said with a dry chuckle, though there was no humor in his voice. He sank into the chair by the window and ran a hand through his hair.

"I've got to tell you something, Jimmy. Hollister's not just after the painting. He's after me."

Jimmy narrowed his eyes, leaning against the counter. "You figured that out all by yourself?"

Max looked up, locking eyes with his old friend. "And I think someone else is in the game now. Someone who doesn't want me dead yet."

David Hollister stared at his phone screen, his hand trembling in a rare display of emotion. The news was worse than he'd anticipated. Max Worthington had escaped.

The silence in his office felt oppressive. He slammed the phone down onto his mahogany desk, the echo of the impact reverberating off the glass walls. His jaw clenched so tight it hurt, but he didn't care. The frustration swirled in him like a storm he could barely contain. Across the room, Evelyn stood by the window, watching the skyline of Atlanta. Her back was to him, but David could sense her tension.

"So," she said quietly, her voice almost lost in the hum of the city below. "It didn't work."

David didn't answer at first. He stood, pacing, trying to shake the anger that coursed through him like wildfire. "No, it didn't work," he growled. "Our boy Max slipped through the damn cracks."

He moved toward the large painting that hung on the wall — one of his private stash of contemporary art collected over years, most of it gained through connections that never saw the light of day. It was a reminder of the power he'd accumulated, of how far he'd climbed to get where he was. And yet, some amateur novelist had just walked right through his carefully laid plan.

"How the hell did he escape?" David muttered under his breath, as if the painting might give him an answer. He clenched his fist, wanting to smash something, anything.

Evelyn turned to face him now, her eyes calm, composed. "Max is proving to be more resourceful than you thought." She crossed her arms, her tone was measured, but there was a flicker of something behind her eyes. Worry, perhaps.

David laughed bitterly. "Resourceful? I thought I had him cornered. I thought I had everything in place."

"You did. But you underestimated him."

His eyes flicked toward her, narrowing. "You were the one who lured him to the warehouse, Evelyn. This was your idea. Don't forget that."

She didn't flinch. "I did exactly what you asked. I sent the email, I set the bait. Max took it, but someone tipped him off. It wasn't my fault the execution fell apart."

David stopped pacing, his mind churning. Someone tipped Max off? He replayed the events in his head, trying to figure out where the leak could've come from. Was there a mole in his operation? Or was Max getting help from someone unexpected? He glanced at Evelyn again. Her face was unreadable, and that bothered him. She'd always been loyal, but lately, he wasn't so sure about anyone.

He moved closer to her, his voice dropping into a low, dangerous tone. "I don't like failure, Evelyn. And I don't tolerate mistakes."

She raised an eyebrow, her lips curving into a faint smile. "Neither do I. That's why this won't happen again. But you need to stop underestimating Max. He's not as easy to crush as you thought."

David's eyes blazed with fury, but he held back. She wasn't wrong. Max had become a problem — one that wouldn't just go away with a single trap. He needed to up the stakes. Go bigger. Deadlier.

"You're right," he said, his voice cold. "This was just round one. But next time, Max won't be so lucky."

He turned back to the window, looking out over the vast expanse of the city he controlled. Somewhere out there, Max was regrouping, probably thinking he'd won a victory. But David knew better.

He wasn't finished yet.

And when he came for Max again, he'd make damn sure there was no escape.

Evelyn's heels clicked softly against the hardwood floor as she moved closer. Without a word, she reached out and traced her fingers along David's jawline, her nails lightly grazing his skin. His breath hitched, but he didn't pull away. She stroked his hair, her fingers weaving through the dark strands, and his eyes drifted shut, as the tension in his shoulders eased somewhat.

"You need to relax, David," she whispered. Her voice was smooth, almost playful. "You're no good to anyone when you're wound this tight."

Before he could respond, she was straddling him, her body pressing against his as she settled into his lap. He let out a low growl, feeling her quickly getting wet. His hands instinctively found her hips and she yawped brassily. For a moment, everything faded — the failed plan, the frustration, the nagging sense that Max was slipping through his fingers. Evelyn leaned in, her lips grazing his ear.

"Forget about him," she murmured, as a mischievous smile played at her lips. "At least for now." Her buttocks twisted unpredictably, making him blurt out with the thrill.

"Agreed?" she said as she threw back her head and her meaty hips began to buck and lurch.

David exhaled, letting himself sink into the moment, his hands roaming her curves. But even as she coaxed him into a rare moment of surrender, a dark thought stirred at the back of his mind. Beneath the surface, the wolf inside him was waking, and it wouldn't stay quiet for long.

CHAPTER XIII

Max Worthington sat at his desk with the unfolding situation pressing against his skull like a vice. The coffee had long gone cold, and from outside the muffled sounds of late-morning Atlanta crept through the open crack in the window. He'd been staring at the same paragraph in his manuscript near to two hours now, but the words refused to settle. His mind was somewhere else. With her.

Felicity.

Max's mind could not stop playing and replaying her behavior in the days leading up to the theft. Every small detail felt sharper, more pointed. Why had she asked so many questions about the paintings in his family?

She'd slipped out of bed the morning *The Silent Watch* disappeared with nothing more than a kiss on his forehead and a murmured excuse about a photography job. At the time, he thought nothing of it. His mind had been on the manuscript he needed to push ahead with. Even when he woke up later and saw the article in the morning paper, it hadn't sparked anything in him. But the name *The Silent Watch* was not one he did not fully recognize. Of course, the levee of his memory had flooded while sitting at Liam's desk and actually seeing the photograph of the artwork in another newspaper.

He knew that the painting had been passed down through his family, at times it felt like it was an old secret, but he hadn't paid much attention. After seeing it in his parents' house as a teenager, the next he'd laid eyes on it was at the time of inheriting tangible personal property. Another one of his heirlooms, *The Silent Watch* had been sitting in his safe for years.

"Why do you keep so many old paintings around, Max?" Felicity had asked a few nights before he discovered that his safe contained a fake. Her voice was light but probing. "Do you even know where they all came from? What's their story?"

Max remembered kneeling in front of the open safe, carefully rearranging the items he had inherited from his parents. The safe was a small vault of family history — old documents, jewelry, and a few framed photographs that had seen better days. Among them were paintings, each wrapped in protective layers of cloth. As he tidied up, he ran his fingers over one of the smaller frames, feeling the weight of the past it represented. The heirlooms didn't often come to mind, but every so often, he found himself drawn to them, wanting to keep his parents' legacy in some kind of order.

Behind him, Felicity sat at the desk, her fingers clicking away on the keyboard, working on one of her photography projects. But her attention soon drifted toward him. He could feel her eyes on his back as he gently set down one of the wrapped paintings on the floor beside him.

"What's that one?" she asked, getting up and walking over to where he was working. Her gaze lingered on the canvas tucked beneath its protective layers. Curiosity had gleamed in her eyes. Before he could respond, she reached out to lift the corner of the cloth.

Max's hand shot out to stop her. "Don't touch that," he said, more forcefully than he intended. Felicity pulled back, surprised but smiling in that easy way of hers.

"Okay, okay," she said, raising her hands in mock surrender. "I'm just curious. You have all these old paintings, and I never see you talk about them."

He shrugged, refocusing on the safe. "They're just family stuff. Passed down. I don't even know much about most of them."

Felicity had lingered, her fingers absently brushing a stray lock of hair behind her ear. "You ever think about changing the combination on this thing?" she asked, almost casually. "You know, just in case?"

Max chuckled softly. "Nah, it's fine. No one's getting into this thing."

"Not even me?" she teased with a mischievous glint in her eyes.

He looked over his shoulder, smiling but not quite taking her seriously. "You don't need to know what's in here."

She pressed a little more, but Max parried the questions easily, distracted as he moved the heirlooms around and closed the door of the safe with a dull, metallic thud.

Why had she seemed so interested in the painting's security?

At the time, he hadn't connected her curiosity with the painting's disappearance. He had simply shrugged off her questions as idle conversation. Nothing more than Felicity's usual playful inquisitiveness. But now, thinking back, the timing gnawed at him. She had left early the morning of the day he became aware of the theft, claiming she had a photography job lined up, and in his sleepy haze, it had all seemed part of the routine.

Now, thinking again … She had kissed him goodbye, the light brush of her lips barely pulling him from sleep before she slipped out the door. Of course, it wasn't until later that day when the weight of the world finally allowed him a pause. The painting he had inherited, carefully wrapped and stored for years, was gone, replaced by something hollow, something that shouldn't have been there. That was when he had scrambled to find answers to the questions starting to pile up. But even then, nothing in it had concerned Felicity. Then desperate to see who might have entered his private space, Max only found the security footage as empty as a blank canvas. He had two cameras — one in the main hallway inside the apartment, aimed at the front door, and another trained on the porch outside. They should have caught Felicity leaving, at the very least, if not anyone else coming or going. But when he reviewed the footage after his first meeting with Jimmy, there was nothing during that morning. Neither camera had captured her leaving that morning. Max had failed to pay attention to this part of the footage until now.

At first, he thought it had to be a glitch, some technical error that erased the footage. But the more he thought about it, the more unsettling it became. Both cameras? Failing at the same time? It didn't add up. He even called the security company, but they insisted the cameras were functioning normally. The hallway footage should have shown her opening the door, stepping out. The porch camera should have picked up her leaving the apartment. But it was like she had vanished into thin air after that morning kiss.

And then everything had felt wrong in an instant.

Dust devils of doubt were sprouting through his thoughts as he replayed the moment in his mind. Had the cameras been tampered with? The timing of her leaving, the cameras failing, and the painting disappearing — it all felt too coincidental now. Felicity had always been tech-savvy, adept with her photography equipment and electronics. Could she have known how to avoid the cameras? Or worse — could she have disabled them herself? He hated even thinking it, but the pieces weren't fitting together any other way. Each time they did, he averted his gaze.

Her departure that morning was starting to feel more like a carefully calculated exit than a simple goodbye.

Max leaned back in his chair and rubbed his temples. He didn't want to think this way. Felicity wasn't just his girlfriend — she was the woman he loved, the woman who brought light into his life. The idea of her being involved in something so sinister, so calculating was unthinkable. But the seed of doubt was beginning to take root.

He glanced at his phone, and his finger hovered over Jimmy Callahan's number. Jimmy was one of his oldest friends, but also a detective with a nose for bullshit. If anyone could help him make sense of these feelings, it was Jimmy. But calling him would make it real. It would mean admitting that he suspected Felicity.

Max dropped the phone back onto the table and stood up. He couldn't sit still any longer. Maybe a walk would help clear his head.

Outside, the autumn sun hung low, casting long shadows across the narrow streets. Max walked aimlessly, his feet carrying him through Grant Park without any real destination. His mind churned over the same questions, trying to find a logical explanation, some way to exonerate Felicity in his head.

But then he remembered something else. Something small, but strange. After she'd asked those odd questions, and after she had left early on the fateful day, she claimed she had a shoot on the other side of town. But hadn't she mentioned earlier that she didn't have anything lined up that week?

It was nothing — just a small inconsistency — but it added to the pile. And that pile was growing.

Max was so lost in thought he didn't notice the child until she nearly crashed into him.

"Whoa, easy there!" Max stepped back just in time as Mackenzie swerved her bike to avoid him. She skidded to a stop, her face flushed with the exertion.

"Mr. Worthington!" She grinned up at him, breathless but excited. "I didn't see you!"

Max forced a smile. "It's alright, Mackenzie. You're getting better on that bike, huh?"

She beamed, bouncing on her toes. "Yeah! I'm getting super fast now. I ride past your place all the time."

Max's smile faltered, a memory bubbling to the surface. The last time he'd seen Mackenzie, she'd been sitting on the curb, her bike overturned. It had been the same day *The Silent Watch* disappeared, the day he'd driven out to his publisher's office. He'd helped her up before heading to his car, and Felicity had already been gone by then.

"Hey, Mackenzie, remember when you fell off your bike? I was getting into my car and saw you. Did you notice anything strange around my place that day after I left?"

"Strange how?" Mackenzie asked, tilting her head. "Like ghosts?"

Max forced a laugh. "Not ghosts. Just… anything unusual, like something that didn't belong."

Mackenzie ran her fingers absently over the bike's handles. "Well, I saw a woman outside your place. But that's not unusual."

Max's pulse quickened. "Wait, what woman?"

"I don't know. I thought she was your girlfriend."

Max blinked. *Girlfriend?* "Can you describe her?"

"Huh?"

"What did she look like? Chestnut hair? Blue eyes? Ties her hair high but lets one lock fall loose?"

Mackenzie squinted, then nodded. "Yeah, that's her. She was over by the curb, talking to someone."

"Talking to who?" Max's voice tightened.

"I dunno. Someone in a car."

"A man?"

"Maybe." Mackenzie shrugged. "Didn't see him too well."

"What kind of car? Light yellow Nissan Versa Note?" Max's hand gripped the bike's handlebar hard enough to make the girl flinch.

"I don't know cars, Mr. Worthington. It wasn't yellow, though."

Max exhaled sharply. "Thanks, Mackenzie."

"Sure thing," she said, flashing a grin as she pedaled off, wobbling slightly. Her pink helmet bobbed as she disappeared down the street. His mind raced, trying to piece it all together. Why had Felicity been near his house, talking to someone on the day the painting disappeared? And more importantly, why hadn't she told him?

Max paced his living room, his mind a whirlpool of suspicion and confusion. The questions swung at him from different angles. Felicity had been secretive that day, no doubt about it. Mackenzie's innocent comment had stirred something deep in his gut. Damn it, it was a sense of betrayal he wasn't ready to accept.

He paused to look at his phone resting on the table. He snapped out of his thoughts, hesitated only for a second before dialing up. When a voice answered at the other end, he said, "Jimmy, you got a minute?"

"Max? Yeah, sure. What's going on?"

Max felt the words stick in his throat. He didn't know how to explain it, didn't know how to tell his best friend that he was starting to suspect the woman he loved. But Jimmy wasn't the type to sugarcoat things. If anyone could help him sort this mess out, it was him.

"It's about Felicity. My girlfriend," Max finally said in a low voice.

There was a pause on the other end. "What about her?"

Max swallowed, starting to pace again. "I don't know, man. I've been getting these ... these feelings. Like something's not right. She's been acting weird lately. Asking questions about the painting, leaving at odd times. And today, I found out she was at my place the day the painting disappeared — talking to some guy in a car."

Jimmy didn't respond right away, and when he did, his voice was calm but firm. "Max, you're not crazy for thinking that something's off. I mean, hell, the painting goes missing, and now you're hearing all these little things that don't add up. It's enough to make anyone suspicious."

Max clenched his jaw. "I don't want to think that she had anything to do with it, Jimmy. I love her. But... I don't know."

Jimmy sighed on the other end. "Listen, man, love makes things messy. It's easy to let your feelings blind you to what's right in front of you. But you've gotta be smart about this. If Felicity's involved in this, and I'm not saying she is, but if she is … you need to find out. Quietly. Don't confront her yet."

Max sank onto the couch, his fingers massaging his temples. "I just … I don't know where to start."

"I'll help you," Jimmy said. "I'll start looking into her connections. If there's anything shady, I'll find it."

"Thanks, Jimmy."

"Don't mention it. And Max? Be careful, okay? Don't let your heart get in the way of your head."

Max sat for a long time after the call ended, the room growing darker as the sun slid downward the meridian. He knew Jimmy was right. He couldn't let his feelings for Felicity cloud his judgment. But as much as he tried to think logically, the idea of her betraying him felt like a knife twisting in his gut.

He stood up, heading over to his bookshelf where a collection of photo albums sat. He flipped through one, scanning the old photos from various events. He wasn't sure what he was looking for, but something was tugging at the back of his mind. It was a nagging feeling that there was something he had missed, something buried in the past that might make sense of the present chaos.

His fingers moved mechanically through the pages, photos of parties, gallery openings, and dinners flipping by in a blur. Felicity was in many of them, always smiling, always surrounded by people — sometimes other photographers, sometimes artists, or the occasional patron. But nothing about the pictures seemed out of place. Max sighed, frustrated with himself. He was grasping at straws. There was no way these old memories held any answers.

Setting the album aside, Max absentmindedly grabbed his phone and opened his social media feed, and began scrolling aimlessly. It was a habit more than anything. Just something to distract himself. He paused when he saw an old post that one of his contacts had shared, tagging him in an art exhibition years ago. It was from a time when he and Felicity had only just started seeing each other. Curious, he clicked on the event. He remembered that night vaguely. It had been an upscale art show in Buckhead, filled with high-society types, the kind of people who seemed more interested in being seen than appreciating the art.

As the event page loaded, he saw the names of several people who had been tagged — artists, curators, a few gallery owners — and then there appeared one name that froze him in place: David Hollister. His eyes widened as he stared at the screen, his pulse quivering. David had been at the same event? Max's finger hovered over the image attached to the post, and as he opened it, he saw David standing near the back of the gallery, talking to someone Max didn't recognize.

His stomach twisted. Felicity had never mentioned knowing David, never said a word about crossing paths with him in all the years they'd been together. How could she leave that out? He zoomed in on the photo, and there, near the front of the frame, was Felicity, smiling and leaning in toward another photographer. Max felt his chest tighten. The post was innocent enough. It was an art exhibition, after all, and Felicity had been a photographer long before he met her. But why hadn't she ever mentioned this? He stared at the image, a knot forming in his gut as he tried to piece together how deep their connection could go.

Scrolling down the post's comments, he saw a few congratulatory messages, people complimenting the show and tagging others. And then it appeared. A comment Felicity had left years ago, thanking someone for introducing her to "such an influential figure in the art world." Max's mind began to race. Was she talking about David? Had they been connected longer than he thought? It seemed ridiculous, but the coincidence was gnawing at him.

The pieces of the puzzle were there, but the picture they were forming was one Max didn't want to acknowledge.

The paranoia was starting to creep in, but he shook it off. It had to be nothing more than an odd overlap in their worlds. After all, Atlanta's art scene was small, and people ran into each other all the time. He told himself that he was overthinking things, letting his imagination get the best of him. And yet, as he closed the post and set his phone down, the first crack in his trust had already begun to form. Subtle but unmistakable, it was like the quiet splintering of glass before it shatters.

As the night deepened, Max sat in his apartment, the suspicion pressing down on him. He knew he had to be careful, had to tread lightly. But with every new discovery, every small detail, it was becoming harder and harder to ignore the truth.

He didn't want to believe it, didn't want to move any closer to the point where there might be no denying the evidence.

CHAPTER XIV

The glow from the phone's screen illuminated Max Worthington's furrowed brow as his fingers hovered over it in the dim light of his study. The message that had pinged moments ago seemed to pulse with an ominous energy:

40°45 ' N, 84°06 ' W. The truth hides in plain sight. Come alone if you want answers.

The coordinates, when punched into his map app, pointed to an abandoned warehouse on the outskirts of Atlanta. "Another warehouse," Max said and muttered a curse. It reeked of a setup, but the promise of answers was too tempting to ignore.

Max's eyes flicked to the framed photo on his desk. Felicity's smile was frozen in time, her camera slung around her neck. The memory of her laughter echoed in his mind, starkly offsetting the knot of suspicion growing in his gut. He reached for his phone again, Jimmy Callahan's number highlighted on the screen.

"Damn it all," Max growled, hitting the call button.

Jimmy's gruff voice answered on the third ring. "Worthington, it's ass o'clock in the morning. This better be good."

"I've got a lead, Jimmy. Coordinates, a cryptic message. Smells like a trap, but—"

"But you're going anyway," Jimmy finished, a hint of resignation in his tone. "Where?"

Max rattled off the details, then added, "I'm going in alone. If I'm not back in touch within three hours—"

"I'll bring the cavalry," Jimmy promised. "Max, be careful. This Hollister character, he's not playing games."

"Neither am I," Max replied, ending the call.

In the quiet of his apartment, Max gathered his tools: a voice recorder disguised as a pen, a small canister of pepper spray, and a flashlight that could double as a baton if things went south. He paused at the safe in his closet, considering the weight of the pistol inside. After a moment's hesitation, he closed the door. If this was a trap, firepower wouldn't be his salvation. Wit would.

While driving down to the warehouse district, the world outside the Fairlady's window melted into a kaleidoscope of streetlights and electric anticipation. Max's mind raced to piece together the puzzle that had consumed his life. The stolen painting, the auction, Felicity's possible involvement … it all swirled together in a maddening vortex of questions.

As he pulled up to the designated address, killing the engine and lights, everything went deathly quiet. The building was a hulking shadow against the pre-dawn sky. Max's eyes scanned the perimeter, noting the absence of other vehicles. Either he was walking into an extremely well-laid trap, or someone had gone to great lengths to appear invisible. Max slipped from his car, gravel crunching softly under his feet. He approached the building, every sense on high alert. A faint scraping sound from inside froze him in his tracks. Pressing himself against the cool metal siding, he inched towards a dirty window, and peered inside.

The interior was a maze of crates and forgotten machinery, but what caught Max's eye made his breath catch. In a cleared area at the center stood several easels, each draped with cloth. Beside them, a figure hunched over a table, working with meticulous care on what appeared to be a painting.

"Son of a bitch," Max whispered, realization dawning. This wasn't just about one painting. It looked like an operation. He crept towards a side door, testing the handle. It gave way with a soft click, and Max slipped inside, the darkness enveloping him. The smell of paint and chemicals swelled in the air.

As his eyes adjusted, details emerged from the gloom. Stacks of canvases leaned against walls, their subjects obscured but their frames ornate and aged. On a nearby table, documents were spread out — shipping manifests, Max realized with a start.

A floorboard creaked behind him. Max whirled, heart pounding, to find himself face to face with a man he recognized from society pages and whispered rumors.

"Mr. Worthington," David Hollister's voice was smooth as aged whiskey, but his eyes were cold. "I must admit, I'm impressed. You're more resourceful than I gave you credit for."

Thoughts charged through Max's head, his adrenaline surging. This was the mastermind, the puppeteer behind it all. "Hollister," he managed, forcing calm into his voice. "I suppose I should be flattered by all the attention. The stolen painting, the auction, the traps. It's all been about me, hasn't it?"

Hollister's laugh was devoid of humor. "Oh, Max. You're a piece of the puzzle, certainly. An interesting piece, but just one among many." He gestured around the warehouse. "You see, your little painting was just the tip of the iceberg. We've been at this game for years, replacing masterpieces with forgeries so perfect even the owners don't know they've been robbed."

As Hollister spoke, Max's peripheral vision caught movement in the shadows. Silent figures emerged, surrounding them. The magnitude of the operation began to sink in.

"It's not just you," Max realized aloud. "It's a network. Forgers, smugglers, auction houses. How deep does this go?"

A slow smile spread across Hollister's face. "Deeper than you could imagine, my friend. And far too deep for you to escape from."

Max's hand inched towards his pocket, fingers closing around the object inside. "I wouldn't be so sure about that," he said, tensing for action. What happened next was a jumble of motion and sound. Max feinted left, then ducked right, spraying the pepper spray in a wide arc. Shouts of pain and surprise erupted as he bolted for cover behind a stack of crates. Chaos erupted in the warehouse. Max caught glimpses of men in suits grappling with the effects of the spray, while others rushed to secure paintings and documents. Through the mayhem, he spotted Hollister making for a back exit.

"Oh no you don't," Max growled, giving chase.

They burst out into the pre-dawn light, Hollister a few paces ahead. Max's longer stride was closing the gap when the wail of sirens split the air.

Hollister stumbled, surprise evident on his face as he glanced back. It was all the opening Max needed. He lunged, tackling Hollister to the ground. They grappled, rolling in the gravel, each fighting for dominance.

"It's over, Hollister," Max panted, pinning the man down. "The police are here. Your whole operation is about to be blown wide open."

For a moment, fear flashed in Hollister's eyes. Then, with a strength born of desperation, he bucked, throwing Max off balance. In the split second it took Max to regain his footing, Hollister was up and running. Max gave chase once more, but Hollister disappeared around a corner. By the time Max reached it, the sound of screeching tires told him Hollister had found an escape route.

Cursing, Max turned back to the warehouse. Police cars were pulling up, officers pouring out with weapons drawn. Among them, Max spotted a familiar face — Jimmy Callahan.

"Max!" Jimmy called out, jogging over. "What the hell happened here?"

Max, still catching his breath, gestured towards the warehouse. "It's big, Jimmy. Bigger than we thought. Hollister, he's part of an entire forgery ring. They're replacing real artworks with fakes all over the place."

Jimmy's eyes widened. "Christ," he muttered, then turned to bark orders at his team. "Secure the building! I want every painting, every scrap of paper catalogued!"

As the police swarmed the warehouse, Max filled Jimmy in on the details. The forgers they'd caught red-handed, the evidence scattered throughout the building, and Hollister's narrow escape.

"We'll get him," Jimmy assured Max. "This is enough to put out an APB. Every cop in the state will be looking for other members of the ring."

Max nodded, the adrenaline finally starting to ebb. As it did, a familiar nagging thought resurfaced. "Jimmy," he said quietly, "what about Felicity? Did you find anything?" *Wish you didn't.*

A shadow passed over Jimmy's face. "Max, I—" He was cut off by a shout from inside the warehouse.

"Detective! You need to see this!"

Jimmy held up a hand to Max. "Hold that thought. Let's see what they've found."

They entered the warehouse to find an officer standing by an open crate. Inside, nestled in packing material, was a painting Max recognized instantly. The Silent Watch.

"It's the original," the officer said. "We found shipping documents. It was meant to go out today, headed for a private collector in Dubai."

Max stared at the painting, and emotions warred within him. Relief at its recovery mingled with a renewed sense of betrayal. Whoever had stolen it from his apartment had been part of this larger scheme all along. As the implications sank in, Max's phone buzzed in his pocket. He pulled it out to find a text from an unknown number:

You're closer than you think, but still so far. Watch your back, Worthington. And watch those closest to you.

Max's grip tightened on the phone, his gaze drifting to Jimmy, who was coordinating the evidence collection. The warning in the text echoed in his mind, along with all the unanswered questions about Felicity.

The sky over Atlanta was cloaked in deep shades of indigo and violet, with the first faint glow of dawn creeping along the horizon. But for Max Worthington, the arrival of a new day brought not clarity, but deeper shadows and more dangerous secrets. His instincts said that the game was far from over.

"Hold your horses, Jenkins," Jimmy said. "Just because it looks right doesn't mean it is right. These bastards are good. Damn good. For all we know, this could be another smoke and mirrors act."

Jimmy turned to another man in uniform, his voice gruff but steady. "Get this painting to the lab, pronto. I want every test run on it. Spectral imaging, pigment analysis, the works. And those shipping docs? Could be as phony as a three-dollar bill. Check every signature, every stamp. Nothing leaves this warehouse until we're 100% sure what's real and what's fool's gold."

As he watched the flurry of activity around him, Max's writer's mind was already careering to string together the possible next steps in this real-life thriller. Hollister was in the wind, the forgery ring was exposed but not fully dismantled, and the question of Felicity's involvement still hung over everything like a storm cloud.

Max's fingers itched for a keyboard, the urge to write almost overwhelming. But first, he had a mystery to solve — one that had become far more personal and perilous than any novel he'd ever penned.

With a deep breath, he turned to Jimmy. "I need you to know what I'm thinking about Felicity," he said, his voice steady despite the turmoil within. "And if you've found out something about her, I can take it whatever it may be."

Jimmy's expression was grim as he said, "Let's go somewhere quiet."

As they walked out of the warehouse, leaving behind the bustling crime scene, Max couldn't shake the feeling that he was walking into yet another trap. And this one was laid not

by Hollister or his gang, but by fate itself. And this time, he
wasn't sure he had the tools to escape unscathed.

II

Blood Whisper

CHAPTER XV

The neon sign of Margo's 24-Hour Diner flickered weakly in the pre-dawn hours. Its dim light pooled unevenly over the nearly empty parking lot. Inside, the buzz of fluorescent lights and the soft clink of dishes from the kitchen set a muted backdrop to the tense conversation unfolding in one of the corner booths.

Max Worthington sat hunched over a steaming cup of black coffee, his fingers drumming an anxious rhythm on the worn Formica tabletop. Across from him, Detective Jimmy Callahan leaned back against the cracked vinyl seat, his weary eyes fixed on his friend.

"Alright, Max," Jimmy said, breaking the silence. "We're here. Tell me what's really going on with Felicity."

Max took a deep breath, then launched into the story. He told Jimmy about the missing security footage, the social media posts linking Felicity to David Hollister, and the growing pit of dread in his stomach.

"I know how it sounds, Jimmy," Max said, his voice low and strained. "But I can't shake this feeling. It's like … like I'm seeing her clearly for the first time, and I don't recognize what I'm seeing."

Jimmy nodded slowly, processing the information. "I hear you, Max. But we need to be careful here. Suspicion isn't proof, and love … well, love can play tricks on the mind."

"You think I'm imagining things?" A hint of desperation crept into Max's voice.

"No, I'm not saying that," Jimmy replied, leaning forward. "But we need solid evidence before we can accuse anyone, especially someone as close to you as Felicity. Bring me that security footage tomorrow. I want to see it for myself."

Max felt his breath coming easier. "Thanks, Jimmy. I just, I needed someone else to know, you know?"

"I get it," Jimmy said, his tone softening further. He held both forefingers against his upper lip, weighing a thought. "What date was it when you found out the painting in your safe was a fake?"

"Saturday, August 10th," Max said. "Why?"

"I'm thinking about the morning of that day. Your camera throws up nothing at the time it should show Felicity leaving. So, it should do the same for you, if you went out someplace that day."

Max's eyes narrowed as he drew in a breath. "That's right, it should, and we should check. Because I did go out later in the day. And I know that whoever broke in … well … whoever David sent to pull it off, must have done it while I was in Inman Park."

"Inman Park?"

"Redbrick. My publisher wanted to see me."

"Right. And we're sure the theft didn't happen before the 10th?"

"It couldn't have. I'd been in the safe a few days before and the canvas was there and so were the ownership papers.

Wasn't until I saw the auction story in the paper and checked again that I noticed all the ownership papers were gone. That immediately sparked suspicion and I found out the real painting was gone. I'd had a few friends over the evening before, and the camera shows their arrival and departure. The times match."

"And Felicity was there?"

"Yeah, she joined us a little late, after we got through with dinner. But she was there."

"Right, and you checked the footage for the days before then?"

"Sure. It seems normal."

"We'll find out when we have a look," Jimmy said. "Look, I'll dig deeper into Felicity's background, but discreetly. We don't want to tip her off if there is something going on."

Max's phone buzzed and he pulled it out. Somehow, he had received the same message he saw back at the warehouse. "The same message twice?"

Jimmy saw his face paling and said, "What message?"

Max read the message aloud: "You're closer than you think, but still so far. Watch your back, Worthington. And watch those closest to you."

Jimmy's eyes narrowed. "That's new. Any idea who might've sent it?"

Max shook his head. "Could be David, could be someone else."

Jimmy's detective instincts kicked in. "The mystery man you mentioned before?"

"Maybe," Max said, absently scratching the stubble on his chin.

"You've got two," Jimmy said.

"Two?"

"What happened at the Steel River Warehouse. The guy who led you away from danger."

"Wait… " Max held up a finger and tapped the air with it, "you think they're connected somehow?"

The detective's mouth curled conspiratorially. "I'll go one step ahead and say the two are the same man."

"How can we be sure?"

"Who is this man, what does he look like?"

"Both times I met him, I didn't see his face. I don't understand why he wants to hide and help at the same time." With this Max proceeded with the details about the conversation that had transpired between him and this mystery man in Piedmont Conservatory.

Jimmy leaned forward and spoke slowly. "He's hiding his face for a reason, Max. If this man has ties to the feud between the Worthingtons and the Hollisters, it might not be safe for him to show who he really is. But if he's helping you, he's not working with David."

Max frowned and leaned back. "Or maybe he's just playing both sides. How do we know he's not setting me up?"

"We don't," Jimmy said. "But the fact that he's warned you twice, saved you from one of David's traps — there's something more going on here."

Max's eyes darted toward the diner's window. "He said there's a family secret. Something I don't know. What if this isn't just about the painting? What if it's personal?"

Jimmy's expression hardened. "It always is, Max. But until we know for sure, we need to be careful. This man may be your ally. Or he could be your biggest enemy."

"This whole thing is a hell lot bigger than just a stolen painting, isn't it?"

Jimmy nodded grimly. "I'm starting to think so. The forgery ring at the warehouse, Felicity's possible involvement, this unknown player." Jimmy paused and took a few sips from his mug before he added, "Max, I think we're just scratching the surface here."

Max leaned back, his mind reeling. "What do we do next?"

"We stay cautious," Jimmy said firmly. "I'll look into the footage and Felicity's background. You keep your eyes open, but don't confront her. Not yet. And Max?"

"Yeah?"

"If half of what we suspect is true, you're in the middle of something dangerous."

The situation was as thick as it could ever get and Max knew it. While they sat in silence, the soft clatter of the diner faded away, replaced by the quiet hum of two minds working overtime, trying to piece together a puzzle that seemed to grow more complex with each passing moment.

Max Worthington sat alone at a corner table in the dimly lit bistro. He had promised to be here at half past noon, but taking a detour up to Callahan's office to give him the footage took up a half hour. It was almost half past one when he messaged that he had arrived. His eyes constantly flickered between the doorway and the steam rising from his untouched coffee. He glanced at his phone again. He didn't see any new messages, but several old ones from Liam Corcoran stared back at him unanswered. A familiar knot of anxiety tightened in Max's chest as he scrolled through them, each more urgent than the last.

When can we meet, Max?

I need an update. You're running out of time.

This can't wait. Call me.

He had dodged Liam's calls for too long. The distraction of the stolen painting, the chaos surrounding Felicity, had kept him from facing the one task he had control over — finishing his novel. And now, here he was, finally about to face the music.

The door swung open, and in stepped Liam Corcoran. Max's editor was just as he always remembered him — tall, wiry, with a sharpness about him that seemed to slice through the noise of the room. The history between them was built on long nights and shared ambitions, poring over manuscripts and drinking cheap beer. Max remembered when Liam had been slinging scripts in the cutthroat world of Hollywood before trading that chaos for the steadier ground of publishing. Back then, Max was still drifting after the lukewarm reception of his first novel. It was Liam's faith in him that had made a difference, offering a contract with Redbrick just when Max needed it most. As he watched Liam walk into the diner, Max traced the invisible thread of the dreams they'd chased together over the years. Corcoran's eyes immediately found Max, and without breaking stride, he moved toward the table.

The woman Max remembered seeing behind the reception at Redbrick followed a few steps behind. Max barely recognized her. Gone was the frumpish librarian look she'd worn during their last meeting. Now, her dark hair was loose around her shoulders, and her figure was elegantly wrapped in a sleek, form-fitting dress that somehow managed to be both classy and provocative. The way she walked demanded attention with a deliberate, unhurried, quiet confidence.

"Max." Corcoran greeted him curtly as he slid into the seat across from him. The secretary took the chair next to her boss. Her eyes lingered on Max for just a moment too long. Liam said, "This here's Pauline. I believe you two met before."

"Liam. Pauline." Max nodded at both of them. He heard the tightness in his voice as he braced himself for the inevitable.

A table attendant appeared, silent and efficient, setting down a napkin before each of them. Liam flicked a glance at the menu and gestured for a crimson-hued mocktail garnished with a curled orange peel, while Pauline opted for a glass of dry red. Max barely glanced up. He didn't order.

When the attendant was gone, Corcoran didn't waste any time. "You're late. Not just today. With the book. I've been patient, Max, but the patience is running thin. What the hell's going on?"

Max exhaled, running a hand through his hair. "I know, I know. Look, I've had some personal stuff going on. It's been a bit chaotic lately, but the book—"

"The book isn't finished," Corcoran interrupted, his voice as sharp as his gaze. "You've been promising me this final chapter for close to two months now. And you're still dragging your feet."

"I'm almost there," Max said quickly, though he wasn't sure if he believed it himself. "It's just—"

"Just what?" Corcoran leaned forward, eyes narrowing. "Let me guess. You still don't want to kill the female lead. The character you're so damn attached to, the one who's holding up the entire ending."

Max shifted uncomfortably in his seat. "It's more complicated than that. I don't think the story needs to end that way. I don't want to—"

"You don't want to what? Follow through? Finish the damn thing?" Corcoran's voice was low, but the frustration was unmistakable. "This isn't about what you *want*, Max. This is about what the story needs. It needs an ending. You're too close to it to see that."

Max felt the words like a punch to the gut, but before he could respond, Pauline chimed in, "You've always been a bit of a perfectionist, haven't you, Max?" The softness in her voice had an edge of playful amusement. Her lips curled into a small, knowing smile. For a fresh second, Max was taken aback by how different she seemed. Her tone and posture gave off a quiet allure that hadn't been there before. She tilted her head slightly, with her gaze lingering on his, and in that moment, Max couldn't help but notice the way her lips parted; as if she were on the verge of saying something more intimate.

"Yeah, I guess you could say that," Max said, feeling an odd mix of discomfort and curiosity. Was she really flirting with him, or was it just his imagination? The attendant returned to deftly set down Liam's garnished mocktail and Pauline's glass of wine before slipping away.

Pauline leaned in ever so slightly, her fingers tracing the rim of her glass in slow, deliberate circles. "Sometimes, perfectionism can hold you back. You know, keep you from finishing what you started."

The subtle suggestion in her words wasn't lost on Max. Her eyes flicked up to meet his, and she offered him a slow, sultry smile before handing him a business card. He didn't need it, since he already had her contact information. Her fingertips brushed his hand lightly as she passed it to him. Her lips curled into a slight pout, her eyes lingering on his face.

Max swallowed, feeling the weight of Pauline's attention, but Corcoran, oblivious or uninterested, kept his focus on the conversation.

"You've been dodging me for weeks, Max," Corcoran continued, his voice now steely. "You've let this personal stuff get in the way of your career. You've got talent, I've always said that, but remember what I told you? Talent without discipline is a tragedy."

Max shifted in his seat. "I haven't forgotten about the book, Liam. It's just... everything's happening at once. Felicity, the pain—"

"Felicity," Corcoran echoed, his expression darkening. He glanced at Pauline, then back at Max. "There's something I need to tell you about her. I've never trusted her."

Max blinked in surprise. "What do you mean?"

"I mean, you're not the first person to have doubts about her," Corcoran said bluntly. "Something felt off when you first introduced her to me. I didn't say anything because it wasn't my business, but now, with everything that's going on, Max, you might be onto something with your suspicions."

A chill ran down Max's spine. "So you think she's involved?"

"You know the guy?" Corcoran said.

"Guy?"

"You said you suspected she was involved with someone."

"No, I meant my painting got stolen and I've be—"

"Stolen?" Corcoran's brows knitted. "Wait, wait," he instructed with a confused shake of his head. "What *are* you talking about?"

Max launched into the story: the missing painting, the connection to David Hollister, and the growing pit of doubt regarding Felicity. As he spoke, he noticed Pauline's eyes narrowing slightly. Her lips parted as though she was listening to every word with more than just casual interest. Her hand rested on the table, fingers tapping lightly, and when Max glanced at her, she met his gaze with a slow, deliberate sweep of her tongue across her lips. Subtle, but unmistakable.

"So, you think Felicity's involved?" Corcoran's voice cut through Max's growing discomfort.

"What would you say?"

Corcoran waved dismissively. "She always struck me as … how do I put this? Calculating. Like she was playing a role. I saw it at those book launches she came to with you. Always so perfect, so polished. But there was something behind the act. I've been in this business a long time, Max. You learn to read people faster than you can read a book."

"But you never said anything."

Liam shrugged. "You seemed happy enough with her. Who am I to question it?" Then leaning back in his chair, he sighed and his expression softened slightly. "I don't know what to say to all this. But it's dangerous, Max. You're in over your head. David Hollister, I've heard about him. He's powerful, well-connected. If Felicity's tied up in this, you need to tread carefully."

Max felt the familiar tension return, tightening around his chest. "I just want to get the painting back, Liam. That's all. Once I've done that, I'll be done with this whole mess. I'll finish the book. No more distractions."

Corcoran shook his head, his eyes hard. "You're playing a dangerous game. This isn't some plot in one of your novels, Max. This is real life. People like Hollister don't just let things go. If Felicity is involved, you're in deeper than you realize."

Max clenched his fists under the table, his voice strained. "I can handle it."

"No, you can't," Corcoran said flatly. "Not alone. You need to be smart about this. Get the painting back, but don't let your emotions cloud your judgment. And for God's sake, don't go charging into something you're not ready for."

There was a heavy silence between them. Pauline, still watching Max, broke it with a soft purr. "You always were a bit of a risk-taker, Max. That's what makes you exciting."

Her flirtatious tone, the slow way she licked her lips as she spoke, it was almost too much. Max shifted uncomfortably, feeling the heat rise in his cheeks. He had always been good at reading people, but Pauline? She was harder to figure out now. Was she just toying with him? Or was there something more?

Corcoran cleared his throat, pulling Max's attention back. "Look, I've extended your deadline as far as I can. But this is it, Max. Get me the book. Finish it. Or we're done. Redbrick can't wait forever."

Corcoran's words were unavoidable. Max said, "I understand. I'll get it done."

Corcoran stood, signaling the end of the meeting. "Good. But Max, don't let this thing with Hollister derail you. And keep your eyes open. There's more going on here than you probably realize."

CHAPTER XVI

Piercing through the gathering dusk, the city lights caught David Hollister's face as he stood at the window of his penthouse suite. The streets sprawling beneath were oblivious to the turmoil that churned within the mind of one of Atlanta's most influential residents. His fingers tightened around the scotch when the knock came. He knew it was perhaps the last piece of his ill-fated plan. The wild card he hadn't expected to become such a liability. "Come in," he called out.

The door opened, and Felicity stepped inside. Gone was the carefree photographer who had charmed her way into Max Worthington's life and home. In her place stood a woman on edge, whose eyes darted around the opulent room as if searching for an escape route.

"You wanted to see me?" Felicity said.

David turned from the window, his imposing figure silhouetted against the city lights. "I think it's time we had a little chat, don't you?" He gestured to a leather armchair. "Please, sit."

Felicity hesitated before perching on the edge of the seat. Her posture remained rigid with tension. David moved to the bar and poured another drink. "Can I offer you something? To calm your nerves, perhaps?"

"No, thank you," Felicity said curtly. "I'd rather keep a clear head."

A mirthless chuckle escaped David. "Wise choice. We wouldn't want your judgment clouded, would we? Not when there's so much at stake." He settled into the chair opposite her, studying her face.

Felicity met his gaze with a flicker of defiance in her eyes. "I want out, David. I've done what you asked. I want the money you promised me, and then I'm gone."

David leaned back, swirling the amber liquid in his glass. "Is that so? And what makes you think it's that simple?"

"Because it has to be," Felicity snapped. Her composure was cracking. "Your whole operation's been exposed. Max is onto us. I can't … I won't be dragged down with you."

A dangerous smile played across David's lips. "My dear Felicity, you seem to have forgotten one crucial detail. You're already in this up to your neck. Or did you think your role in stealing The Silent Watch would go unnoticed?"

Felicity paled while her fingers dug into the armrests. "That wasn't part of the original plan. You said I just had to get close to Max, feed you information. I never agreed to—"

"And yet you did it anyway," David interrupted smoothly. "You played your part beautifully, I must say. Max never suspected a thing, did he? Not until it was too late."

A flash of pain crossed Felicity's face. "He didn't deserve this. None of it. If I had known—"

"Known what?" David's voice took on a harder edge. "That you were merely a pawn in a game that's been played for generations? That your precious Max is just as much a part of this as I am, whether he knows it or not?"

Felicity's brow furrowed in confusion. "What are you talking about?"

David rose, and began pacing the room with measured steps. "Let me tell you a story, Felicity. A story about two families, the Hollisters and the Worthingtons, bound together by a secret that stretches back to the Civil War."

He paused to refill his glass before continuing. "That painting, The Silent Watch, it's more than just a valuable piece of art. It's a key to a past that some would rather keep buried. A past that could destroy everything my family has built."

Felicity leaned forward, intrigued despite herself. "What does it have to do with the Civil War?"

David's eyes gleamed with a mix of anger and something akin to fear. "Behind the serene façade of that picture is a very different story. A story of my ancestors' role during those dark days. A role that, if revealed, would shatter the Hollister name forever." He turned to face Felicity, and his expression hardened. "That painting belonged to my family for generations. It was our burden to bear, our secret to keep. Until Harrison Worthington came along."

"Max's father?"

David nodded grimly. "Harrison and my father, Robert, they were friends once. But friendship means little when weighed against family legacy. There was a deal, you see. A secret agreement. The painting for a favor … or was it a debt? The details don't matter now. What matters is that Harrison walked away with our family's shame, and my father was too weak to stop him."

Felicity's mind was trying to process this new information. "So all of this … the theft, the auction, setting Max up, it was about getting the painting back?"

A bitter laugh escaped David's lips. "Getting it back? No, my dear. It's about making sure that painting never sees the light of day again. Max may not know the truth, but as long as a Worthington possesses that cursed thing, my family is at risk. *I am at risk.* And I won't be weak like my father. I won't let the sins of the past destroy everything I've built." He fixed Felicity with an intense stare. "That's why you're here, Felicity. That's why I needed someone close to Max. Someone who could gain his trust, learn his weaknesses. And you played your part perfectly."

Felicity stood abruptly, her face a mask of disgust. "I never signed up to be part of your family vendetta, David. I did what you asked because I needed the money, but this … this is insane. You can't just destroy a man's life over some ancient grudge!"

David's hand shot out, gripping Felicity's arm with surprising strength. "Can't I? You've seen what I'm capable of, what lengths I'll go to protect what's mine. Don't make the mistake of thinking you're any different … any less expendable than Max."

Felicity wrenched her arm free. Her eyes were blazing. "Is that a threat?"

"Consider it a reminder," David replied coolly. "Of where your loyalties should lie. Of what's at stake if you decide to have an attack of conscience now."

A tense silence fell between them. Felicity had known she was getting involved in something illegal, but this web of family secrets and some kind of historical intrigue was far beyond anything she had imagined.

"What happens now?" she finally asked.

David moved back to the window, and gazed out at the city once more. "Now, my dear Felicity, we wait. The painting is safe, hidden where even Max's clever friend Jimmy Callahan won't find it. But Max is still a problem that needs solving."

Felicity's blood ran cold at the implication in David's words. "I won't let you hurt him."

David's mouth twisted into a sardonic smile. "And how exactly do you plan to stop me? By confessing your role in all this? I'm sure Max would be thrilled to learn how the woman he loves has been playing him from the start."

Tears pricked at the corners of Felicity's eyes. "It wasn't all a lie. I do care for him."

"How touching," David sneered. "But sentiment won't save you now. You're in this to the bitter end, Felicity. The sooner you accept that, the better off you'll be." He turned back to her, his expression slightly softening. "The money I promised you is in an offshore account. It's yours, as agreed. But remember, that money comes with strings. Your silence, your continued cooperation. That's the price."

Felicity felt the weight of her choices pressing down on her. She had entered this arrangement naively, thinking it would be a simple con. Now she found herself entangled in a generational feud. The lives of those she had come to care for hung in the balance. "What do you want me to do?" Resignation colored her voice.

David's smile was cold and calculated. "For now? You go back to Max. Play the concerned girlfriend. Keep him distracted, off-balance. I'll be in touch with further instructions." He moved closer, his voice dropping to a menacing whisper. "And remember what's at stake. Not just for me, or for Max, but for you. One wrong move, one whisper to the wrong person, and everything comes crashing down. Are we clear?"

Felicity met his gaze with a mixture of fear and determination in her eyes. "Crystal."

As she turned to leave, David called out once more. "Oh, and do try to enjoy your time with Max. After all, who knows how much longer he'll be around to appreciate your charms." The door closed behind her with a soft click, leaving David alone once more. He turned back to the window, raising his glass in a mock toast to the glittering skyline. "To family legacies," he murmured. "And the lengths we go to preserve them."

In the corridor outside, Felicity leaned against the wall, her heart pounding. She had entered David's penthouse looking for a way out. Instead, she found herself sinking deeper into a quagmire of lies and betrayal. As she made her way to the elevator, one thought echoed in her mind: How could she protect Max without destroying herself in the process?

The doors slid shut, carrying her down into the Atlanta night, where the game of cat and mouse between the Hollisters and the Worthingtons was about to enter its most dangerous phase yet.

CHAPTER XVII

Max's eyes fluttered open, and he squinted against the late morning light filtering through the blinds. He reached for his phone on the nightstand, fumbling for a moment before bringing the screen into focus. 8:47 a.m. glared back at him accusingly.

"Shit," he muttered, pushing himself up. As he swung his legs over the side of the bed, the sound of running water caught his attention. The shower was on. A frown creased his brow. He hadn't heard Felicity come in last night. Padding across the hardwood floor, he approached the bathroom door and rapped his knuckles against it.

"Felicity?" he called out, voice still rough with sleep.

The water shut off abruptly. "Max? You're up already?" Felicity's voice carried a note of surprise. "I was hoping to surprise you with breakfast in bed."

Max leaned against the doorframe, a small smile tugging at his lips despite the nagging doubts in the back of his mind. "When did you get in?"

"Just this morning, around seven." Her voice was muffled as she presumably toweled off. "I didn't want to wake you."

"You're sweet," Max said, pushing away from the door. He wandered back to the bed, collapsing onto it with a sigh.

Jimmy's words sounded in his head: *Don't confront her. Let me handle the investigation.*

The bathroom door opened, releasing a cloud of steam. Felicity emerged, wrapped in a towel, her dark hair slicked back and dripping. Her eyes found Max, and something flickered in their depths. He clearly saw a hunger that made his breath catch. Without a word, she crossed the room. The towel slipped to the floor as she slid under the sheets, her skin cool and damp against his. Their lips met, and for a moment, Max forgot about stolen paintings and tampered security footage.

Felicity broke the kiss while her fingers traced patterns on his chest. "God, I've missed this," she murmured. "Ever since that damn painting disappeared, it's like we've barely touched each other."

Max swallowed hard, guilt and suspicion warring in his gut. "I know," he said softly, running a hand down her back. "I'm sorry, I've been—"

The shrill ring of a cell phone cut through the air. Felicity tensed, and Max could have sworn he saw a flash of worry cross her face before she masked it with a smile. "Sorry, I should get that," she said, pressing a quick kiss to his lips before sliding out of bed. She snatched up her phone and disappeared into the hallway. Max strained to hear her conversation, but her voice was too low. A few minutes later, she reappeared, already pulling on clothes.

"I'm so sorry, babe," Felicity said, her voice tinged with regret. "That was work. There's an emergency with one of our clients, and I need to go in."

Max sat up, sheets pooling around his waist. "On a Saturday?"

Felicity buttoned up her blouse and shrugged. "Life of a photographer." Her hands gave off a dramatic gesture. "Crises don't take weekends off, especially when you discover a junior photographer can't make a shoot work the way it's supposed to." She leaned in for a goodbye kiss. "I'll make it up to you tonight, I promise."

As soon as the front door clicked shut, Max was reaching for his own phone. He hit the speed dial for Jimmy, drumming his fingers impatiently as it rang.

"Max?" Jimmy answered on the third ring.

"Felicity just left in a hurry. I think you should follow her. But how will you know where she's going?"

There was a pause, then a low chuckle. "Already on it, buddy. The 2017 Nissan Versa Note, right?"

Max blinked, impressed despite himself. "Yeah, that's the one. Still, you're about nine miles away from my place."

"Already got a little gadget hooked up to that ride, buddy," Jimmy said.

"You can track her?"

"Like a bloodhound, my friend. Don't you worry about a thing. I'll find out where our little bird is flying off to."

"Thanks, Jimmy," Max said.

"I've got news on the security footage …"

Jimmy kicked the sheets off of himself. "And?"

Jimmy's tone turned serious. "Oh, it ain't good. The boys down at the lab confirmed it. That footage from August 10th was definitely tampered with."

Max sat up straighter. "How?"

"It's clever, I'll give 'em that," Jimmy said. "They used what's called a 'loop and blend' technique. Basically, they took a chunk of normal footage, probably from earlier in the day or any other day, and looped it seamlessly. The timestamp keeps running, but what you're seeing is just the same 15 minutes or so played over and over."

"Jesus," Max breathed. "And it's that hard to detect?"

"To the naked eye? Damn near impossible. But the techs, they've got ways. Slight variations in light, shadows that don't quite match up with the timestamp. It's subtle, but it's there."

Max scratched his naked chest frantically. "So whoever did this …"

"Had access to the security system and knew their way around video editing software," Jimmy finished. "Narrows down our suspect pool, don't it?"

"Yeah," Max said quietly, thinking of Felicity's rushed departure some minutes before. "It sure does."

"Alright, I'm gonna tail your girl," Jimmy said. "I'll let you know what I find out." Jimmy hung up and left Max alone with his thoughts and the lingering scent of Felicity's shampoo on the damp pillow beside him.

Half an hour later, Max stepped out of the shower, toweling off his hair as steam billowed around him. The looming deadline for his book pressed on his mind. Liam Corcoran's words boomed in his thoughts: *Get that book finished, Max. Time's ticking.* He was reaching for his laptop when his phone chirped. A message from an unknown number flashed on the screen:

Meet me at the High Museum of Art in one hour. It's about The Silent Watch.

Max's heart raced. The mysterious man again. This time, though, the number wasn't blocked. He hit 'call' immediately. To his surprise, a deep voice answered. "Mr. Worthington."

"Who are you?" Max demanded. "What's this about?"

"Patience," the voice replied. "All will be revealed at the museum."

Max raked a hand through his damp hair. "Look, the last two times we met at Piedmont Park, you barely told me anything. Why should I come?"

"Because this time," the voice said with a hint of amusement to his tone, "I'll tell you what's really going on with the painting."

"At least give me your name," Max pressed.

"Names are earned, Mr. Worthington. I'll see you soon."

The man hung up leaving Max to stare at his phone. Frustration and curiosity wrestled within him. With a resigned sigh, he began to dress.

An hour later, Max found himself wandering through the vast, gleaming interior of the High Museum of Art. The soaring atrium, with its stark white walls and floods of natural light, felt both awe-inspiring and oddly exposing. Every shadowed corner, every lingering patron could be his mysterious contact. He climbed the gently curving ramp, moving from gallery to gallery. Modern sculptures gave way to centuries-old portraits. Abstract splashes of color morphed into painstakingly detailed landscapes. All the while, Max's eyes darted from face to face, searching. His phone remained stubbornly silent. Calls to the unknown number went straight to voicemail. As he entered a gallery dedicated to African art, surrounded by intricate masks and towering wooden sculptures, his nerves began to fray.

Just as he was about to give up, his phone buzzed. "Lower level, storage area C," the voice instructed. "Tell the guard you're here for the Emerson collection review."

Heart pounding, Max made his way to the museum's lower levels. The guard eyed him suspiciously but nodded him through after he mentioned the collection. The storage area was a maze of climate-controlled rooms and long corridors lined with carefully wrapped artworks. He found Storage Area C at the end of a dimly lit hallway. As he pushed open the heavy door, a figure emerged from the shadows.

The mask the man wore was a vision of otherworldly menace. Its base, a deep crimson that seemed to shimmer in the low light, was adorned with intricate whorls of obsidian and gold. These swirling patterns created an illusion of movement, as if scales were rippling across the surface. Amber eyes glowed from within slanted sockets, their gaze piercing and predatory. But it was the lower half of the mask that truly chilled Max's blood. The same gaping maw filled with gleaming, gilt-edged fangs that he had seen in his last meeting with this stranger. Looking at that maw transformed the wearer's visage into that of a snarling, mythical beast.

"Mr. Worthington," the masked figure said, his voice muffled but unmistakable. "I'm glad you came."

Max swallowed hard. "No more games. Tell me what's going on."

The figure nodded slowly, then reached up. With deliberate care, he removed the mask. Max found himself staring into a face that spoke of a rich, complex heritage. High cheekbones and bronze skin hinted at Native American ancestry, while the man's sharp nose and square jaw suggested European roots. His eyes, dark and intense, seemed to hold centuries of stories. A scar, thin but prominent, ran from his left temple to his chin, adding an air of danger to his otherwise handsome features.

"My name," the man said, his voice now clear and resonant, "is Gabriel Thunderhawk. And it's time you learned the truth about The Silent Watch."

The moment Max's gaze settled on the short salt-and-pepper hair, the thought tore through like lightning splitting a tree. "I've seen you before!" he said. Snapping his fingers twice, Max added, "On the day it happened. You drove past the front of my house."

Gabriel's lips curved into a subtle smile. "Perceptive, Mr. Worthington. Yes, that was me. I needed to see for myself what we were dealing with."

Max's brow furrowed. "We? What do you mean? And what exactly are we 'dealing with?'"

"The Silent Watch," Gabriel said, his voice low and intense. "It's not what you think it is, Max. Not even close."

The strange chill that gripped Max deepened his confusion each passing second. "What are you talking about?"

Gabriel's dark eyes bore into Max's. "The painting you've known all your life? It's a lie. A cover-up. Beneath that serene landscape lies a truth that's been buried for generations."

Disbelief etched harder on Max's face as he shook his head. "That's impossible. My father—"

"Your father, Harrison," Gabriel interrupted, "and Robert Hollister. Do you remember them?"

Fragments of memories flickered through Max's mind. Tense silences at family gatherings, hushed arguments behind closed doors. "Vaguely," he admitted. "There was some kind of tension. But I never understood why."

Gabriel nodded. "To Robert Hollister, your father was just an outsider. New money stepping on old territory. But that was only scratching the surface. There was a lot more beneath it. I mentioned this duri—"

"The painting," Max said slowly. "It belonged to the Hollisters before my family, didn't it?"

"Indeed," Gabriel confirmed. "Robert needed a favor. A big one and it was something only your father could provide. In return, Harrison asked for the painting. Whether he knew its true significance …" Gabriel shrugged. "That, we may never know."

The confusion was still a slow-spinning fog around Max. "What significance? What truth?"

Gabriel's expression turned grim. "To understand, we need to go back. Back to the Civil War, to a man named Commander James Hollister."

As the words fall into Max's ears, the storage room fades to give way to another lifetime. The time is 1863 and the place is Blackridge Hollow.

The air is thick with gunpowder and the metallic tang of blood. Commander James Hollister, his Union uniform stained with mud and worse, crouches behind a fallen oak. Beside him, Standing Bear, his Amerindian second-in-command, nocks an arrow to his bow.

"We're outnumbered, sir," Standing Bear says, his voice steady despite the chaos around them.

James nods grimly. "But not outfought. Rally your men. We'll flank them from the east."

As Standing Bear melts into the underbrush, James catches sight of a familiar face across the battlefield — his cousin, Ezra Hollister, wearing Confederate gray. Their eyes meet for a brief, charged moment before the roar of cannon fire drowns out all thought. Hours later, as the smoke clears and the Union flag flows victorious over

Blackridge Hollow, James makes his way to his tent. He is about to enter when he hears hushed voices from within.

" — can't let him find out." It is Ezra's voice, urgent and low.

"He suspects nothing," another voice — James' other cousin, Silas — replies. "As far as James knows, we're loyal to the Union cause."

James feels his blood run cold. Spies. His own family, betraying everything he has fought for. He bursts into the tent, hand on his pistol. "Explain yourselves," he demands.

The shock on their faces quickly gives way to something darker. Ezra's hand inches towards his own weapon.

"James," Silas says in a voice oily smooth. "You weren't supposed to hear that."

"Clearly," James spits. "How long have you been feeding information to the Confederates?"

"Long enough," Ezra growls. "And now, cousin, you've left us no choice."

Everything that happens next becomes a tangle of movement and sound. A gunshot rings out. James feels pain searing his chest. As he falls, he sees Standing Bear burst into the tent, bow drawn. The last thing James Hollister hears before darkness takes him is Silas's voice dripping with malice: "The Indians. They've turned on us. Spread the word... Commander Hollister was murdered by savages."

As the storage room comes back, Max stares at Gabriel with horror and disbelief melding on his face.

"My God," he whispered. "And the painting?"

Gabriel's eyes were hard. "Commissioned to commemorate the bravery of those Amerindian soldiers. A truth the Hollisters couldn't allow to exist. So they buried it, literally and figuratively."

"And you?" Max asked. "How do you fit into all this?"

A sad smile played on Gabriel's lips. "Commander James Hollister married an Amerindian woman. My great-great-grandmother, Aiyana. I am the last of his line, Mr. Worthington. The last keeper of a truth that's been silenced far too long."

"You too are a Hollister," Max said.

"Same family name, branching down vastly different paths."

Max sank onto a nearby crate. His mind felt like a manically shaken snow globe. "David," he murmured. "He knows, doesn't he? That's why he wants the painting so badly."

Gabriel nodded. "The Hollister shame, passed down through generations. And now, it's time for that shame to see the light of day."

Max looked up with a new determination in his eyes. "Tell me everything," he said. "Every last detail."

Listening to Gabriel's story, Max realized that *The Silent Watch* was about to break its long silence. And the strident echoes would change everything. While buried secrets slowly opened out before him, his phone buzzed insistently in his pocket. He fished it out and muttered, "Jimmy." He held up a finger to Gabriel to silently ask for a moment.

"Hey, Jim. What's up?" Anxiety and relief colored Max's voice.

There was an undercurrent of excitement in Jimmy's gruff voice. "Max, buddy. Got some news about your girl. And let me tell you, it's a doozy."

Max's heart skipped a beat. He turned away from Gabriel and lowered his voice. "Felicity? What about her?"

"Not over the phone, pal," Jimmy replied. "Can you swing by my office in about an hour? We need to talk face-to-face."

Max scratched his temple. "Yeah, sure. I'll be there."

"Good," Jimmy said. "Oh, and one more thing before you go. Remember that painting we saw at the warehouse? The one where David tried to spring his little trap?"

"How could I forget?" Max said dryly.

"Well, turns out that one's a fake too."

Max felt the blood drain from his face. "What?"

"You heard me," Jimmy confirmed. "We had it analyzed. It's good work, I'll give 'em that, but it's definitely not the original. Looks like you've seen two fake copies of The Silent Watch now, buddy. The one in your safe and this one."

"Jesus, Jim. This thing goes deeper than we thought."

"You're telling me," Jimmy agreed. "Anyway, we'll dig into all of it when you get here. See you in an hour."

Max pocketed his phone and Gabriel said, "Troubling news, Mr. Worthington?"

Max turned back to Gabriel, almost having forgotten the man's presence. "That was my friend, Jimmy. He's a detective, been helping me with this whole mess."

Gabriel nodded, his expression unreadable. "And what did your detective friend have to say?"

Max hesitated, studying Gabriel's face. There was something in the man's eyes, a glimmer of what? Knowledge? Expectation?

"He wants to meet," Max said carefully. "Says he has information about someone involved in all this."

A ghost of a smile played on Gabriel's lips. "Your girlfriend, perhaps? Felicity, isn't it?"

Max stiffened. "How did you—"

"I make it my business to know these things, Mr. Worthington," Gabriel said smoothly. "Especially when they pertain to The Silent Watch."

How much did this man really know? Max thought. *And could he be trusted?*

"There's more," Max said, deciding to test the waters. "The painting we found at David's warehouse? It's a fake too."

For the first time since they'd met, genuine surprise flashed across Gabriel's face. "Another forgery? Interesting. Very interesting indeed."

"What does it mean?" Max pressed. "Why would David have a fake copy?"

Gabriel stroked his chin thoughtfully. "It seems Mr. Hollister is playing a deeper game than we realized. Perhaps he's trying to muddy the waters, create confusion about which painting is the real one."

"Or maybe," Max said slowly, a new thought occurring to him, "he doesn't have the real painting at all."

Gabriel's eyes gleamed. "An intriguing theory, Mr. Worthington. So, which painting did Anastasia Chen pay for?"

Max glanced at his watch. "I need to go. Jimmy's waiting." He paused at the door and turned around. "I'm sorry I forgot to thank you."

"What for?"

"For leading me out the vents from the Steel River warehouse."

Gabriel smiled. "You guessed."

"It looks like everyone in this game has something to hide," Max said, his hand on the doorknob.

A look of intense focus replaced the smile on Gabriel's face. "Hide, yes. But remember, Mr. Worthington, sometimes we hide things to protect them, not to deceive."

Max nodded slowly. "And sometimes," he replied, "what's hidden is more valuable than what's on display."

As Max slipped out of the room, Gabriel's voice followed him. The words were almost a whisper: "The question is, are you prepared for what you might uncover?"

As Max made his way through the museum's winding corridors, he thought, *Two fake paintings. Felicity's possible involvement. David's increasingly Byzantine schemes. And at the center of it all, the enigmatic Gabriel Thunderhawk ...*

This man seemed to have stepped out of the pages of history itself. *The Silent Watch* was proving to be anything but silent. Its secrets were beginning to speak, and soon it seemed they would be shouting. He stepped out into the Atlanta sunshine, squinting against the glare. As he hailed a cab, he thought, *Whatever lies ahead, I'm committed now. The truth must come to light, no matter who or what stands in my way.*

CHAPTER XVIII

The faint scent of old leather and cigar smoke greeted Max as he pushed open the door to the office. Jimmy was slouched behind his desk, flipping through a small notebook, his hat tipped low over his brow. The blinds were half-closed, letting in just enough of the afternoon sun for the shadows to slash the room.

"Max," Jimmy greeted without looking up as Max shut the door behind him softly, "was startin' to wonder if you'd get here before sundown."

Max dropped into the chair across from Jimmy's cluttered desk. "You said you had news. I'm here."

Jimmy leaned back in his chair, finally looking at Max with his piercing blue eyes. "Yeah, I've got somethin'. You ain't gonna like it."

"Try me."

Jimmy set the notebook down and leaned forward. "Felicity. She ain't on your side, Max."

Max's stomach tightened, but he kept his face neutral. "What do you mean?"

"I followed her, like you asked. Girl went straight to The Velvet Lounge, over on Peachtree and 10th. High-end spot, lotta money changin' hands there. Real classy place to hide in plain sight, y'know? Anyway, she met someone."

Max raised an eyebrow. "Who?"

Jimmy sighed, sliding a hand over his greying head. "David Hollister."

Max's heart skipped a beat, but he stayed silent, waiting for Jimmy to continue.

"I couldn't get too close, place was packed. But I managed to slide in close enough to hear bits of their conversation." Jimmy's voice was lowering. "She's workin' for him, Max. I heard her say somethin' like, 'I'll stay close to him—he doesn't suspect a thing.' Then she talked about reportin' back to Hollister, keepin' you in the dark."

Max clenched his fists, feeling the betrayal like a punch to the gut. "You're sure?"

"Clear as day," Jimmy said. "She's playin' you. Has been for who knows how long. But that ain't all I heard."

Max narrowed his eyes. "What else?"

"They started talkin' 'bout the paintin'. Something about how it originally belonged to the Hollisters, not the Worthingtons. Sounded like some kinda old family beef. Felicity said somethin' about not lettin' you get too close to findin' out the truth."

Max leaned back, exhaling slowly. The painting again. He'd heard this story before, but now, pieces were starting to fit together. "I know what she's talking about."

Jimmy looked at him curiously. "You do?"

Max nodded. "I met the mystery man."

Jimmy blinked. "You what?"

"Yeah, finally. He decided to show his face. His name's Gabriel. Gabriel Thunderhawk."

"Thunderhawk? Sounds like somethin' outta an old western," Jimmy quipped.

Max ignored the comment and continued. "He told me something about the stolen painting. It's not what it seems. The picture you see? It's just a cover."

Jimmy frowned. "A cover? What do you mean?"

"The real painting is hidden underneath," Max explained, his voice steady. "Gabriel said it was painted over, like some kind of secret was buried underneath it."

Jimmy shook his head in disbelief. "Why the hell would anyone do that?"

"I'm not sure yet," Max admitted. "But Gabriel gave me a history lesson. It goes back to the Civil War. Blackridge Hollow, near the Tennessee border, just north of the Chickamauga battlefield."

Jimmy whistled low. "Chickamauga? Man, that was a bloodbath, from what they taught us in school."

"Yeah, but Blackridge Hollow was different," Max continued. "It was a smaller skirmish, but important. Union forces, including an Amerindian regiment, fought off a Confederate advance. Gabriel's ancestor was one of the regiment soldiers—a leader, actually. His name was Hollister, too, but he was on the Union side."

Jimmy raised an eyebrow. "A Hollister on the Union side?"

"Yep. Commander Hollister, Gabriel's ancestor, was loyal to the Union. But he was betrayed. By his own cousins—David's ancestors. They were Confederate sympathizers, and they framed the Amerindians for Commander Hollister's murder to cover up their own treachery."

Jimmy sat back, letting the story sink in. "So the Hollisters screwed over Gabriel's family, and that's what this is all about?"

"Exactly," Max said. "After the war, Blackridge Hollow was supposed to be given to Gabriel's family as reparations for their service. But the Hollisters—David's ancestors—used their political connections to take the land for themselves. They pushed Gabriel's family out, stole their heritage."

Jimmy shook his head in disgust. "So that's what this painting is about? The land, the history?"

Max nodded. "That's what Gabriel believes. He thinks the real painting—the one hidden underneath—depicts the battle at Blackridge Hollow. The Amerindian soldiers standing tall against the Confederates. It's a part of history that's been erased, and Gabriel wants to expose it."

Jimmy's eyes narrowed. "And David doesn't want anyone findin' out about it."

"Exactly. If the truth comes out, it could ruin the Hollister legacy."

Jimmy leaned back in his chair, rubbing his chin thoughtfully. "Well, damn. That explains a lot. So this whole thing—this theft, the painting—it's not just about the money. It's about buryin' the past."

"And making sure it stays buried," Max agreed. "Gabriel sees this as his chance to reclaim his family's honor, and he thinks I'm the key to doing that."

Jimmy let out another low whistle. "Man, I gotta say, I didn't see that one comin'. You've got yourself in the middle of a real mess, Max."

"Tell me about it," Max said, shaking his head. "But now we know what we're up against."

The detective in Jimmy was on guard. "So what's the plan? You gonna confront Felicity?"

Max paused for a moment, then shook his head. "No, not yet. She doesn't know I'm onto her. That's my advantage."

Jimmy gave him a long look. "You sure about that? She's got Hollister in her ear."

"I'm sure," Max said firmly. "But I do have an idea."

Jimmy raised an eyebrow. "Oh yeah? What's the play?"

Max stood up from the chair, grabbing his jacket off the back. "Come with me."

Jimmy blinked. "Wait, what? Like, right now?"

"Yeah," Max said, already heading for the door.

Jimmy groaned as he pushed himself up from his chair. "Max, what the hell? Where are we goin'?"

Max stopped in the doorway and looked back at his friend with a determined glint in his eyes. "I'll explain on the way. Let's go."

Jimmy grumbled something under his breath but grabbed his hat and followed Max out of the office. *Whatever he has in mind, it's going to be big. And real dangerous*, Jimmy thought.

The engine of the faded vermillion Fairlady 300ZX hummed beneath the old but sleek hood as it glided through the streets of Buckhead. The posh neighborhood's manicured lawns and sprawling estates spoke of wealth that went back generations. Max gripped the wheel tightly as he weaved through the winding roads, his thoughts miles away. Beside him, Jimmy Callahan sat back, his hat tipped low over his eyes, watching the world blur past. "Alright, Max," he said, breaking the silence. "Where are we headed, exactly?"

"To see Anastasia Chen," Max replied in a clipped tone.

Jimmy straightened up and a frown creased his weathered face. "Anastasia Chen? You mean *the* Anastasia Chen? The one who bought that painting at Sotheby's?"

Max nodded. "Yeah, that's the one."

Jimmy scratched the side of his jaw. "What's the sense in goin' to see her? She already bought it. She's got no idea what's goin' on with Hollister, or you for that matter."

"I'm going to tell her she might have bought a fake," Max said, eyes focused on the road ahead.

Jimmy let out a low whistle. "A fake? Max, Sotheby's don't sell fakes. You know that. How's it gonna be fake if it's from them?"

Max sighed, frustration bubbling just under the surface. "I don't know, Jimmy. I'm not saying I have all the answers. But I've seen two versions of this painting already. One was in my safe, and it's a fake. The second one, the cops found in that warehouse after Hollister tried to trap me — fake. So, what are the chances the one Anastasia got is real?"

"Hell, man, those are long odds," Jimmy replied, shaking his head. "But I get it. You're doin' what you think is right." They turned down a wide, gated drive, and the opulent mansion came into view.

They waited outside on a large, sun-soaked lawn, where a small table had been set up beneath the shade of a massive oak tree. The tea service was laid out meticulously, silver gleaming in the soft afternoon light. Max's mind wandered as he scanned the estate, lost in thoughts about the painting and David's ever-tightening noose.

"Gentlemen."

The voice was soft, lilting, and Max turned to see Anastasia Chen approaching. She was dressed casually, but the light fabric of her thin dress clung to her curves, fluttering slightly in the breeze. Her dark hair was loose around her shoulders, and she carried herself with the same effortless grace that had caught Max's eye the first time they met. Even now, he couldn't quite keep his gaze from trailing over her.

"Mrs. Chen," Max greeted, standing as she reached the table. He caught a subtle whiff of her perfume, a mix of jasmine and something darker. It clung to the air like a lingering secret.

Anastasia smiled, the corners of her mouth curling upward in a way that felt more playful than polite. "Max, what a surprise. I didn't expect you to be here with a friend."

"This is my friend, Detective Jimmy Callahan. I hope this isn't an inconvenient moment."

"Not at all," she said and shook Jimmy's hand. "Please, sit." She gestured toward the chairs.

Max caught the faintest hint of a smirk on Jimmy's face as they both took their seats, but his friend said nothing. He hid it well, but Max could feel Jimmy's eyes on him, waiting for the next move. "I'm afraid I didn't come here for tea," Max said, cutting straight to the point. "I need to talk to you about that painting. The Silent Watch."

Anastasia raised an eyebrow, feigning surprise. "The painting? Really? I thought by now we'd be talking about something more … personal."

Max ignored the subtle tease, though he could feel the temperature rising. "I believe the painting you bought might be a fake."

Her laughter was soft and incredulous. "A fake? Sotheby's doesn't sell forgeries, Max. You must know that."

Jimmy leaned forward, breaking the silence. "Look, Mrs. Chen, we've got reason to believe Hollister's tied up in a pretty high-stakes forgery ring. Expensive stuff. The kinda thing that'd fool anyone, even the best."

Anastasia's face shifted as her surprise gave way to intrigue. "David Hollister? Forgery?"

Max nodded. "I've already seen two fakes. One in my own … I mean I came across one during my investigation, and the other was found in a warehouse. Both were copies of The Silent Watch. It stands to reason that the painting you bought might be the same."

The woman's playful smile faltered for some seconds. A small but unsettling possibility seemed to creep into her mind. Was there some truth buried in this accusation? Could what these men were saying be more plausible than she was willing to admit? She opened her mouth to respond, but before she could, an older man's voice called out from across the lawn. "Darling, I'll be inside if you need me."

Anastasia waved back to the man, who Max assumed was her husband. The older gentleman offered a polite wave to Max and Jimmy before disappearing into the house.

Jimmy stood up suddenly, straightening his jacket. "Excuse me for a moment, folks. Nature's callin', and I'd rather not answer right here."

Anastasia rang a small bell, and a servant appeared almost immediately, bowing slightly. "Please show Mr.

Callahan to the restroom," she said, before turning back to Max with a smile that held more than a hint of mischief.

Jimmy tipped his hat and followed the servant, leaving Max and Anastasia alone in the shaded stillness. Anastasia crossed her legs slowly. Distracted by the movement, Max's eyes were drawn to the delicate anklet fastened about her ankle. It was a thin chain of silver resting against her smooth skin. Her foot, curling toward him, was slender and graceful, the arch perfectly formed. Her polished nails gleamed in the soft light, and for a moment, Max found himself staring, mesmerized by the sight.

When he looked up, Anastasia's lips were curled into a suggestive smile. "You've been looking at me like that since the first time we met, Max. Careful, or people might start to talk."

Max cleared his throat, struggling to keep his focus. "I think you should really consider looking into the painting. There's a lot of money involved, and if you bought into David's scheme —"

She leaned forward, lowering her foot, and as she did, her toes grazed against Max's leg, sliding down with deliberate, slow pressure. Max froze, his breath catching as the sensation shot through him. He tried to maintain his composure, but the touch left him flustered, fumbling for the right words.

Anastasia chuckled softly, and leaned back into her chair with an amused glint in her eyes. "You're cute when you're nervous, Max. But you don't need to worry about me. I've handled my fair share of art deals before. I know what I'm doing."

Max straightened in his seat, forcing his voice to remain steady. "This is different. David Hollister isn't just some art dealer. He's dangerous, and if you're tangled up in his world —"

Before he could finish, Jimmy reappeared, adjusting his belt as he walked back to the table. "Well, that was a relief," he muttered, flashing Max a knowing look. "We good to head out, Max?"

Max rose to his feet quickly, eager to escape the charged tension of the moment. Anastasia stood as well, and suddenly they were closer than he'd anticipated. The faint scent of her perfume washed over him again. Intoxicating, it made his head swim.

"Leaving already?" Anastasia asked in her soft voice, as her lips spoke just inches from his. "You always seem to rush off when things start getting interesting."

Max swallowed hard, stepping back just enough to regain his composure. "I'll be in touch. About the painting."

Her eyes gleamed as she smiled. "I'm looking forward to it."

With that, Max turned on his heel. Jimmy followed close behind as they made their way back to the car. He could still feel the weight of Anastasia's eyes on him as they walked away. Once they were out of earshot, Jimmy let out a low whistle. "Man, you better watch yourself. That woman's gonna eat you alive."

Sliding into the driver's seat, Max quietly started the engine. He needed to get out of there — away from Anastasia's lingering touch, her perfume, her dangerous smile. But even as he drove off, heaviness grew within his chest as if something was about to unravel soon.

David Hollister floated on his back in the cool water of his pool. The gentle ripples were lapping against the sides and the night sky above was dotted with stars. As warm bourbon slowly settled in his chest, the only things he was aware of were the wobbly shadows under him and the glow of Atlanta's lights dominating the horizon in the distance. On the edge of the pool, the phone lit up with an incoming call. He reached out without leaving the water.

"Evelyn." His voice was sharp as he answered.

"Mr. Hollister," came the crisp reply. "I've made the necessary arrangements. Spoke to the contact you requested. They said they'll handle it."

A nervous tick pulled at the corner of David's mouth. "Are they satisfied with the payout?"

"Yes, sir," Evelyn replied smoothly. "He's agreed to the terms. Said he's done things like this before. Clean work. He won't leave any trail behind."

David swirled the bourbon in his glass, staring out into the night as if it held all the answers. "That's good to hear, but I want more than promises. Remind them that nothing can go wrong, Evelyn. This needs to be airtight. I don't want to hear about it again. Ever."

"Of course, Mr. Hollister," Evelyn said without hesitation. "I made it clear. He's aware there's no room for error."

David's eyes remained cold. "Max Worthington. That slippery bastard. He's gotten away from me twice already. Now I'll give him something to die for." He paused, the twitch in his mouth returning before he forced it away. "No more delays."

"I understand." Evelyn's voice was steady. "He said he'd take care of it swiftly. There won't be anything left to tie back to us."

David closed his eyes and let the water cradle him as he exhaled slowly. "Tell them this is their last chance to prove they're worth what I'm paying. No mistakes, not with Max sniffing around."

"I'll pass the message along. They're professionals."

He ended the call and dropped the phone back on the concrete ledge. His fingers trailed lazily through the water. There was something final in the way the plan had fallen into place, something inevitable. His laugh echoed across the still surface of the pool as he imagined the aftermath, knowing that this time, Max wouldn't be able to slip the pieces into place.

CHAPTER XIX

Morning light streamed through the trees to create a patchwork of shadows across Max's backyard. Felicity stood near the edge of the property, with her camera raised to the sky. Her lens was tracking something above. Max watched her from the small back porch, coffee mug in hand, studying the way she moved. He saw the practiced grace, each motion carefully measured. *Just like everything else about her lately*, he thought bitterly.

A flock of common grackles wheeled overhead, their iridescent black feathers catching the sunlight as they shifted and swayed in fluid patterns against the pale blue Atlanta sky. The camera's shutter clicked rapidly as Felicity captured their aerial drift.

"There's something about the way they move." She sensed Max's presence without lowering her camera. "Like they're all connected by invisible threads, you know?"

"Invisible threads," Max repeated softly, as he let a hint of irony color his voice. "Yeah, I know all about those."

She lowered the camera to turn to him, with a slight smile hovering over her lips. "Didn't realize you were so philosophical this early in the morning."

Max drew a slow sip of his coffee, watching her over the rim of his mug. "I've been doing a lot of thinking lately.

About loyalty. Trust. The way things aren't always what they seem."

"Oh?" Felicity's smile remained steady, but something flickered in her eyes. "Sounds serious."

"Could be." He descended the steps to move closer. "You ever notice how grackles stick together? They're loyal to their flock. Until they're not." He gestured toward the birds above. "Sometimes one breaks away, joins another group entirely."

Felicity's camera lowered slowly. "I didn't know you were into bird behavior."

"I'm interested in all kinds of behavior." Max kept his tone light. "Haven't seen much of you lately. Been busy with work?"

Felicity's smile wavered just a hair. "Yeah, sorry about that. Had a bunch of assignments back to back." She fiddled with the settings on her camera. "But I'm here now."

"Right here," Max agreed in a soft voice. "Safe and sound in my backyard. Like always." He paused, watching her hands move across the camera's controls, remembering Jimmy's words from yesterday. Those same hands had worked to pass information to David Hollister, finding ways to betray him piece by piece. "Getting any good shots?"

She brightened, seemingly relieved by the change in subject. Turning the camera's display toward him, she said, "Look at this one. The way they're spread out, it almost looks like—"

Max's phone buzzed in his pocket. He glanced at the screen, and saw Jimmy's number. "Sorry, need to take this. Back in a minute."

He walked into the house, and didn't answer the call before the door had closed behind him. "Hello, Jimmy?"

"Max." Jimmy's voice was tight. "You sitting down?"

"What's wrong?"

"The Chen place. It's gone."

Max's breath hitched. "What do you mean, gone?"

"I mean gone, Max. Burned to the ground last night. Fire department's saying it started around three a.m. Spread fast. By the time they got there …" Jimmy's voice trailed off.

The coffee mug nearly slipped from Max's fingers. He set it down on the counter with a shaky hand. "The Chens?"

"Dead, Max. Both of them." Jimmy's voice was heavy. "Fire department found two bodies in the master bedroom. Place went up like kindling in the middle of the night. By the time anyone spotted it …" He paused, before saying. "Nothing survived. Not the Chens, not any of the artwork at the place, not a damn thing. Just ash."

The implications hit Max like a physical blow. The painting. The evidence. All of it, reduced to ash. This wasn't coincidence. This was Hollister, cleaning house, erasing traces. "Jesus Christ," he whispered.

"I'm heading over there now," Jimmy said. "Gonna see what I can find out. Max, be careful, where's Felicity?"

"Here, at my place."

There was a pause at the other end before Jimmy's voice came through. "This isn't just about art anymore." As the call ended, Max stood staring at nothing. Behind him, he heard the back door open, followed by Felicity's footsteps.

"Max? Everything okay?"

He turned slowly to face her, seeing her concerned expression, the camera still hanging from her neck. In that moment, everything crystallized; the betrayal, the fire, the web of lies he'd been tangled in. And at the center of it all, the woman standing before him, waiting to hear what he would say next.

With his mind reeling from Jimmy's call, he observed the morning light catching Felicity's face. It highlighted a concern that seemed so genuine it made his chest ache. How many times had he seen that same expression and believed in it completely?

"Need a drink?" The words came out before he could stop them.

He could tell the frown on Felicity's face was genuine. "It's not even ten, Max."

"Yeah." He moved to the liquor cabinet anyway, and pulled out a bottle of bourbon. "One of those mornings."

She watched him pour two glasses, hesitated, then took the one he offered. "Who was it on the phone."

"A close friend of mine. Jimmy Callahan."

There was no hint in her eyes she knew who he was talking about. He had never gotten the chance to introduce Jimmy to her before. "What did he want?" she said.

Max took a long sip and waited to let the burn steady him. "The Chen estate burned down last night. Anastasia Chen and her husband died in the fire."

Felicity's glass stopped halfway to her lips. "What?"

"Everything destroyed. All the artwork. Nothing left but a smoldering ruin." He watched her face carefully. "At least, that's what they want people to think."

"They?" Her voice wavered slightly.

"Come on Felicity." Max set his glass down. "You know exactly who I'm talking about."

"Max, I don't—"

"The security cameras." His voice remained steady, but his fingers tightened around the glass. "August 10th. They didn't pick you up leaving that morning. Or coming back later."

Color drained from her face. "I don't understand."

"The safe. The painting. All of it." He took another drink. "You've known Hollister longer than you've known me, haven't you?"

Felicity set her untouched drink on the counter. Max saw her hand was trembling. "Max, please—"

"I know about your meetings at the Velvet Lounge with him." The words felt like stones in his mouth. "All this time, I thought I could trust you. Thought what we had was …" Instead of saying it he sucked loud on his lips. "Was any of it real?"

"Max." Her voice cracked. "It wasn't supposed to be like this."

"Then tell me what it was supposed to be like." An edge crept into his voice now. "Tell me why the woman I love has been playing me for a fool."

Tears welled in her eyes. "I did love you. I still do. But David … he had things on me. From before. And the money—" She stopped, pressing her hand to her mouth.

"The money." Bitter laughter broke forth. "That's what it comes down to? What was the price tag on us, Felicity?"

"No!" She stepped toward him, but he moved back. "It wasn't like that. At first, it was just supposed to be information. About your work, your contacts. Then the painting …" She swallowed hard. "He said nobody would get hurt."

"Tell that to the Chens." His voice was ice.

Felicity's face went white. "The fire," she said and paused. Max's gaze was nailed on her. She went on, "That wasn't part of the plan. The painting isn't destroyed, Max. David had it moved before—" She stopped, realizing what she'd admitted.

"Where is it?"

"I don't know." She wrapped her arms around herself. "I swear I don't know where he keeps it. But I can help you find it."

Max studied her face. "Why should I believe anything you say now? After you broke into my safe and stole it because he told you to?"

"It didn't happen like that."

"Really? You were here that day, after I drove away. You were talking to someone right past the front." He gestured with a hand toward the front door. "You told me you had to be on a shoot, but you were here. You're the one who put that replica in my safe."

Felicity screwed her eyes shut and shook her head at him. "Believe me. I passed on the information. I didn't lay hands on that painting or anything else in your safe."

"Believe you, my ass," he said. "After everything, you still think I'm too stupid to see through you?"

"It's the truth. I didn't take it," she said. "Please belee—" Her words were cut short by glass smashing against the counter. Max glared at her, the wrecked half of the glass still in his hand. He'd been careful not to cut himself.

"Give me a good reason why I should," he spat.

"Because I'm telling the truth." Tears spilled down her cheeks. "I know I betrayed you. I know I can never make that right. But let me help fix this. Please."

"Two people are dead, Felicity. This isn't just about a painting anymore." He fought to rein in his breathing.

"I know." She wiped her eyes. "That's why I want to help. David's gone too far. The things he's doing … I never wanted any part of this."

Max set the broken glass down and turned to look out the window, at the garden where moments ago she'd been photographing birds. The morning felt like a lifetime ago. "You were supposed to be the one person I could trust," he said quietly. "Do you have any idea what that feels like? To realize the person you're in love with has been lying to your face?"

"I hated every minute of it." Her voice was trembling. "Every time I had to report back to him, every lie I told you, it was killing me. But I couldn't see a way out."

He turned back to her. "And now?"

"Now I want to make it right." She met his eyes. "David still thinks I'm working for him. We can use that. I can help you get the painting back."

Max was quiet for a long moment. He brought out a fresh glass and poured from the bottle. The bourbon caught the morning light, throwing amber shadows on the counter. Her desperation had a familiar ring to it — he'd heard that same note in too many voices over the years, echoing through the dog-eared chapters of his life and the hardboiled fiction that paid his rent. But desperation made people predictable, and predictable he could use. Maybe she was playing him, maybe she wasn't. Either way, the painting was closer now than it had been in weeks.

"If we do this," he said finally, "I need to know I can trust you. One hundred percent. No more lies, no more games."

"I promise." She took a tentative step toward him. "Whatever it takes to prove it to you."

He didn't move away this time. "We'll need a plan. A good one. David's already shown what he's willing to do to keep his secrets."

"I know." She nodded. "But I know things about his operation. Things that could help."

Max picked up his glass and drained it. "Start talking."

Felicity drew a shaky breath. "Okay. But Max? I need you to know something first."

He waited.

"What I feel for you was never part of the act. I fell in love with you for real, and that's why this has been tearing me apart." Her voice caught. "I know I don't deserve your forgiveness, but—"

"You're right," Max cut in. "You don't." He set the glass down with a soft clink. "But right now, we have work to do. The rest we'll figure out later."

Felicity nodded as she wiped away fresh tears. "Where do we start?"

"With everything you know about David's operation. Every detail, no matter how small." Max's voice was professional and focused now. But inside, his heart felt like broken glass. "And Felicity?"

"Yes?"

"If you're playing me again …" He left the threat unspoken.

"I'm not." Her voice was steady despite the tears. "I promise you, Max. Never again."

CHAPTER XX

The parking garage was nearly empty at this hour. Felicity's heels echoed off concrete as she walked to her car. She'd stayed late at the gallery again, something that had become a habit since the whole mess with Max began. The fluorescent lights buzzed overhead, creating pools of harsh white light between long stretches of shadow. She heard them before she saw them. Footsteps that weren't quite in sync with her own. Before she could reach for her keys, a hand clamped over her mouth. The world tilted sideways as consciousness slipped away.

She awoke to the musty smell of old wood and wine. Her head throbbed as she tried to orient herself. Her vision swam into focus and she saw she was in what appeared to be a wine cellar. Though, it was one that hadn't been used in years. Empty racks lined the walls, their wood warped with age and humidity. A single bulb hanging from the ceiling splashed a sickly glow over everything. Her wrists were bound to the arms of an antique wooden chair, but not particularly tight; as if whoever had tied her wanted her uncomfortable rather than truly restrained. The air was thick with the peculiar stillness that comes with being underground.

"Welcome back." David Hollister emerged from the shadows at the far end of the cellar. He was dressed impeccably in a charcoal suit that seemed to absorb what little light there was. He carried a crystal glass of what looked like brandy. It looked like blood in the yellow light. "I hope my associates weren't too rough with you."

Felicity tested her restraints subtly. "This seems excessive, even for you."

"Does it?" He moved closer, free hand trailing along the dusty wine racks. "I thought it rather appropriate. This cellar belonged to one of Atlanta's oldest families. They used to host the most exclusive parties here during Prohibition." His fingers brushed against her hair, letting a strand slip through them. "So many secrets buried in these walls."

She jerked her head away from his touch. "I assume there's a point to all this theater?"

"Always so direct." David circled behind her, his hand sliding to her shoulder. "That's what I liked about you, Felicity. No games. Until recently." His fingers tightened painfully. "Tell me about your conversation with Max."

"If you're going to kill me, just get it over with."

He chuckled, but there was no warmth in it. Coming around to face her again, he took a slow sip of his brandy. "Death can be so final. I prefer to explore all my options first." His free hand moved to her chin, forcing her to look up at him. "And you're far too valuable to waste. Unless you give me no choice."

She could smell the brandy on his breath, see the dangerous glint in his eyes. His thumb brushed across her lower lip, a gesture both intimate and threatening. "So tell me, dear Felicity, what exactly did you share with your righteous boyfriend?"

"Everything." She kept her voice steady despite the revulsion his touch sparked. "About the painting, about working for you. About the Chens."

The glass shattered in his grip, brandy and blood dripping onto the dirt floor. David barely seemed to notice, though his other hand tightened on her jaw. "You stupid, ungrateful little—"

"He has proof." She cut him off to force the words out against his grip. "Documents, recordings, everything. If anything happens to me, it all goes public."

His bloody hand wrapped around her throat. Warm liquid smeared against her skin. "You think that frightens me? You think I haven't buried worse than some paperwork and recordings?"

"I think …" She struggled to speak, heart pounding against her ribs. "I think I can give you something better than killing me."

"And what's that?" His grip tightened fractionally.

"Max." The name crawled out as a thin whisper. "I can bring him to you."

David's hold loosened slightly. "Go on."

"He trusts me now more than ever." The words tumbled out in a rush. "He thinks I've had a change of heart, that I'm helping him recover the painting. I can lead him wherever you want."

That hand moved from her throat to her hair. His fingers tangled in it as he studied her face. Blood matted the strands together. It was a detail that seemed to amuse him. "Why should I believe you?"

Felicity forced herself to not flinch away from his touch. "Because I want to live. And because I know which side is going to win this."

"And you think that's my side?" A dangerous smile played at his lips as he leaned closer, his bloody hand sliding down to rest against her collarbone.

"I know it is." She met his gaze steadily. "Max is smart, but he's not like you. He still believes in justice, in doing the right thing. That makes him predictable. Vulnerable."

David released her abruptly and walked to one of the old wine racks, running his fingers along the dusty wood. "You'd really serve him up to me? Just like that?"

"Just like that." Her voice was firm.

When he turned back, the dim light cast deep shadows across his face. Blood still dripped slowly from his cut hand. Each drop hit the dirt floor with a soft pat. "Tell me your plan."

"Not yet." Felicity's voice hardened. "First, I want your word. After this is done, I walk away. Clean slate, fresh start, whatever you want to call it."

David laughed, the sound echoing off the stone walls. "You think you're in a position to negotiate?" He moved back to her, hands coming to rest on the arms of the chair as he leaned down to bring his face close to hers. "Tied up in my cellar, covered in my blood?"

"I think I'm offering you exactly what you want." She didn't back away from his proximity. "Max Worthington, handed to you on a silver platter. All you have to do is let me disappear afterward."

The silence stretched between them, heavy with possibility and threat. Finally, David straightened and pulled out his phone. "Clean up the mess upstairs and get a car ready," he spoke into it before returning his attention to Felicity. "You have seventy-two hours to make this happen. After that …" He began untying her restraints.

"I'll need details." Her voice was businesslike now, though she couldn't entirely hide her relief at being freed. "Where you want him, when. And I'll need to know he'll be alone."

David pulled a handkerchief from his pocket and wrapped it around his bleeding hand. "I'll text you the location tomorrow. Make sure he comes alone, or the deal's off." His eyes were cold despite his smile. "And if, by any chance, you're playing both sides here …"

"I know." She stood, rubbing her wrists. "Seventy-two hours."

"One more thing." His voice stopped her as she headed for the stairs. "The painting. Where does he think it is?"

"He doesn't know." She paused with her foot on the first step. "That's why he'll go wherever I tell him to look for it."

Satisfaction slowly crept across his features. "Good." He gestured to the stairs. "Someone will drive you back to your car. Clean yourself up before you go home. You're covered in blood, my dear." After her footsteps faded up the wooden stairs, David smiled at the silence of the cellar. "Seventy-two hours," he hummed. "And then it all ends."

III

Edge of the Blade

CHAPTER XXI

The early evening heat clung to Atlanta like a fever. Max's ceiling fan spun lazy circles, doing little more than pushing the stale air around his Grant Park living room. The ice in his untouched bourbon had melted, leaving rings of condensation on the side table. He'd loosened his tie an hour ago, rolled up his sleeves, but sweat still gathered at his collar as he watched Felicity pace between the windows.

"David talked to me about the painting," she said, stopping to face him. "About a week ago, before everything with the Chens."

"Did he now?"

Felicity sank into the armchair. "He'd been drinking." Her photographer's hands began to twirl against each other in her lap. "Started talking about your families, the Hollisters and the Worthingtons. About the Civil War. It was a little confusing."

"What exactly did he say?" Max kept his voice level, though his pulse quickened. He needed to hear how much David had revealed, how it matched against the history Thunderhawk had passed to him.

She recounted David's story, whatever he had said about family legacies and buried secrets, about Harrison Worthington and Robert Hollister's fractured friendship. As she spoke, Max cataloged each detail against what he already knew, searching for discrepancies, for hints of what David might still be hiding.

"The way he spoke about that painting," and Felicity shook her head. "He called it more than just valuable art. Said it was the key to a past that could destroy everything his family had built."

Max moved to the window, using the movement to hide whatever might show on his face. "And you believe him?"

"I believe he's terrified of what that painting could reveal." Felicity stood up and crossed to the drink cart. Her hands shook slightly as she poured herself a measure of bourbon. "That's how I know it couldn't have been destroyed in the fire. He needs it too much."

"How can you be sure?"

"David's been different since getting his hands on it. Calmer, almost satisfied." She took a slow sip. "And yesterday his assistant called me about a private viewing. Some European collector flying in next week."

Max turned from the window. "His assistant called you?"

As she spoke, Max studied the way shadows played across her face, looking for tells, for signs of deception layered beneath deception. "He still thinks I'm useful." The words came out bitter. "Wants me to photograph the piece for the buyer's insurance records. Guess he figured keeping me involved would look less suspicious."

Max crossed his arms. His brow furrowed in thought. "Wait. If David's holding a private viewing, it sounds like he's planning to sell. But he doesn't want to part with the original, does he?"

Felicity gave him a knowing look. "He's too possessive. That piece is like his trophy. But he knows the buyer wants to see something authentic."

Max paced, running a hand over his jaw. "Then he must've arranged for another fake. But with his forgery ring taken down, how would he pull that off? There's no way he could get a copy good enough to fool a collector."

Felicity shrugged, a pout playing around her mouth. "David always has another card up his sleeve."

"Where's this viewing happening?"

"The Buckhead gallery. After hours." Felicity met his eyes. "I can get us in. It's our best chance to get it back."

Max paused pacing and turned to her. "How?"

"Even if David is planning to slip in a replica later on, he would not risk a display of something that's not the real thing for the viewing. How do you think he managed to pull off the Sotheby's auction without a hitch?"

Max began to weigh the words of the woman standing before him. There was a sliver of truth in what Felicity was saying. He could feel it but it was just as likely she was stringing him along, setting him up for another fall. She could be lying to him outright, every word crafted to keep him off balance. But he'd played this game before; one more gamble wouldn't break him. The only way to be sure was to step in, take the plunge. Risks had gotten him this far; what was one more if it got him closer to the truth? He'd taken dangerous chances before and come out breathing. This one, though murky and reckless, might be worth the price.

"I want a real chance to study it, front and back. Not a rushed glance."

That caught her off guard. "Why both sides?"

"Authentication." Max's lie came smooth and practiced. "Need to be sure it's the real thing, not another forgery."

"David's obsessed with that painting," she said. "Whatever secret he's guarding, it's worth another forgery to him." She set her glass down. "You already knew that though, didn't you?"

Before Max could respond, his phone buzzed against the coffee table. Jimmy's name flashed on the screen.

"Need to take this," he said and stepped into his kitchen. "Jimmy?"

"Max." Jimmy's voice was rough. "Got something on the Chen fire. Insurance report just came through. They're calling it electrical failure. Natural causes."

"Natural causes? The whole place went up in the middle of the night."

"Gets worse." Papers rustled on Jimmy's end. "Chen's will got updated three months back. Guess who's listed as beneficiary for their entire art collection?"

Max closed his eyes and waited some moments before he said, "David."

"Bingo. He's about to collect millions in insurance money for artwork he already stole. Plus whatever he gets from the estate." Jimmy's disgust carried through the line. "My contact at the insurance company's been going through old claims. Looks like there might be a pattern here. Other collections, other convenient accidents."

"You think you can prove it?"

"Working on it. But listen…found something else. There's a private viewing scheduled at the Buckhead gallery next week. European buyer, very hush-hush."

Max's grip tightened on the phone. "How'd you hear about it?"

"Got a friend in the security company they use. Thought it was weird, scheduling extra coverage for what's supposed to be a closed night."

"Send me everything you've got on the security detail."

"Already on it." Jimmy paused, before saying, "But keep this in mind: guy like that, sitting on that kind of money? He's not going to let anything stand in his way."

Max ended the call and stood for a moment, letting the rage settle into something cold and focused. When he returned to the living room, Felicity was standing by his bookshelf, studying an old photo of his father. "Everything okay?" she asked.

He moved to the window beside her, watching darkness creep across his backyard. "The Chens' will," he said. "David had it changed three months ago. Made himself beneficiary of their art collection."

Felicity turned, her face turning pale. "What?"

"Insurance is calling it an accident. He's about to get paid twice for the thing he already stole." Max watched her carefully. "Including pieces that might not have burned at all."

"That son of a bitch." The words came out as a whisper. Her hands were trembling. "I knew what he was capable of...but this? Those people..." She sank onto the couch, genuine shock written across her features. Or a convincing performance of it. Max thought of Jimmy's warning, of the growing stack of coincidences that always seemed to benefit David Hollister.

"The viewing," he said. "We need every detail; security patterns, cameras, exits. Tell me everything you know."

Felicity nodded, composing herself. "I'll get everything." She looked up at him. "Whatever's hidden behind that painting, it's big enough that David killed for it. Are you sure you want to know what it is?"

Is she playing me? he thought. *How many lies could dance on the head of a heart?* In the growing darkness, neither could quite make out the other's expression. Perhaps that was just as well.

And if she was playing him, the question was whether he could play her right back, and whether the truth behind *The Silent Watch* was worth the risk of walking into what was almost certainly a trap. Max thought of his father, of generations of carefully guarded truth. "I already know. The question is, whose side are you really on?"

"I told you, I want to make this right." She stood and began to gather her camera bag. "I'll have the security details tomorrow. After that it's up to you."

Max watched her head for the door, and wondered how many layers of falsehood they were both swimming in. Somewhere in the city a painting hung that could bring down an empire. All they had to do was survive long enough to reach it.

"David's going to pay," Felicity said softly, pausing at the threshold. "For the Chens. For everything."

"Yes," Max said, noting how the fading light caught the tension in her shoulders. "He will." After she left, Max poured himself a fresh glass of bourbon with no ice this time. Wednesday night at the gallery. Either he'd uncover the truth protected by all the lies, or he'd join the growing list of David Hollister's inconvenient accidents. Which side of that equation would Felicity end up on?

CHAPTER XXII

Felicity sat at the small kitchen table, the hum of the refrigerator almost too loud in the quiet surrounding her. The rhythm of her fingers drumming absently on the wood matched the frantic pace of her thoughts. She had become accustomed to the silence, to the way her life had started to feel like a series of quiet moments before the storm hit. But tonight, her choices hung over her, and she couldn't shake the feeling that the ground beneath her was shifting. She studied the lies she was juggling. They were too many, too close, and ready to collapse in on her if she let her guard down. This was a game that kept her close to both men, and now, it seemed, close enough to make a choice.

But what choice do I have?

She swallowed down the bitter taste in her mouth as she thought about Max — his intelligence, his charm, the way he'd pulled her in before she even realized it. The buzz of the phone cut through her thoughts.

We need to talk.

A message from David.

With a resigned sigh, she grabbed her purse and left the apartment in a rush, as always. Stepping out into the sticky night air, still heavy with the remnants of an afternoon storm, she glanced over her shoulder. It had become second nature — the constant need to stay ahead of whoever might be watching her every move. She was playing the long game now, and it meant that her movements, her choices, had to be precise.

The window of the black sedan that pulled up just as she rounded the corner was too dark to see inside, but she didn't need to check. She opened the door and slid into the back seat without a word. David didn't look at her immediately. His gaze focused on the darkened streets.

"Everything in place?" The calmness in his voice betrayed none of the tension between them. The car lurched forward into the night.

"The story's been planted. Jimmy's got the tip, the one about the private viewing. Max is already biting."

David's lips quirked up in a half-smile. "Good. Let's see if he's foolish enough to walk into it."

Felicity's stomach churned. She could feel the tension creeping up her spine. It wasn't the kind of discomfort that came from being followed or suspected. It was the kind that accompanied the weight of betrayal. "Max won't just walk in. He'll investigate. He'll want to get close to the painting."

"Let him," David replied, his voice flat, like the plan was already settled. "The more he believes he's uncovering something, the easier it will be for us."

Felicity glanced out of the window, feeling the unease coil in her gut. The painting was a means to an end, she knew that. But somewhere along the way, it had become more than that. The game had changed, and so had the stakes. She wasn't just worried about the painting anymore — she was worried about Max, and about herself.

She shifted in her seat. "You're sure about this?" she asked, her voice quieter now. "Everything's ready?"

David didn't answer right away, his gaze fixed ahead as if calculating every detail. Finally, he spoke. "Max will walk in. He won't suspect anything. Your job is to make sure he's focused on the gallery."

Felicity swallowed hard, nodding, but the question lingered in her mind. *What if he doesn't?* She didn't voice it. Instead, she asked, "And if he catches on?"

"He won't. Not unless you give him a reason to. He trusts you, doesn't he?" David's cold gaze flicked to her. "Make sure he doesn't see what's coming."

She nodded, but the doubt remained. Max was smart, and she knew that better than anyone. Her mind raced as they continued driving, the weight of the plan pressing down on her chest. She had planted the tip. She had made sure everything lined up perfectly. But what if it wasn't enough? The car slowed to a stop in front of an inconspicuous building. It was a low-rise office with dark windows, nestled in a quiet corner of the city. It wasn't the kind of place you would expect to find an art dealer or a mastermind pulling strings behind closed doors, but Felicity knew better. This was where David liked to talk business out of the spotlight, where no one would be listening. It was also where he could put everything in place without interference.

The door clicked open, and David stepped out first, his posture rigid and controlled. Felicity followed, heels tapping sharply against the pavement as they entered the building.

Inside, the air was cool, and the faint scent of leather hung in the atmosphere. David led her down a corridor to a small, dimly lit room. A large table sat in the middle, covered in maps and photographs, the pieces of their plan laid out in front of them.

"Everything's ready," David said, his voice steady, almost serene. "Max will walk right into this." His palm hovered flat over a map before he tapped a finger on a spot circled in blue. "This is where he should be."

Felicity took a seat at the table, her hands clenched tightly in her lap. The words sounded too simple, too certain. She forced herself to remain calm, even as a small voice in the back of her head reminded her how easily things could unravel.

"I've made sure Jimmy's looking into the gallery's security. He's got the details. If Max suspects anything, it'll be too late."

David's gaze was sharp. "Good. The less he knows, the better. Everything's been set in motion. I trust you've handled the rest?"

Felicity took a breath. "Max believes the viewing is real. The buyer is a European collector looking to authenticate the painting."

David's lips curled into a thin smile. "Perfect. He won't question it. He won't be looking for trouble unless he catches any hints from you. Your part's simple: lead him there."

Felicity felt his words settle inside her chest like an iron nail. She had done her part, but she couldn't shake the feeling that this wasn't as painless as it seemed.

What if Max doesn't follow the plan?

David's voice cut through her thoughts. "If he tries anything, we'll deal with it. But I don't think he will."

She stood, her pulse quickening. "I'll make sure he gets the message. He'll walk in."

David didn't say anything else, just turned toward the door with the faintest smirk on his lips. Walking out, Felicity knew that whatever happened next, there would be no turning back. She only hoped that the man standing behind her would be the one to take the fall when everything inevitably came crashing down.

Felicity sat across from Max at the small, polished table in his loft. He leaned forward, his eyes sharply focused on her, waiting for her to speak. She knew better than to show the weight of her own nerves. His trust was a fragile thing now, but it was still hers to control. She breathed in slow to steady herself. The plan was set and the trap was nearly ready to spring. But for Max, it was all still a game of reclaiming the painting, a piece of his past he'd never let go. Felicity had to keep him believing that, right until the very end.

"I got what you asked for," she said, keeping her voice steady as she pulled out a small notebook. The leather cover was worn, making it look more authentic, more trusted. "The viewing's set for Wednesday night at the Buckhead gallery. They're keeping it quiet. Invitation only."

Max's eyes narrowed slightly. "Security?"

"Two guards on rotation." Felicity flipped through her notes, the lies flowing smoothly now. "One at the main entrance, one patrolling the back corridor. They switch positions every hour, on the hour. Between 10:15 and 10:30, there's a gap. The first guard checks the loading dock while the second makes his rounds through the east wing."

She watched Max absorb this, knowing he was already forming plans around the false information. Her stomach tightened.

"Cameras?" His voice was soft, but she could hear the intensity behind it.

"Four in the main gallery." She sketched a quick diagram on a fresh page, her hands steady despite the tremor in her chest. "Two are fixed…here and here." She marked Xs that would lead him exactly where David wanted him. "The others pan on a thirty-second rotation. But there's a blind spot." She circled a small area on the paper. "Right behind the Renaissance exhibition. The camera closest to it has been glitchy, cutting out for several minutes at a time."

Max took the notebook and studied her diagram. His fingers traced the path she'd drawn, and she could almost see him plotting his route in his mind. "The painting?"

"North wall of the main gallery. They're keeping it separate from the other pieces. Special lighting, climate control." She paused, before adding the detail that would seal it, "They're paranoid about authentication. The collector's bringing in an expert, but they're handling it like it's already priceless."

"Entry points?"

"Main entrance on Peachtree, service entrance in the back, and a fire exit on the east side." She leaned forward. "The fire exit's interesting. It's tied to the alarm system, but the gallery's been having issues with it. False alarms. They've had to disable it twice this month already."

Max sat back with a slight smile. It was the look she'd been waiting for; the one that said he believed every word. "You've done well," he said softly.

Felicity felt the praise like a knife-twist. "There's more," she added, maintaining her momentum. "The collector's flying in from Vienna. He'll be there at eight, but the real viewing doesn't start until nine. They're clearing the gallery at seven. That gives us a window."

He nodded slowly, still studying her diagram. "And the staff?"

"Minimal. They're keeping it exclusive. Two curators, the gallery owner, and a handful of assistants. Most of them will be focused on the collector." She hesitated, then added, "I can get you the staff rotation schedule by tomorrow."

Max finally looked up from the notebook, his eyes meeting hers. There was something in his gaze—trust, appreciation, maybe even affection—that made her chest ache. "This is exactly what we needed," he said.

She smiled back, ignoring the cold sweat at the base of her spine. Every detail she'd given him was orchestrated to lead him precisely where David wanted him to go. The blind spot she'd described would put him in perfect position for the trap. The security gap she'd invented would ensure he moved at exactly the right time.

"Just be careful," she said softly. The warning was genuine despite everything. "Even with the gaps in security…"

He reached across the table and took her hand. His touch was warm and sure. "I've got this under control. Thanks to you."

Felicity squeezed his hand back, hoping he couldn't feel how cold her fingers had become. In the dim light of his loft she could almost pretend this was real; that she wasn't leading him into a trap that would destroy everything between them.

"I should go," she said and gently pulled her hand away. "I'll get you that schedule tomorrow."

As she stood to leave, Max caught her arm. "Felicity." His voice was gentle. "We're close. After Wednesday, everything changes."

She nodded, not trusting herself to speak. He was right about one thing: after Wednesday, everything would change. Just not in the way he imagined. Walking to the door, she felt his eyes on her back. The weight of her deception pressed down on her shoulders, but she kept her posture relaxed, casual. It was only when she was in the street that she let out the breath she'd been holding. She pulled out her phone and typed a quick message to David:

"It's done. He's in."

The response came almost immediately: "Good girl."

Felicity stared at those two words until the screen went dark. A stray wind whipped a lock of her hair against her eyes and she thought, *I just signed Max's death warrant and my own.*

CHAPTER XXIII

Max checked his watch, then the entrance to Krog Street Market, where people drifted in and out like leaves caught in a midday breeze. It was one of those clear Atlanta afternoons with a low tense hum in the air, like the city was waiting on some kind of storm. Max took a deep breath, smelling roasted coffee, fresh bread, and something fried wafting from a stall nearby. It was busy, loud enough that two guys could talk without anyone caring to listen.

He spotted Jimmy coming through the door, hands stuffed in his coat pockets, his shoulders hunched against the world like he was expecting a punch that never came. Jimmy's eyes met his, and he gave a tight nod, moving over to where Max had claimed a table near the back, partially hidden by a big steel column. Jimmy sat down with a sigh, cracking his neck.

"Busy place for a secret meet-up," Jimmy said, his mouth twisting in a half-smile.

Max shrugged. "Figured it's safe enough here. Too many people around, nobody's gonna notice us."

Jimmy grunted, eyeing a group of teenagers laughing loudly as they jostled each other past the tables. He leaned forward, resting his elbows on the table, and pulled out his phone. "So, you ready to hear this or what?" He had been trailing Felicity, tracking her every move like a bloodhound, and Max needed to know what he'd found. Still, part of him didn't want to hear it.

Jimmy glanced around, leaned in a bit closer. "So, about Felicity," he said, his voice low but cutting through the background noise like a knife. "She's been up to her old tricks, no surprises there. Meeting with David, like you two planned. All of that's been going like clockwork. But three nights back, something weird happened."

Apprehension coiled at the base of Max's stomach. He raised an eyebrow. "Go on."

Jimmy rubbed a hand over his face, a habit he had when he was sorting through the facts, deciding what to say first. "Alright. Three nights ago, I'm following her, like you asked. She's leaving the gallery late, heading to her car in the parking garage. Place is nearly empty. Just as she stops beside her car, two guys walk up, suits, real quiet-like. Next thing she knows, someone's got her—hand over her mouth. They've got her by the arms, and she's looking… well, let's just say she wasn't planning on a joyride with those goons."

Max's hand rolled into a fist on the table. "You're saying she was kidnapped?"

"Looked that way," Jimmy said, nodding slowly. "They haul her to a spot a little off the grid—way over near the West End. Old, boarded-up house, kind that's been in some family since Sherman's march, probably. Place looks like it hasn't had life in it for decades. I'm thinking it's some kind of safe house, and I keep my distance, watch from down the block."

"And?" Max's voice was a strange mix of dread and anger boiling under his skin.

"She's in there a while, maybe a little over an hour. Then she comes out, no fuss, looking like she's walked out of a spa. They put her back in the SUV, drop her right back at her car." Jimmy leaned back, folding his arms. "So whatever went down in that house, she went along with it. Didn't even put up a fight."

Max shook his head, a flicker of doubt gnawing at him. "Maybe she didn't have a choice."

"Could be," Jimmy said with a trace of skepticism in his voice. "But the next night? She leaves her place again, gets into another car—same tinted windows. This time, she's riding with David. They go to some building downtown, real hush-hush. She's in there with him, and it ain't a five-minute trip, either. I'm sitting out there watching the whole time. Finally, they come out, and she's walking down the street like nothing's happened."

Max listened to the noise of the market as it churned around them: dishes clinked; a baby was crying somewhere; conversations thrummed and blended into a radiophonic mélange of urban life. It felt surreal, sitting here, hearing all this like he was just some guy listening to gossip, when everything in him was screaming that things were going sideways.

"So, what do you make of it?" he asked, keeping his voice casual, like they were talking about last night's baseball game.

Jimmy glanced down at his phone, tapping the screen idly. "I dunno, Max. It's messy, that's for sure. She's meeting with David like you two planned, sure, but she's not exactly playing it safe. There's more here than just a simple meet-and-greet. And the way she's walking in and out of these places, it's almost like she's got more skin in this game than you thought."

Max clenched his jaw. The words felt heavy, like a weight settling in his gut, pressing down on everything he thought he knew. "Well, Felicity told me about the viewing at the Buckhead gallery. Said it's happening tomorrow night. Some big European buyer's supposed to show up, authenticate The Silent Watch," he said, his eyes narrowing. "She gave me the layout, the security gaps, even the camera positions."

Jimmy's brows shot up. "She fed you all that?"

"Yeah," Max said, nodding. "And get this—I heard it from you too. Remember? Your buddy at the security company. He mentioned something about the gallery wanting extra coverage for a closed night."

Jimmy leaned back, looking thoughtful. "Yeah, that's right. He said they were beefing up security, which only made me think the intel was solid."

They sat in silence for a moment, the noises of the market drifting over them like a wave, voices and laughter mingling with the clattering of china. Somewhere nearby, a barista shouted out an order, and a couple at the next table broke out laughing.

Max tapped the finger of one hand against the knuckle of the other. "Felicity told me the security's going to be light at the gallery. Just two guards on duty, rotating shifts. She said one's at the main entrance, the other patrols the back corridor, and they switch every hour. Supposedly, there's a gap between 10:15 and 10:30 when one guard's checking the loading dock while the other's doing rounds in the east wing." He paused, brow furrowing. "That doesn't exactly line up with what you heard, does it?"

Jimmy met his gaze, a glint of doubt in his eyes. "No, it doesn't. If David's playing you, he's covering all his bases. He's got enough brains to pull it off, and Felicity…well, she's proving she can dance to his tune when it suits her."

Max frowned. "You think she'd go that far?"

Jimmy sighed, looking out over the bustling crowd, his expression hardening. "It's hard to say. People do things they never thought they'd do when they're in a bind, when someone's holding something over their head. And David? He's ruthless. He's already got more money than God, and here he is, playing these twisted games with people's lives like it's nothing."

Max's gaze drifted to the floor, his mind racing. Every instinct he had told him to trust Felicity—that she was playing David's game because she had no choice. But after everything Jimmy had just told him, he couldn't shake the feeling that he was missing something, that maybe Felicity's game was more complex than he'd thought. And tomorrow night, he'd be walking into that gallery, thinking he was one step ahead, when maybe he was right where David wanted him to be.

Jimmy reached over, giving his shoulder a firm squeeze. "Max, you're walking into his backyard. Whatever you think you know, David's probably five steps ahead. Just make sure you've got an out, alright? This guy doesn't play by anyone's rules but his own."

Max nodded, his jaw set, his eyes steely. "Don't worry, Jimmy. I'll be ready."

Jimmy watched him for a long moment, then pushed back from the table, giving Max a nod as he got to his feet. The sounds of the market seemed to swell, louder and more chaotic, filling the silence they left behind as Jimmy walked away.

Max stayed there a moment longer, feeling the world around him buzz with life, with the laughter and shouts of people who had no idea what was at stake tomorrow night. With a final click of the tongue that signaled the stage of his own personal Rubicon, he got to his feet. The world might be a mess of noise and confusion, but his resolve was set. He was going to that gallery.

CHAPTER XXIV

This members-only joint tucked away in Midtown's heart was trying so damn hard to be impressive with its velvet curtains blocking out the real world, mahogany tables polished to within an inch of their lives, and that sharp stink of cologne that probably cost more than most people's rent. The club wasn't her usual hangout. Not by a long shot. Sure, she'd been in her share of upscale joints over the years, but the low hum of conversation mixed with the clink of overpriced glasses and that fancy jazz drifting from the corner made Felicity want to laugh. Even when she wasn't sticking out like a sore thumb, the place had a way of making her feel like an outsider looking in. Not that it mattered. She wasn't here to fit in.

David took a slow pull from his whiskey, watching the amber liquid catch the light from those pretentious overhead sconces. Across from him, Felicity was doing her best impression of someone with a guilty conscience, her fingers tracing the edge of her glass like she was trying to read its fortune. He'd seen her rattled before, but this was different. The cool, collected mask she usually wore was cracking around the edges, and that set off every alarm bell in his head.

The shadows in the room stretched out like hungry things, swallowing up the corners where rich folks traded their precious little secrets like baseball cards. David shifted in his seat, studying Felicity over the rim of his glass. Her eyes were darting around the room like a trapped animal, never settling on him longer than it took to draw breath. After all the time they'd spent playing this game, he knew when something was off, and right now, everything about her was screaming that she was hiding something bigger than usual.

"What's going on with you, Felicity?" he finally asked, keeping his voice just above the quiet murmur of the club's ambient noise.

She started like someone had jabbed her with a pin, her fingers stumbling before finding their rhythm again. The smile she flashed him was about as genuine as a knockoff Rolex. "Nothing. Just tired, I guess."

Bullshit, David thought, watching the tension ride her shoulders like a weighted vest. Her hands trembled slightly as she adjusted her position.

"You sure about that?" he pressed. *Because you look about as relaxed as a long-tailed cat in a room full of rocking chairs.*

"I told you, I'm fine," she snapped, then caught herself. "It's just been a long day."

Yeah, pulling double duty can do that to a person, he thought, without letting the implication hang in the air between them.

"Everything's fine." She took a long sip of her martini. "Max doesn't suspect anything. I told you I'd handle it."

Before she could spin another story, something caught his eye across the room. At first, it was nothing worth noting—just another suit at the bar nursing what was probably some overpriced scotch. Nothing unusual about him, except for the way he was staring. Not at the fancy paintings some decorator had picked out, not at the parade of wealth strutting around in designer labels. No, this guy's eyes were locked on David like he was memorizing him for a police lineup.

David wasn't the paranoid type—couldn't afford to be in his line of work—but something about that stare set his teeth on edge. He tried to redirect his attention to Felicity, but those eyes followed him like a sniper's laser sight, drilling into the back of his skull.

Felicity was running her mouth again, probably another carefully crafted lie, but David had stopped listening. The figure across the room had him hooked, the way those dark eyes seemed to pin him down with an intensity that felt wrong in a place built for polite fiction. The guy wasn't even trying to be subtle about it. It was deliberate, calculated, like he was waiting for something specific to happen.

Then the stranger did something that kicked David's pulse into overdrive. The observer—who'd barely registered as a potential threat before—started moving with the kind of precision that spoke of practice. Slowly, deliberately, like he was following a script he'd rehearsed a thousand times, he reached up and produced something that turned David's blood to ice water. It wasn't just that the man was staring anymore—it was that he was putting on a mask that looked like it belonged in some ancient temple, not a Midtown social club. The mask's deep red base caught the low light from the chandeliers, seeming to pulse with its own inner fire. Gold and black patterns swirled across its surface like living things, creating the illusion of scales that might start moving any second. The bottom half of the mask was pure nightmare fuel—golden fangs sharp enough to tear through flesh, arranged in a permanent snarl that transformed the man's face into something primitive and dangerous. David blinked hard, trying to process what he was seeing. The transformation wasn't just physical—it was like watching someone shed their humanity piece by piece.

David's jaw clenched tight enough to crack walnuts. The whole scene dragged up memories he'd buried years ago— being eight years old, staring painfully at the ornate Venetian masks in his father's study, each one seeming to mock him with empty eyes and frozen smiles. Even then, he'd known there was something terribly unsettling about people who hid behind beautiful things. And the fear that his father had tried to cure by lining the family estate's hallways with ceremonial pieces from Asia, each one of which was a lesson in facing fear. He hadn't thought about those days in years, but right now, that old familiar itch between his shoulder blades was back with a vengeance.

Felicity's voice faded to white noise as David stared, completely transfixed by the scene playing out across the room. His grip on his glass turned his knuckles white, but he barely noticed. There was something about the cold, mechanical precision of the man's movements that sent ice water running down his spine. It felt like watching someone load a gun—a warning that something ugly was about to go down. He tried to shake it off, but the more he watched, the stronger the feeling grew that he was missing something crucial.

The masked figure seemed to be sending him a message written in a language he couldn't quite grasp but understood on some primitive level.

David rubbed his eyes, fighting the fog settling in his brain.

The mask now covered almost all of the man's face, but just before David could look away, those gleaming golden eyes locked onto his. The cold intensity of that stare cut through him like a winter wind, raising goose bumps that had nothing to do with the club's carefully controlled temperature.

Then, like some cosmic editor had cut the frame, everything blurred. A group of people walked past, the usual parade of rich drunks, blocking his view for several seconds. David's heart hammered against his ribs as he leaned forward, straining to keep sight of the stranger.

When the crowd cleared, the man had vanished like smoke.

"Son of a bitch," David muttered, exhaling sharply as unease settled in his gut like bad seafood. His pulse was still racing, hands shaking just enough to notice. The whole room felt different now, like someone had cranked up the gravity and thickened the air with promises of violence. He stood up so fast his chair screamed against the floor. Felicity shot him a look that mixed surprise with something else fear, maybe, or guilt—but David was already moving. He needed answers more than he needed her lies right now.

He cut across the room, eyes scanning the spot where the man had been holding court. The bar was packed with the usual crowd, but there wasn't a mask in sight. He cornered one of the staff—some woman with a clipboard who looked like she alphabetized her sock drawer—who was quietly talking to a couple by the entrance.

"The guy who was sitting there," David said, forcing his voice level despite the adrenaline pumping through his system. "Who is he?"

The woman's smile was professional grade, empty as a politician's promise. "I'm sorry, sir, but we don't provide information on our members."

Frustration rolled through him like a wave. Of course they didn't. He was already swimming in waters too deep for comfort, and now he couldn't even get a straight answer about what kind of sharks he was dealing with. He leaned in closer, eyes narrowing to slits.

"I didn't ask for his life story," he stated through clenched teeth. "Just tell me who the hell was sitting there a minute ago."

The woman didn't even blink. "I'm afraid I can't help you with that, sir."

David's fist clenched at his side, but he knew a dead end when he hit one. The woman's smile was a wall he wasn't going to break through, no matter how hard he pushed.

With a tight nod that felt like admitting defeat, he turned away. Walking back to his seat, his mind spun like a crooked roulette wheel. Doubt, suspicion, and the unseen played pinball in his head. Had he imagined it all? The man, that mask that belonged in a museum of nightmares, the way those eyes had stripped away every layer of protection he'd built up over the years? The reality of being watched, of being known, sat in his gut like old lead.

As he dropped back into his chair, Felicity was watching him with eyes that gave away nothing and everything at once. He couldn't bring himself to meet her gaze, too busy staring out across the room while his vision blurred at the edges, mind tangled up in questions he couldn't answer. Something was definitely wrong. And now, looking at Felicity's carefully composed face, he wasn't sure if he could trust anyone at all—including this woman who'd promised to help him trap Max Worthington.

CHAPTER XXV

The Buckhead gallery's façade punctured the darkness with squares of artificial light, its windows casting bright rectangles onto the empty sidewalk. Max Worthington observed the scene from across the street. He counted three dark sedans with diplomatic plates parked out front. Through the glass doors, he could make out the occasional movement of security personnel. Two were stationed in the lobby like sentinels, another one was making methodical rounds past the first-floor exhibitions.

His shoes clicked on the pavement as he crossed over, the summer heat still lingering in the night air even at this hour. Inside, the lobby's marble floors reflected the stark overhead lights, making the space feel larger and emptier than it was. A guard at the front desk looked up from his crossword puzzle and straightened his posture as Max approached.

"I'm looking for Felicity Blackwood," Max said the last name he had been told to give. He noticed the guard's fresh-pressed uniform and the way his eyes kept darting to the stairwell. "She's involved with the viewing tonight," Max added.

The guard consulted a tablet, his fingers moving with exaggerated precision. "There are several private viewings scheduled. Which room were you headed to?"

Several? Max thought for a moment before saying, "The Silent Watch presentation. I believe that's the only one on for tonight."

"Sir, I don't have that listed specifically." The guard scrolled through his screen, the blue light reflecting off his face. "And I'm not seeing a Felicity Blackwood on any of tonight's lists."

Why's he saying that? Is he supposed to be saying that? Should I ask it some other way? Max thought as he drummed his fingers on the desk. He watched another guard walk past with an earpiece, speaking quietly into his collar. Something about this place looked like a stage waiting for the wrong play to begin. He nodded his thanks and headed back outside into the thick night air, already pulling out his phone to call Felicity.

"Max."

He spun around, startled. Felicity emerged from the side of the building. Her silhouette was sharp in the faint glow of the streetlight.

"What are you doing here?" he asked, his voice cutting through the stillness.

"I was waiting for you." Her tone was calm but with a faint edge. "Come on, I'll get us inside."

"Why did that man at the desk say you're not listed?" Max said.

She hesitated before giving him a placating smile. "Don't worry about that. He's not supposed to know what's really happening."

"What's really happening?"

She stepped closer and her hand brushed his arm. "This is your chance to see the painting again, Max. Isn't that what you wanted?" Her touch was light, her smile faintly disarming.

"Follow me," she said, heading toward a side door.

Max glanced toward the street before following. Felicity led him inside into a part of the gallery that was vast and eerily quiet. The silence was broken only by the soft hum of the climate control system. They moved through shadowed halls, their footsteps muffled by the thick carpet. Max kept his voice low. "Why is it so quiet in here?"

She glanced back at him and her eyes were unreadable. "Trust me."

"Has the collector arrived yet?" Max said. "I saw some State Department plates outside."

She quickened her pace instead of answering. They reached a set of double doors. Felicity paused, her hand on the handle. "The painting's inside," she said in a soft voice. "But there's someone else you need to meet first. Someone who's representing David."

Max's stomach tightened. "Who?"

"You'll see." Before he could press further, she pushed open the doors and stepped inside.

"Why didn't you tell me about this before?" Max said.

"Because the truth is not always simple," she said as she led him inside.

The room was as quiet as the hallway they'd just walked down. Large, dimly lit, with landscapes, portraits, abstractions hanging on the walls, it let each one draw a momentary glance. And then, hung on a freestanding easel in the center of the room was the one he had come to see. The spotlight cast a dramatic glow over the painting, highlighting every detail: the stormy sky, the windswept grass, the lone boy standing sentinel. Max froze as his eyes settled on the artwork. It was real. He knew it instantly. The brushstrokes, the colors, the subtle imperfections in the frame. It must be the same painting that had belonged in his parents' home before it was stolen from his safe.

"It's the real one," he murmured, stepping closer.

As Felicity shifted behind him, her nervousness was palpable. "How can you tell?"

Max shot her a look, but she avoided his gaze. Her attention flitted to a door on the far side of the room.

"Why are you so jumpy?" he asked, his voice sharp.

"I'm not," she said quickly, her tone unconvincing.

Max turned back to the painting, and began to circle it slowly. His eyes scanned every inch. "This was in my safe," he said, his voice low but certain. "It was stolen, and now it's here. I don't care who's 'representing David.' I'm taking it back."

Felicity flinched, her gaze darting to the door again. Before Max could question her, it swung open and a man walked in. The stride was confident, the features were unfamiliar. He wore a tailored suit while his face was unremarkable but for the faint sheen of sweat on his brow.

"Good evening," the man said smoothly. "I understand you've come to see the painting too."

Max studied him and his unease deepened. The man carried an aura of unsettling ambiguity. His skin looked too perfect, too smooth, like it belonged to someone younger.

"Who are you?" Max asked.

"Call me Andrew," the man said with a tight smile.

Max crossed his arms. "And you're here on David Hollister's behalf?"

Andrew's smile widened, though it failed to show through those eyes. "I'm here to ensure the painting's authenticity. Flew in just yesterday, as a matter of fact. I couldn't pass up the chance to examine it in person before deciding whether to finalize the purchase."

Max raised an eyebrow. "And where did you fly in from?"

"Vienna," Andrew said in a casual tone. "Though my collection spans far beyond Austrian borders. Art doesn't recognize nationalities, does it?"

Max tilted his head, studying him. "Your English is impressive for someone raised outside an Anglophone country."

Andrew gave a subtle smirk. "Let's just say art isn't my only field of study. If you spend years negotiating for a Pieter Bruegel or a Modigliani, mastering a language becomes an afterthought."

Max's skepticism deepened. "Bruegel and Modigliani, huh? That's quite the collection you're boasting."

"Boasting?" Andrew's tone remained light, though the undercurrent was sharp. "Hardly. But I do own *Landscape with the Fall of Icarus*. Not the one in Belgium, of course—the better version in Vienna. And a Modigliani reclining nude that's drawn its fair share of controversy over provenance. I'd rather not see this painting meet a similar fate."

Max shifted his weight, turning his gaze back to the boy in the windswept field. "You're sure this piece is worth the trip, then? Considering it was stolen from someone's private collection." He gave the man a sly sideways glance as soon as he said it.

Andrew only stepped closer, his gaze fixed on the painting with a near-reverent intensity. "The boy's attire, early 19th century, wouldn't you say? The grass, that's definitely not European. Too wild, too raw. That sky, though, has the brush of Constable's influence, wouldn't you agree? But the palette is far more muted, somber. Perhaps American."

Max frowned as he followed Andrew's line of sight. "If it's American, it might explain its presence in my family's collection. Though that doesn't explain how you plan to prove it's real. Or do you simply trust the word of the one you're 'representing'?"

Andrew chuckled softly with an almost condescending sound. "Provenance, my friend. A painting is more than oil on canvas. It has a history, a journey. This piece has been whispered about for decades. Stolen during the mid-20th century, supposedly found again in the '80s. Its journey alone makes it valuable. But authenticity? That requires expertise."

Max was thinking, *What is this man talking about? He doesn't seem to fucking care about hearing it's stolen goods.*

The other man leaned closer to the painting, his head tilting slightly. "The brushstrokes here are crucial. See the way the artist layers the sky, blending shades without losing the turbulence? That's not the hand of an amateur. The pigment tells a story too—chemical analysis can trace it to a particular region or era. And the frame…" He moved a hand as though tracing the edges in his mind. "Walnut. The wear patterns suggest it's original to the piece. Replicas rarely get that detail right."

Max stepped beside him, his voice low. "So you're convinced it's the real deal?"

Andrew's expression remained inscrutable. "Convinced? Not yet. The texture of the paint must match the cracking pattern of its age. A UV light examination will show if there have been touch-ups. Infrared reflectography could reveal sketches beneath the paint. That is proof of the artist's process. Only then will I consider trusting my instincts."

Max nodded, unwilling to admit he was impressed. "And you'll go through all this trouble for a painting you're not even certain you'll buy?"

Andrew's smile had returned sharper now. "A true collector isn't buying paint on canvas, Mr. Worthington. We're investing in immortality. And if this boy, with his staff and those windswept fields, can speak to the world the way he speaks to me, then yes, I'll consider it worth every second."

Max turned to the painting, narrowing his eyes as he tried to see it with Andrew's detachment. But all he could feel was a tightening in his chest. "This was my family's immortality once. Now it's just a commodity."

Andrew gave him a sidelong glance. "That depends, doesn't it? On what you're willing to do to claim it again."

Max nodded. "That's right."

Felicity's expression was constantly shifting. Her composure faltered with each passing second. Tiny tremors of unease betrayed her desperate attempt to appear calm. Her gaze was nailed on Andrew. Her eyes narrowed and adjusted as if she was trying to see past something.

Max caught the look and turned back to Andrew. "Why isn't David here himself?"

Andrew's light chuckle grated on Max's nerves. "David has many priorities. I'm here to ensure everything proceeds smoothly."

Max stepped closer. "Smoothly? None of this is smooth. You're here to inspect a painting that's supposed to be stolen. Care to explain?"

Andrew's smile faded. "The painting is authentic, Mr. Worthington. Surely Harrison Worthington's son would recognize that."

The words carved through Max's defenses. His father's name. Only David Hollister would know that. He stepped back, his gaze locking onto Andrew's face, scrutinizing every detail. The perfect skin, the faint sheen, the calculated movements—it wasn't the man's real face. It was a realistic face mask.

"You," Max said, his voice low and dangerous. "It's you."

The man was smiling thinly, his hand twitching ever so slightly. "What gave me away?"

Max's jaw tightened. "Only one person would bring up my father. You couldn't help yourself, could you?"

As the smile on the stranger's face widened, the guise of civility slipped. "Ah, well. Old habits die hard."

Felicity stepped forward, her voice trembling. "David, what are you doing?"

The man turned to her and his expression darkened. "What I always do, Felicity. Taking control."

Her eyes darted to the painting as panic crept into her tone. "You said you'd put the copy here."

David smirked, his voice lacing with mockery. "And let him walk away thinking he'd won? That's not my style."

Felicity's voice rose, sharp with fear. "You didn't have to do this. You're risking everything!"

David's gaze turned icy. "No, Felicity. I'm *ensuring* everything. And I suggest you remember where your loyalties lie."

Max squared his shoulders, his anger boiling over. "I came here for the painting, Hollister. It's mine. My family's. And I'm not leaving without it."

David's chuckles sounded cold and sharp. "Oh, Max. You think this is about the painting?" He leaned closer, his voice dropping to a maniacal cackle. "It's about what the painting represents. And if you think you can just walk out of here with it," he straightened with a venomous smile, "you've underestimated me." It was a threat veiled in control, a reminder that David held all the cards, and with one decisive act, he could erase Max's hopes entirely.

David's move was calculated cruelty, a masterstroke of dominance. By bringing the real painting he had cornered them both. If he destroyed it now, right in front of Max, he would have already been paid by the insurance company. But it would obliterate everything Max was fighting for: the painting, his family's legacy, even the fragile thread of trust with Felicity.

Max's fists clenched at his sides. He wasn't leaving without the painting and he wasn't backing down.

CHAPTER XXVI

Liam Corcoran cradled the phone between his ear and shoulder with a faint scowl pulling at the corners of his mouth.

"Look, Marcia," he said, pacing his office, "I don't have a concrete date for Max Worthington's manuscript. He's caught up in personal matters at the moment."

Marcia O'Donnell, the sharp-tongued editor at Redbrick, didn't miss a beat. "Caught up? Liam, the buzz around *Poison Dusk* is already fading. His readers are loyal, sure, but they're restless. We're seeing preorders cancel. You know as well as I do that it's not just about sales. It's momentum. If this book isn't out by the end of the quarter, his brand—*your* brand—takes a hit."

"I'm aware," Liam replied tersely. "And believe me, no one's more frustrated about this than I am."

"You might want to remind Max of that," she said. "I'll be expecting an update next week."

The woman hung up before Liam could respond. He pulled the phone away and stared at it for a moment before slamming it down on his desk. The sudden jolt sent a stack of papers cascading to the floor.

"Dammit!"

He stood there for a moment, breathing heavily, then grabbed his phone again and dialed Max.

Three rings. Four. Then voicemail.

"Max, it's Liam. We need to talk. Call me back as soon as you get this."

He hung up and thrust a hand through his wiry hair, muttering under his breath. "Where the hell are you, Worthington?"

A light knock on the door drew his attention. Pauline, in her usual horn-rimmed glasses and an impeccably pressed blouse, peeked in. "Everything alright, Mr. Corcoran?"

Liam waved her in, motioning to the mess of papers on his desk. "Not really, Pauline. I need you to try Max again. He's not answering."

Pauline hesitated, her hands clasped in front of her. "Actually, there's something I need to tell you about Max."

Liam narrowed his eyes. "What is it?"

She stepped inside, closing the door behind her. "It happened a couple of mornings ago. No, actually sometime toward the end of last week. I was driving up to the office and stopped at a red light near Inman Park. That's when this guy—some scruffy-looking bum with a matted beard and a jacket about three sizes too big—appeared at my window. I thought he was begging for money and told him, 'Move along, buddy,' but he didn't. Instead, he asked if I was Pauline Tremont. When I said yes, he asked if I knew Max Worthington. I barely had time to answer before he dropped a parcel into my lap and vanished before I could say anything else."

Liam straightened, his focus sharpening. "A parcel? What kind of parcel?"

"I didn't know what to do at first," Pauline admitted, fiddling with her glasses. "The light turned green, and I had to pull over to check it. There was a note attached. It said, *This is about the Theft at Max's place.*"

Liam's brow furrowed. "And you didn't think to tell me this sooner?"

"I was scared! For all I knew, it could've been a setup. But I opened it when I got to the office. There was a letter inside. I still have it—I'll get it."

Pauline disappeared briefly and returned with a folded envelope. Liam took it from her, his eyes scanning the faded ink as he pulled out the letter. The handwriting was neat but hasty, the words weighted with history and bitterness.

To whomever this reaches,

What transpired at Max Worthington's home goes much deeper than some burglar getting their hands on a rare painting. It's about the old wounds between two families: the Worthingtons and the Hollisters.

Harrison Worthington and Robert Hollister were friends once, but their bond dissolved over ambition and betrayal. Robert needed a favor, a big one—something only Harrison could provide. A critical land deal tied to the Hollister legacy was about to fall through, and only Harrison's connections in the state legislature could secure its approval. But the strings attached to that assistance were heavier than Robert had imagined. In return, Harrison demanded the painting, The Silent Watch. Was it for its beauty? Its mystery? Or something deeper? That, no one knows for sure. But Harrison's demand came at a price.

The painting became a symbol of shame for Robert, a reminder of what he owed and what he lost. While Harrison paraded it as a triumph, Robert's resentment festered. And when Harrison passed, Robert's son, David, swore he'd take back what he believed was rightfully his.

Now David Hollister holds the painting, but it's more than just revenge. There's something in that piece of art, something your friend Max may not even know he's chasing. Secrets have a way of surfacing, whether they're invited or not.

Be cautious. This isn't just about art anymore.

Liam read the letter twice, his jaw twitching upon each word. He looked up at Pauline, who was watching him nervously. "Did you show this to anyone else?" he asked.

She shook her head. "I promised Max I wouldn't. But if he's in danger…"

"He is," Liam said, his voice grim. "This changes everything."

Pauline bit her lip, then hesitated. "I— I've been worried about him, you know? He's been distracted. But that's part of his charm, isn't it? He's brilliant, but he's also reckless. It's why people like me can't help but…well…" She trailed off, her cheeks flushing slightly.

Liam arched a brow but said nothing. He grabbed his coat. "We're not sitting here waiting for another cryptic letter. Let's go. If Max is tangled up with David Hollister, he might not have much time."

Pauline scooped up her bag, a flicker of determination replacing her nervousness. "I'll drive."

The words of the letter were heavy between them as they left the office together and stepped into the night.

CHAPTER XXVII

Jimmy Callahan leaned back in the driver's seat of his unmarked Crown Vic, watching the blinking red dot glide through the grid of the city streets. Felicity's Nissan Versa Note was heading south, cutting a line that should've taken it toward the Buckhead gallery. But it didn't.

"You're off script, lady," Jimmy muttered, his gravelly voice barely rising above the hum of the engine. He tapped the dashboard. His unease grew.

Max had told him about the meeting at the gallery, and Jimmy had known Felicity would double-cross him. It wasn't a hunch; it was a fact. So when the car veered away from the gallery's direction and ended up at a high-rise on Peachtree, Jimmy's suspicions sharpened.

"She's not driving," he said aloud, as his mind pieced it together. "Clever."

The red dot came to a stop at the high-rise, a gleaming tower that reflected the city like a polished knife. A place built for people who thought themselves untouchable. The kind of place where people like Felicity—or whoever was driving—thought they could disappear.

Jimmy snorted, shaking his head. "Not from me."

He grabbed his jacket and slid out of the car. The humid Atlanta night wrapped around him like a damp shroud. The tracker's signal had gone dead as soon as the car had entered the underground garage, but that was no surprise. "Signal blockers. Fancy." He smirked, tugging his jacket tighter.

Crossing the street, Jimmy's eyes scanned the building. The glass lobby reflected the city's lights, but the real action wasn't up there. It was in the shadows below. He headed down the ramp leading to the garage, each step slower than the last.

It was quiet. Too quiet. The kind of quiet that made his instincts bristle. Reaching the garage, he found the Versa Note parked near the far wall, its dull gray paint blending into the dimly lit space. His eyes darted left and right, watching for movement. Nothing. He crouched by the car, and his fingers found the small tracker he'd tucked beneath the rear bumper weeks ago. The casing was intact, but the signal had cut clean. He pulled out a pocket light to inspect the device. Jimmy examined the tracker. The signal blocker had cut the live transmission, but these models stored a backup record. If he could extract the data, he'd know exactly where they'd stopped before coming here.

And then he heard it. A soft scrape, like leather shifting against concrete.

Jimmy stood quickly, spinning around, and his hand instinctively moved to his hip. But before he could react, a shadow lunged from the corner of the garage, and pain exploded at the base of his skull.

David Hollister's hand moved with deliberate slowness to reach his face. Almost theatrically, his fingertips met the edge of the skin-like mask. A sharp tug followed; the artificial face peeling away to let the true features through. Max watched the faint smug smile on David's face coming into focus. It wasn't the disguise that unsettled him; it was the sheer arrogance radiating off the man, as if he'd wangled the entire world to bow to his will.

Felicity took a half-step back, her breath twisting within her chest. She said nothing, but the way her eyes darted to Max betrayed her inner turmoil. She knew. She'd known all along.

"Well, now that the theatrics are out of the way," David said as he folded the mask neatly to tuck it into his pocket, "shall we get to the heart of the matter?" He gestured casually toward the painting hanging in the center of the room.

Max's nails dug into his palms. "You've been playing games since the beginning, David. But now I'm here, right here. You made a big mistake when you sent one of your errand boys to pull that painting outta my safe. No more running, I swear, no more. I'm here to take what was mine an' still is."

Laughter from the other side came across thin and sharp, like breaking glass. "Ah, Max. Always so straightforward. It's almost endearing." He stepped closer to the painting, his gaze sweeping over its surface with a strange mix of reverence and disdain. "It was I who came to get it, boy-uh. Settled some of my doubts about having been out of practice."

"You bastard," Max said.

With a smirk spreading from ear to ear, David's voice was a silken drawl laced with venom. "A bastard? Oh, Max, how unoriginal. If you only knew how much worse I can be." Mockery made his eyes glitter. "You should've seen me, strolling through your so-called safe haven, cracking open that vault of yours. Honestly, I haven't had that much fun in years. And the best part? Watching it all slip through your fingers without you even knowing. All about who's got the leash, pup."

Max matched David's step, circling the painting on the opposite side. "Oh, I know exactly what it's about, *Big Man*. It's about erasing the truth. It's about your family's betrayal and your desperation to cover it up."

Felicity flinched. "Max, maybe this isn't the time—"

"No, Felicity. This is exactly the time." His gaze never left David, his voice steady but filled with steel. "You've spent your whole life building on lies, David. Lies about what your family did. Lies about who they destroyed to get where they are. And this painting—" he pointed at *The Silent Watch* "—is proof of all of it."

A cold, calculating stare snuffed the smile on David's face. "You think you've figured it all out, don't you?"

"I don't need to figure it out," Max shot back. "I know. I know what your family did during the war. I know how they stole the land from the Amerindian soldiers who fought and died for it. I know about the lies your father told to keep the painting hidden." He leaned forward, his voice dropping. "And I know that you'll do anything to stop the truth from coming out."

David's jaw twitched, and for the first time, unease flickered over his face. But he recovered quickly, getting the smirk back on like a shield. "You're right about one thing, Max. I *will* do anything to protect my family's legacy. Because unlike you, I understand the value of power. Of control."

"How long can you go on walking all over anyone and everyone to feed your vile ego? All the time wanting to go around stunting on everybody," Max rolled out. "Why'd you even need to play the Chens in your weak-ass crappy game of chess when you might as well sell the damn painting on the low without all that flashy mess you made?"

"The Chens were never the point, Max. They were just another variable in a carefully calibrated equation. Some might call it a scheme, but I call it optimization. Every move, every calculated gesture – it's about maximizing value. Selling that painting wasn't about showmanship; it was about extracting the maximum potential from a single moment. The thrill isn't in the simplicity, my boy, it's in the intricate architecture of success."

Hearing that, Max stopped circling and gave the other man a leery smile. "The truth of what happened at Blackridge Hollow is going to be a hit. And when it lands, Davey, it'll tear through your fucking legacy like ink bleeds through cheap paper."

"Oh, Max, ever the wordsmith. You think your little words could strike even the smallest dent in history? Let me tell you something: words are all you've ever had. Leaves swirling in the wind," — David jiggled his hands in front of himself like he was conjuring the scene — "and just like that, they'll scatter long before they ever touch something real." He stepped around the painting, closing the distance between them. "This painting? Seeing the light of day? People coming to know the truth about Blackridge Hollow?" He took on a mockingly innocent tone, "It would destroy everything *I've* built."

Max didn't flinch. "Good. Maybe it's time your lies came crashing down."

David turned to Felicity, who had been silent, her arms wrapped tightly around herself. "And you, my dear," he said smoothly. "How does it feel to stand between two men so utterly at odds? Torn between loyalty to me and whatever it is you feel for Max?"

Felicity's eyes flicked to Max, then back to David. "I didn't… I didn't sign up for this."

"Oh, but you did," David said, dripping disdain. "You chose this the moment you agreed to help me. Don't play the victim now."

Felicity's voice cracked. "I never wanted anyone to get hurt. I thought… I thought I could fix things."

"Fix things?" Max snapped, his anger finally boiling over. "You've done nothing but lie to me, Felicity. You led me here knowing he'd be waiting. You've been working with him all along."

Her lips trembled, but she didn't deny it. "I was trying to protect you, Max. I thought if I could just keep things from getting worse—"

"Protect me?" Max's voice rose, disbelief tangling with fury. "You've been feeding him everything, haven't you? Every move I made, every lead I followed—it all went straight to him."

David watched the exchange with evident satisfaction, his arms crossed as he leaned casually against the painting's frame. "Touching, really," he said dryly. "But let's not waste any more time with sentiment."

He straightened, his eyes locking onto Max's. "Here's the reality, Worthington. That painting isn't leaving this room with you. You can make all the righteous speeches you want, but in the end, you're just a man playing at being a hero."

Max stepped forward. "You think this is about me? This is about the truth. And no matter what you do, it's going to come out."

"Not if I have anything to say about it." David glanced at Felicity, who had retreated to the edge of the room, her face paling. "And not if your trusted confidante keeps fumbling every chance she gets."

Max took one last look at the painting, its stormy skies and resolute figure frozen in time. He couldn't let it end here, not with David standing smugly over his stolen legacy.

"You're not as untouchable as you think, Hollister," Max said, his voice sharp. "This painting is more than your lies. It's a symbol of everything your family destroyed. And one way or another, I'll make sure everyone knows the truth."

A chilling wave of laughter filled the viewing room. "We'll see about that," David said.

Max knew he couldn't act yet. Not with Felicity caught in the middle and David's guards likely waiting just outside.

CHAPTER XXVIII

Jimmy staggered backward. His shoulder slammed into the side of Felicity's Nissan Versa Note. His vision blurred and the garage began to swim in a haze of concrete and shadows. The sharp, throbbing pain at the back of his skull threatened to drag him under, but he clenched his teeth and stayed upright.

Not here. Not now.

"You should've stayed out of this," came a gravelly voice from the darkness.

Jimmy blinked hard, his focus sharpening on the figure stepping out of the shadows. The man was broad-shouldered, with a hard, angular face that looked like it had been carved from stone. He wore a dark jacket, and his knuckles gleamed as he rolled his fists like a boxer warming up for the next punch.

"You're good at sticking your nose where it doesn't belong," the man continued, his casual tone menacing. "But that nose is about to get broken."

Jimmy's lip curled into a smirk, despite the pounding in his head. "You talk like you're working by the hour. Hollister doesn't pay you enough for that."

The man snorted, "Big words for a guy barely standin'."

Jimmy's hand jerked toward his belt, but the man moved fast, lunging forward with a wild swing aimed at Jimmy's head. Jimmy ducked. The fist grazed his hair as he twisted to the side. The car door jammed against his back as he used it to push himself forward, delivering a sharp elbow to the man's ribs.

The grunt that followed was satisfying, but it didn't last. The attacker recovered quickly, spun with surprising agility, and another fist connected with Jimmy's shoulder to send him stumbling back. Jimmy gritted his teeth, his breath ragged, and squared up. Instinct took over like flame catching dry timber.

"You're tougher than you look," the man growled, circling.

"Yeah," Jimmy spat, "and smarter than you." He feinted left, then slammed a right hook into the man's jaw.

The crack of bone on bone echoed through the garage, and the man stumbled. But he wasn't done. He lunged again, his hands grabbing for Jimmy's throat, and the two men grappled. Their shoes scuffed the concrete as they struggled for dominance. Jimmy's head swam, the earlier blow threatening to rob him of balance, but he dug deep, slamming his knee into the man's stomach. The attacker grunted, doubling over slightly. Jimmy pressed the advantage, throwing him against the car. Before Jimmy could land another blow, a sharp whistle cut through the air.

"Enough."

The voice was calm with authority, and it froze both men mid-movement. Jimmy's attacker turned, his expression hardening as a third figure stepped into the light.

The newcomer was sturdy, compactly built. His features were sharp, his skin a sun-weathered tan, and his jet-black hair was tied back in a loose tail. His eyes, a piercing gray, locked onto the attacker with quiet intensity.

"I don't think you'll want to finish that fight," the man said evenly, his voice carrying a faint hint of an accent Jimmy couldn't place. "Not with me here."

Backing away slightly, Jimmy's attacker cursed under his breath before he rumbled, "Who the hell are you?"

The newcomer didn't answer. He moved almost imperceptibly to close the distance in a heartbeat. His fist struck the attacker's jaw with a crack that echoed like a gunshot. The man crumpled to the ground, groaning, and didn't get back up.

Jimmy leaned against the car, breathing heavily. His eyes flicked between the fallen man and his unexpected savior. "And you are…?"

The man turned to Jimmy, offering a hand. "Gabriel Thunderhawk. I think we have some common enemies."

Jimmy hesitated, then clasped the man's hand, allowing himself to be pulled upright. "Yeah? You don't exactly look like you're on Hollister's payroll."

Thunderhawk smirked faintly. "That's because I'm not. But I know who he is. And I know you're trying to stop him."

Jimmy winced, rubbing the back of his head. "That obvious, huh?" Then the name clicked in his foggy mind, sharp and sudden. *Thunderhawk.* "Hey, I've heard about you. Max mentioned he'd met the mystery man."

The detective rubbed his temple as he sized the stranger up. "Didn't expect to run into you here," he said. "Didn't think you were this hands-on."

Thunderhawk nodded toward the unconscious attacker. "He wasn't here by chance. Hollister sent him to slow you down. Same reason I'm here—to keep this mess from getting worse."

"Hell of a way to introduce yourself," Jimmy muttered, shaking off the dizziness. "You sure know how to make an entrance."

Thunderhawk shrugged. "It gets the job done." He stepped back, scanning the garage. "We don't have much time. If Hollister's making his move, we need to be at the Buckhead gallery."

Jimmy worked his shoulders in quick, sharp jerks to shake off the starburst of pain from the blows. "You know about that too?"

"Let's just say I've been keeping an eye on things." Thunderhawk's gaze was serious. "If we don't get there soon, Max could be in real trouble."

Jimmy nodded, already moving toward his car. "Then let's go. You can explain the rest on the way."

CHAPTER XXIX

Liam Corcoran's sedan screeched to a halt at the curb of Max's garden apartment, tires spitting gravel onto the sidewalk. Before the engine finished its growl, he threw open the door and climbed out.

"Max!" he called, his voice sharp in the stillness of the street.

Pauline followed, her heels clicking on the pavement as she stepped out and scanned the quiet row of houses. She adjusted her horn-rimmed glasses with a trembling hand. "Doesn't look like anyone's home."

Liam glanced at the windows. No lights. No movement. The unease that had been gnawing at him since they left the office now clawed at his chest. He pulled out his phone and jabbed at the screen.

"No answer," he said after a few moments, slipping the phone back into his pocket. "Let's take a closer look."

They approached the front door together. Liam rapped on it, hard enough to make the frame shudder. "Max! It's Liam! You in there?"

Pauline bit her lip, her gaze flicking to the neighboring houses. "Maybe we should leave a note. He's obviously not here."

Liam ignored her, moving to the nearest window and cupping his hands around his face to peer inside. The living room sat undisturbed. Books on shelves, a few mugs on the coffee table, but no sign of Max.

"Nothing," Liam muttered, stepping back. "Let's check the side alley."

Pauline hesitated, then followed as Liam strode toward the narrow path leading to the backyard. The alley was shaded, bordered by a high wooden fence on one side and Max's house on the other. At the back of the house, they found a glass door overlooking a modest yard. Liam grabbed the handle, his brow furrowing when it gave way easily. He slid the door open and stepped inside.

"This doesn't feel right," Pauline murmured, hesitating at the threshold.

"Nothing about this does," Liam replied, scanning the room. The kitchen was to the left, tidy but with signs of recent use: a kettle on the stove, a plate in the sink. To the right, a short hallway led to what looked like a study.

The study was cluttered but organized in a way that spoke to Max's habits as a writer. Liam pointed to the papers lay spread across the desk, along with a few open books and a notepad filled with scribbled lines. Pauline moved to the desk, picking up a loose sheet.

"Looks like notes for his novel," she said, skimming a few lines. "Nothing about where he... wait."

Her eyes caught on another piece of paper, half-hidden beneath a corner of the notepad. She pulled it free and held it up.

Liam leaned in, frowning as he studied the sheet. It wasn't ordinary paper; it was thick, glossy, and printed with sharp, angular lines. "That looks like a floor plan."

Pauline nodded, pointing to the top of the page. "It's marked Buckhead Gallery."

A chill ran through Liam. "Why would he have this?"

Pauline traced a finger over some annotations in the margins, written in Max's familiar scrawl. "Security arrangements," she read aloud. "Staff rotations... exit routes... This is detailed."

Liam's stomach sank. He looked at Pauline and said in a tight voice, "He's gone there. He's gone to the gallery."

Pauline swallowed hard, her fingers tightening on the paper. "You think he went after the painting? Alone?"

"I don't know," Liam admitted, heading back toward the door with urgency in his step. "But if Max is involved in this mess, and David Hollister's in the picture, he could be walking into real trouble."

Pauline hurried after him. "The gallery's in Buckhead, right? That's at least twenty minutes from here."

"Then we better move," Liam said, already pulling out his phone to call for directions. They didn't waste another second.

The viewing room at the Buckhead gallery was getting to feel more suffocating by the minute. It smelled of antagonism and malice. As the two men were bent on staring each other out, Felicity looked like an animal trapped between converging forest fires. Her muscles were coiled but there was nowhere to flee.

David stepped up circling the painting and his smirk was corrosive. "You know, this painting has always belonged to the Hollisters," he said. "My father may have let it go temporarily, but its rightful place was never in your father's hands. Or yours."

"Rightful?" Max returned with agonizing sharpness. "That's rich, coming from the family that signed it away like it was nothing. My dad didn't steal The Silent Watch. Your father handed it over. Don't try to rewrite history."

David stopped pacing and his shoulders hunched like he'd decided to let an unseen photographer capture his pose. "Rewrite history? You think you know the first thing about what my father sacrificed? Harrison took advantage of Robert when he was desperate. He forced that painting out of him, knowing exactly how much it meant to our family."

Max took some minutes, his nostrils flaring, as he set the next words out. "And what about what Redwood Plains meant to *your* family, huh? Did Robert care about that when he begged my dad for help? Harrison made him a fair deal. It was a way out of a mess your father created all on his own. If anyone sold out your family's legacy, it was Robert."

David's face suddenly sported a Philadelphia lawyer's smile. "You're so sure of yourself, aren't you? So proud of how your father played the big man. But you weren't there. You didn't see the way he lorded it over my father, rubbing his nose in it every chance he got."

A thin laugh spurted out of Max. "Sounds like your father couldn't handle the price of the favor he asked for. But that's the difference between Harrison and Robert, isn't it? My dad knew how to hold onto power. Yours just gave it away."

The smile on David's mouth gave way to a glare. "You really think you're better than me, don't you? Just like

Harrison thought he was better than Robert. That arrogance is why this painting will never stay in your hands. Never."

Max began to nod like an old dashboard doggie. The consistent motion seemed to mock Hollister's pain. "You know, it's funny, Hollister. Your father sold out his precious Redwood Plains for a quick payout and handed over the painting as a trophy for my dad. A trophy! And here you are, decades later, chasing after scraps of your family's dignity."

"Watch your mouth, Worthington." David raised a warning finger at the other man.

"Oh, I get it," Max went on as Felicity winced. "It's not just about the painting, is it? It's about undoing what your father couldn't—taking back what he handed over like some desperate beggar." Max smirked, his voice sharper now. "But here's the truth: no matter what you do, the Hollister name will always be tied to failure. To shame."

"You don't know a damn thing about my family," David said.

A deadly calm spread over Max's face as he took a step toward the man who was now visibly shaking. "I know enough. I know that every time my father showed off The Silent Watch, your dad stood there pretending not to care, but he was dying inside. And now you're trying to fix what he broke. But guess what, David? It's not going to work. The truth about Blackridge Hollow is coming out, and when it does, it'll rip your legacy apart. Just like my dad ripped your family's pride to shreds."

"You little piece of fuck!"

David's hand moved faster than Max expected, reaching into his jacket. When the gun came out, Max recognized it immediately: a Colt Python, six-inch barrel, gleaming nickel finish. The long barrel seemed to glint in the gallery's soft light, catching Max's novelist-trained eye. He knew its reputation—powerful, intimidating, lethal. This wasn't a threat. It was a warning shot about to be fired.

"David no!" came Felicity's voice, and the next moment her eyes bugged as she saw the barrel jerk away from Max to point at her.

"Wha—" came out of her mouth before the deafening blast shook the room.

The crack of the gunshot was ringing in Max's ears as he saw Felicity stagger, her mouth opening in shock but with no blood visible. He didn't wait to check for a second shot. His hand darted to the nearest object, closing around the side of a heavy bronze sculpture perched on a display pedestal. With a desperate shout, Max hurled it across the room. The sculpture struck David's forearm with a dull thud and the Colt Python skidded across the polished floor.

"Bastard!" David snarled, clutching his arm.

Max didn't hesitate. He lunged at David, the momentum of his charge slamming them both into another display pedestal. The impact knocked over a framed canvas, which crashed to the floor, its glass shattering around them.

David twisted and brought an elbow up that clipped Max's jaw and sent him reeling backward. Max's back hit another pedestal, nearly toppling a delicate porcelain vase. He grabbed the vase without thinking, whipping it toward David.

David ducked, and the vase exploded against the wall behind him.

"You really wanna do this, Worthington?" David growled, grabbing a long, wrought-iron stand that had been holding a spotlight. He swung it like a club. The air hissed as it cut toward Max.

Max barely dodged, the stand grazing his ribs as he staggered to the side. He grabbed a chair—sturdy and modern, designed more for form than comfort—and rammed it into David's chest.

David stumbled but didn't fall. He snarled, tossing the stand aside and charging at Max like a linebacker. The force of the hit sent Max sprawling onto his back, the air rushing out of his lungs. For a moment, everything blurred. The room tilted, the gallery lights swirling like a fractured kaleidoscope.

But David wasn't done. He grabbed Max by the collar, hauling him up, and threw him against the wall. Max's shoulder collided with the surface, sending pain lancing down his arm.

"You think you can take me?" David spat, his face twisted with rage. "You're nothing but your father's shadow!"

Max's teeth clenched. His hand shot out, fingers curling around a small marble bust on a low pedestal beside him. He swung it upward in a wide arc, catching David under the chin.

David staggered, his head snapping back as he stumbled into the center of the room. He fell to one knee, blood dripping from the corner of his mouth.

Max didn't waste the opportunity. He pushed himself off the wall, breath heaving, and crossed the space to where David knelt. His body ached, his pulse thundered in his ears, but his focus was razor-sharp.

Before Max could close the distance entirely, David tried to rise, reaching blindly for something (*anything!*) to use as a weapon.

But Max was faster. He kicked out, catching David square in the chest to send him sprawling onto his back. David groaned, as he rolled onto his side; his movements sluggish as he tried to catch his breath.

Max's eyes darted to Felicity, who was slumped against the far wall, her face pale, her hands clutching at her chest.

"Felicity!" he shouted, the panic breaking through his rage. The next moment he was rushing to her side, sliding to his knees.

———————————

Jimmy Callahan slammed the car door shut, his boots crunching against the gravel driveway of the Buckhead Gallery. The grand building loomed ahead, its glass-and-steel facade glowing faintly under the dim streetlights.

"Quiet place for a gunshot," he said, his sharp ears still taping the distant report they'd heard as they pulled up.

Thunderhawk stepped out of the passenger side, his sturdy frame casting a shadow over the car. "That wasn't a quiet gun. Someone's in trouble."

Jimmy nodded grimly. "No time to waste."

The two men approached the gallery's main doors, where a broad-shouldered guard stood with his arms crossed. His posture was stiff as granite. His cold eyes tracked their every step.

"Detective James Callahan, Atlanta PD," Jimmy said, flashing his badge with practiced precision. "We've got reports of a disturbance inside."

The guard didn't budge. "This is private property," he said flatly. "You're not getting in without authorization."

Jimmy narrowed his eyes. "There was a gunshot. Either let me in, or I call in backup, and this place gets swarmed with uniforms in five minutes."

The guard smirked, leaning forward. "I don't see any backup here, pal. Maybe you should go find some."

Jimmy sighed, slipping his badge back into his jacket. "Always gotta do this the hard way," he muttered, then drove his fist straight into the man's gut.

The guard doubled over with a grunt, but recovered quickly, swinging a meaty fist toward Jimmy's face. Jimmy ducked, pivoted, and sent a sharp elbow into the man's ribs.

Thunderhawk was already moving. Another guard emerged from the side of the building, but Thunderhawk intercepted him with brutal efficiency, his fist connecting with the man's jaw in a crack that echoed through the night.

Jimmy grabbed the first guard by the collar and slammed him into the doorframe. "Open it," he growled.

The guard hesitated, his lip bleeding, but a glare from Thunderhawk sent him fumbling for the keys.

The door swung open, and Jimmy shoved the man aside. He and Thunderhawk stepped into the gallery, their senses heightened as they moved through the silent, sterile halls.

"Max!" Jimmy shouted, his voice cutting through the still air.

A distant voice shouted back. "In here!"

Jimmy's pulse quickened. He followed the sound, his footsteps echoing against the marble floor. Thunderhawk stayed close, his eyes scanning every corner, every shadow. They reached the viewing room. Jimmy burst through the door to find Max crouched over Felicity, who was pale and gasping, with blood spreading on her shirt below her chest.

David Hollister stood near the center of the room, a Colt Python clutched in his hand, the barrel gleaming under the soft lights.

"Stay right there," David said to Callahan. His tone was cold as the steel in his grip. Flanking him were two men, their features shadowed but unmistakably threatening. One cracked his knuckles with deliberate menace, while the other let a switchblade catch the light, its edge gleaming like a predator's grin.

Jimmy's eyes flicked to Max, who looked up briefly, his face etched with panic and fury. "She needs help," Max said. "She's bleeding out!"

David smirked, the gun steady in his grip. "Maybe you should've thought about that before you decided to meddle in my family's business."

Felicity's voice was a reedy whisper, but it cut through the tension like a razor. "Max…" She coughed as blood flecked her lips. "I'm sorry… I didn't want it to end like this…"

Max gripped her hand tightly, his jaw quivering. "Don't talk like that. Stay with me."

She turned her head weakly toward David, her eyes narrowing despite the tears streaming down her face. "You're a monster," she rasped. "No matter what happens, you'll die with nothing. Just like your father."

David's smirk faltered, replaced by a flicker of rage. "Say what you want, darling," he said with a hollow laugh. "You won't be around to see it."

"Jimmy, we need to call an ambulance," Max said.

Before anyone could respond, the door behind David creaked open. This was a different entrance to the one Jimmy had come in through. The air in the room seemed to shift, growing heavier and colder. David's head snapped toward the noise, and his expression twisted into confusion, before devolving into fear.

The man who stepped into the room wasn't the man Jimmy had entered the gallery with. He wore a mask. It was a horrifying creation of lacquered wood, painted black and red, with jagged teeth carved into a perpetual snarl. The hollow eyes seemed to glow faintly, and the intricate patterns around the edges gave it an aura of ancient menace. It was unmistakably from Japanese culture, resembling an Oni; a demon that strikes fear into the hearts of those who dare to face it.

The two men flanking David wasted no time. One lunged forward, the switchblade flashing in a precise arc aimed at the masked man's throat, while the other reached for a concealed firearm beneath his jacket.

The masked man moved with frightening speed, his hand snapping out to catch the knife-wielder's wrist mid-strike. The sound of bone crunching echoed through the room as the man let out a guttural scream. Without pause, the masked figure twisted the broken wrist, forcing the blade to reverse course and plunge into the attacker's own throat. Blood spurted in a violent arc, and the man crumpled, gurgling his last breath.

The second man had barely drawn his gun when the masked figure turned on him. In one swift motion, he grabbed the barrel of the weapon, wrenching it upward as it discharged a deafening shot into the ceiling. The masked man drove a brutal elbow into the attacker's face, shattering his nose in a burst of crimson. As the man staggered back, clutching his face, the masked figure yanked the gun free and, with an eerie precision, slammed the butt of the weapon into the side of the man's temple. The sickening crack of skull meeting steel was final. The second guard collapsed, lifeless, as the masked man stood over the carnage. His wooden grin unmoving, his hollow eyes glowing faintly in the oppressive silence that followed.

David's hands were trembling. The gun wavered slightly. His jaw started to twitch, his mouth began to open and close as if words had abandoned him.

The stranger's voice was calm, but it carried the weight of centuries, "David Hollister. The truth you've tried so hard to bury has risen to meet you."

David took a shaky step back, his breath hitching. "Wh— Who are you?"

Thunderhawk tilted his head slightly with the mask's snarl seeming to grow wider. "Your family's lies cast a long shadow over Blackridge Hollow. And I'm here to drag everything into the light."

The words struck nails into David's composure like a hammer. His shoulders flagged, his fingers twitched uncontrollably, and his eyes darted around the room as though searching for an escape.

Max's voice broke the thick silence. "It's him," he said hoarsely. "It's Thunderhawk."

The next instant footsteps were heard rushing up the hallway outside. Liam and Pauline burst through the doorway, both panting hard. David pointed the weapon toward the balding publisher. "Don't dare to do anything smart."

Liam halted and screwed his eyes at the man whose face could have been a masterpiece painted with sinister intentions, but now a disturbing pallor smothered it. "Hold on, I know you from somewhere—" he said but broke off at Pauline's sharp intake of breath. Following her fixed stare, he found Felicity crumpled on the floor, blood seeping into the hardwood beside her. "Jesus Christ, what happened here?"

"Just shut the fuck up and remain where you are," David barked.

Then David spun like he'd been standing on ice, his fear twisting into desperation. He raised the Colt Python, his grip tightening as he aimed it—not at Thunderhawk or even Max, but at the painting hanging behind him.

"David, don't!" Max shouted, but it was too late.

The shot rang out, ear-splitting in the enclosed space. The bullet ripped through *The Silent Watch*, tearing a jagged hole through its center. The room fell into a heavy, breathless quiet and the torn canvas swayed faintly in its frame. No sooner than it happened Liam's screechy grunt echoed through the stunned silence as he flew at David's knees. Awkwardly hooking his arms round the man's legs, Liam hit the floor hard with David skidding off his feet like a cowboy off a bucking bronco. Jimmy and Thunderhawk lunged simultaneously. David's hand was wrenched backward, and the gun clattered to the floor as he was subdued.

Callahan quickly produced a pair of handcuffs and latched their quarry's wrists secure. "Watch him for me, would you?" he said to Gabriel and fished out his phone.

"Ambulance, ambulance, ambulance," he hammered as he looked for the number.

"No time," Max cut in, shaking his head in miserable surrender.

In the background, Callahan's voice rose with urgency. "Yes, at the Buckhead Gallery on Peachtree Road, near East Paces Ferry... That's right, 3097 Peachtree... Severe bleeding, possible gunshot wound..."

The moment he lowered his phone, Liam stepped forward. "Forget waiting. My car's right outside. We'll get her to Piedmont faster ourselves. Help me lift her."

Twelve minutes later, Liam's tires scraped against the emergency entrance curb at Piedmont. But in the sudden fluorescent glare flooding through the back window, Max already knew. The weight in his arms had shifted somehow during those final turns; becoming heavier, more absolute. He stared down at Felicity's face, alabaster-pale beneath the harsh lights, and felt something crystallize inside him. It was hard and permanent as diamond. All those shared sunrises walking the streets, all her bright laughter, even the bitter taste of her betrayal — everything compressed into this single, immutable moment.

"She's gone," he said, his voice flat and final as a closing door. Through the rearview mirror, he caught Pauline's stifled sob, saw Liam's hands clench white on the steering wheel. But Max just sat there, still cradling Felicity's cooling form, feeling the last chapter of their story settling like the final grains in an hourglass, never to be turned again.

Once, he had loved her enough to believe in forever. Then came the cracks — small at first, like hairline fractures in glass. Her laughter, her touch, the way she'd once said his name, all of it had eroded under the weight of betrayal, until he convinced himself there was nothing left to mourn. But now, with the last breath gone from her lips, he saw the truth. Love didn't vanish. It only hardened into something unspoken, something lodged too deep to be removed.

And so, he held her a moment longer, not as the woman who had deceived him, but as the girl he had once woken beside, the girl he had once believed in.

CHAPTER XXX

Three weeks later

In Max's bedroom, the venetian blinds filtered a zebra-striped light across the rumpled sheets as the bed began to match the passionate motions they had experienced the night before. Soon, Max froze mid-motion, propped on his elbows, and stared at the stripes the sun made across Pauline's bare shoulders. A thought had struck him, and he couldn't help but laugh.

"What's so funny?" Pauline asked, her breath still quick, as her pudendum squeezed on the hardness joined with her flesh. Her usually pristine hair was splayed across the pillow like spilled coffee.

"I just realized something," Max said, shaking his head. "All those months at Redbrick, watching you work your magic in that corner office in Inman Park. Filing contracts, scheduling meetings, keeping everyone in line… Christ, you looked like you'd walked straight out of a secretary's training manual circa 1955. Those horn-rimmed glasses, every button fastened right up to your throat. Hair pulled back so tight I thought your scalp would scream for mercy."

Pauline raised one eyebrow in a gesture that once would have seemed prim but now held an entirely different meaning. "And?" The squeezing hardened.

"And I figured you'd be about as exciting in bed as a tax audit." He traced a finger along her collarbone, feeling her working under the sheets. "Shows what I know about judging books by their covers."

She laughed with a sound like warm brandy being poured. "Oh darling," she purred, pushing her glasses up her nose in a parody of her daytime self. "Shall we move on to the more intimate parts of your publishing contract? I'm *terribly* detailed with the fine print."

"You're dangerous," Max growled, as he lowered his head to her neck.

"More dangerous than you know," she whispered. There was something in her tone that made him pull back slightly, as he searched her face. Then she smiled that brilliant smile that had been hiding behind pursed lips all those months.

His answering smile was slow and heated. "Hold that thought," he said. "We'll have to continue this conversation later." He reluctantly pulled away. "We should probably get moving. You've got that meeting to get to, and I gotta prep for tonight's get-together. Though I have to say, Pauline, you make it very hard to be responsible."

———————————

Max stared through the hole, silent for a long moment. The evening air in the backyard carried the scent of damp earth and a faint chill, though the whiskey in their glasses kept the men warm. The torn painting stood on an easel under the glow of a patio light. The frayed hole in its center was an open wound, as though the truth had been clawing to escape all along. The novelist's hand brushed the edge of the canvas and he felt the material rough under his fingertips. The world inside the painting felt closer now, stripped of its deception, yet still veiled by layers of betrayal and history.

"You gonna tell us what's on your mind, or are we just here for the ambiance?" Jimmy said as he swirled his glass.

Max's lips twitched into a meager smile. "You ever think about how much blood gets spilled over treasures like this?" He didn't wait for an answer. "This painting, this damn thing, has been at the center of my family's fight with the Hollisters for a generation. And the truth of it? That's even uglier."

As Liam leaned forward in his chair, his wiry frame splashed a long shadow against the fence. "So, what's the full story? You hinted at it before, but I get the feeling we're only scratching the surface."

Max gave a nod, took a sip of his drink and began, "In the early to mid-1960s, Atlanta was undergoing rapid urban development. The city was expanding into neighboring rural areas. The Hollisters owned a vast tract of land on the outskirts of the city, known as Redwood Plains. It was a stretch of untouched forest and farmland that had been in the Hollister family for generations. As the city grew, developers eyed Redwood Plains for a massive project. There was a chance of having a sprawling commercial complex that would bring in millions. The whole idea, if followed through, would cement the Hollisters' name in Atlanta's development history. But there was a problem."

Max took a sip before going on, "A restrictive zoning law. Redwood Plains had been designated a protected area due to environmental concerns. The zoning restriction made it impossible to sell or develop the land without legislative approval, and any attempt to bypass it faced fierce opposition from conservationists and lawmakers."

Max began to pace around the easel. He gazed into his drink like it was a mirror of the past. "Harrison Worthington, a man of considerable charm and connections in Georgia's state legislature, had exactly the kind of pull Robert needed. Harrison had built a reputation as a powerbroker. Someone who could make things happen quietly but effectively. He had friends in high places, including key legislators and legal experts who could sway decisions on land reclassification. Robert was desperate, and though he resented the demand, he agreed to the terms. Harrison used his connections to grease the wheels of bureaucracy. The land was reclassified within months."

Jimmy whistled. "Sounds like your old man Harrison was the kind of guy who could make silk purses out of sow's ears without even wrinkling his suit."

The guests didn't miss the smile on Max's face as he bent his head a little lower to think about his words. He resumed, "That allowed Robert to sell the land to a major developer. The Hollister family received a windfall. But the painting changed hands, and so did the balance of power between the two families."

Jimmy let out another softer whistle. "That's one hell of a price."

"Harrison knew what he was doing," Thunderhawk said, speaking for the first time. His voice was calm, but the weight of his words settled over them like a heavy fog. "He didn't just want the painting for its beauty or value. He wanted leverage. And maybe—just maybe—he knew there was something more to it."

Max's gaze turned to Thunderhawk, who stood near the edge of the light, his sturdy frame blending into the shadows. "Harrison never admitted it, but I think he did know. At least, Robert suspected that he did. See, for Robert, the painting became a symbol of shame and humiliation. Over time, his resentment festered." Max paused to savor a new sip with a smack of his lips. "Especially, as Harrison flaunted the painting in his estate; hosting gatherings where the piece was displayed prominently as a…" Max gave a flourish with one hand, "…*symbol of victory*. Perhaps, he said something to someone at one of these parties, and that turned Robert onto him. Dad was aware this artwork went back to the Civil War. The Hollisters—David's ancestors—had already twisted the history of this painting to cover their treachery. Dad must've figured there was more to the story, but he kept it to himself."

"While his friend instilled his bitterness in his son, David, telling him that the painting was more than a piece of art," Liam pieced the story together, "that it was the key to restoring the Hollister family's honor."

"And here we are," Jimmy said, as he pulled a folded newspaper from his jacket pocket. "Speaking of treachery, you might wanna hear this."

He unfolded the paper, the headline glaring in bold letters: **DAVID HOLLISTER FACES MULTIPLE CHARGES: THEFT, FRAUD, AND MURDER.**

"Nice," Max muttered. "Let's hear it."

Jimmy cleared his throat, reading aloud:

"'David Hollister, 47, was arrested last week and is now facing a slew of charges, including grand theft, art fraud, and the alleged murders of Anastasia and Victor Chen, as well as Felicity Langston—a celebrated Atlanta photographer originally from Florida. Once a respected art dealer and real-life mogul, Hollister built his career on charm and exclusivity, masking the elaborate web of deception that ultimately unraveled around him. Hollister is accused of orchestrating the theft of *The Silent Watch*, a historic painting with ties to the American Civil War, and replacing it with a counterfeit to sell on the black market.'"

Jimmy paused, glancing at the others. "Wait till you hear this part."

"'Investigators have also uncovered evidence linking Hollister to the Chens' revised will, which was updated three months before the fire at their Buckhead estate. The updated document names Hollister as the sole beneficiary of their substantial art collection, including several rare works valued at over $50 million each. While the fire that killed the Chens is still under investigation, authorities have not yet tied Hollister directly to the incident. However, sources close to the case suggest that insurance claims filed after the fire show a troubling pattern tied to Hollister's previous dealings.'"

Jimmy folded the paper, shaking his head. "Guy's a damn snake. My contact at the insurance company says Hollister's name pops up in claims going back a decade— art collections, sudden accidents, suspicious fires. But tying him to any of it? That's the trick. He covers his tracks well."

"And the Chens paid the price," Liam said, his voice heavy. "Makes you wonder how many more there are."

Thunderhawk stepped closer to the easel, his eyes on the torn canvas. "It's not over for him yet. There's another trial coming. The land at Blackridge Hollow—my family's land—was stolen by his ancestors. The painting might finally prove what happened there."

The group fell silent, their eyes following Thunderhawk as he reached for the painting. His hands, steady and deliberate, began working at the edges of the canvas, pulling back the top layer like peeling old skin.

Max held his breath. Even Jimmy stopped fidgeting, his usual sharp remarks swallowed by the gravity of the moment. The process felt like an eternity, every movement precise, every tear a revelation. Finally, the last layer came free, and the hidden painting stood unveiled.

It was breathtaking.

The scene depicted an Amerindian regiment standing firm against a wave of Confederate forces, their courage etched into every line and stroke. In the center stood a lone Union commander. James Hollister, Thunderhawk's ancestor, held his sword raised to lead the charge at Blackridge Hollow.

The silence stretched, broken only by the faint rustle of the wind.

Thunderhawk's voice was quiet but unyielding. "They tried to erase this. Tried to erase us. But the truth always finds its way back."

Max stepped closer, his fingers brushing the edges of the newly revealed canvas. "This is it. The real painting. The truth they buried."

Behind them, the garden gate creaked. Pauline appeared, her honey-blonde hair loose around her shoulders instead of its former severe twist. Gone were the starched collars and rigid posture. She moved like someone who'd finally kicked off their uncomfortable shoes at the end of a long wedding, her sundress catching the amber glow from the compact tiki torches Max had scattered around his yard.

"The office actually feels like it can breathe these days," she said as she crossed the flagstones to stand beside Max. Her smile held none of that carefully measured restraint he'd first encountered.

"Though I still maintain the strictest cataloging standards." She bumped his shoulder playfully, and something in Max's chest warmed at how naturally she'd shed those self-imposed constraints, like some butterfly that has emerged from its too-tight chrysalis.

Liam folded his arms, shaking his head with a smirk. "You know, if Pauline hadn't gotten that anonymous letter, we wouldn't have shown up at the museum when we did. And who knows how that mess with David would've ended?"

Pauline turned to him. "I was thinking the same thing. It's strange, though. Who even sent that letter?"

Thunderhawk, who had been leaning against the wooden railing, straightened. "I spotted Pauline waiting at the red light and figured she was the best shot at getting help to Max in time. So, I threw it at her."

Pauline blinked. "That was you?"

"It would have been near impossible to recover my parents' asset without his help," Max said. "Meet Gabriel, the master of disguise."

Liam let out a low whistle. "Well, Max, now that you've got your painting back, how about finishing that book of yours?"

Max chuckled as he shook his head. "Forget that book. I've got a better idea. *Thieves and Treasures*. That's the story I'm gonna write."

Jimmy laughed, raising his glass. "Here's to it, then. Thieves and treasures—and the bastards who think they can get away with it."

The sound of glasses clinking was a soft streamer in the quiet backyard as the original painting stood between them. And then the Redbrick publisher boomed, "Max, you're going to kill that woman, Liv Hargison, and get the last page ready before that pain-in-the-ass hellcat writes herself into another damn chapter!"

Max let the grin take up one whole side of his gleaming face. "Right now, I'm 'bout to deliver something much more flavorful than that. But if I'm being honest, Liam, I'm still chewing on a few things — pieces that don't quite fit, moves that don't make sense."

"You said during the lunch meeting with Liam that once this adventure was over you'd deliver the final chapters," Pauline pointed out. "That was a promise, Max."

"I know," Max confirmed. "What I promised Liam was just the surface. Besides what I said then might not have been entirely true."

He took a slow sip, eyes locked on the painting like it had just spoken to him. "Funny thing about truth…" he said, almost whispering the words, "is it's not always hiding. Sometimes, it's right there, bold as brushstrokes, but no one's looking in the right place." With that his head tilted slightly, his squinting eyes hinting at a smile as if he had just solved a riddle no one knew was being asked. "The adventure isn't over. Because all that really matters now is that the people of Atlanta deserve to know what really is *The Truth Behind the Canvas.*"